"ROBERT USED YOU, ELISE."

"Don't be ridiculous, Bea." Elise faced her sister. "You don't like Robert because you're afraid that if I fall in love with him, I'll either abandon you or put you in Worthington House. But it's too late, Bea. I've already fallen in love with him and there's nothing you can do about it!"

"Then you love a criminal! Ask him about the old library. Ask him why he was in such a hurry to buy it. With your help, he got the place for a song when it's worth a million, maybe two!"

"I don't believe you," Elise whispered, her color fading.

"And now you tell me that you love him." Bea laughed. "What a joke! If the town was laughing at you before, think what they'll do now. You *love* him!"

With her sister's laughter echoing in her ears, Elise shook her head. "No," she said hoarsely. "No."

Special thanks and acknowledgment to Ginger Chambers for her contribution to the Tyler series.

Special thanks and acknowledgment to Joanna Kosloff for her contribution to the concept for the Tyler series.

Published October 1992

ISBN 0-373-82508-0

BACHELOR'S PUZZLE

BACHELOR'S PUZZLE

GINGER CHAMBERS

Harlequin Books

TORONTO • NEW YORK • LONDON
AMSTERDAM • PARIS • SYDNEY • HAMBURG
STOCKHOLM • ATHENS • TOKYO • MILAN
MADRID • WARSAW • BUDAPEST • AUCKLAND

TYLER

TYLER

American women have always used the art quilt as a means of expressing their views on life and as a commentary on events in the world around them. And in Tyler, quilting has always been a popular communal activity. So what could be a more appropriate theme for our book covers and titles?

BACHELOR'S PUZZLE

This optical illusion pattern of diamonds pieced together to form a series of whirling blocks around the central square could have reflected a quilting woman's vision of the complexity of single life. Once a bachelor found the right woman, everything just fell into place!

Dear Reader,

Welcome to Harlequin's Tyler, a small Wisconsin town whose citizens we hope you'll soon come to know and love. Like many of the innovative publishing concepts Harlequin has launched over the years, the idea for the Tyler series originated in response to our readers' preferences. Your enthusiasm for sequels and continuing characters within many of the Harlequin lines has prompted us to create a twelve-book series of individual romances whose characters' lives inevitably intertwine.

Tyler faces many challenges typical of small towns, but the fabric of this fictional community will be torn by the revelation of a long-ago murder, the details of which will evolve right through the series. This intriguing crime will culminate in an emotional trial that profoundly affects the lives of the Ingallses, the Barons, the Forresters and the Wochecks.

If you've got a little time to spare, the volunteers could sure use some help with the crisis at the library. Right now, the old place is being held together by wishes and prayers.

And it seems Judson Ingalls could use some wishes and prayers as well. A long-awaited announcement from the state coroner's office has sent him to his bed and thoroughly alarmed Alyssa and his grandson, Jeff.

So join us in Tyler, once a month, for the next five months, for a slice of small-town life that's not as innocent or as quiet as you might expect, and for a sense of community that will capture your mind and your heart.

Marsha Zinberg
Editorial Coordinator, Tyler

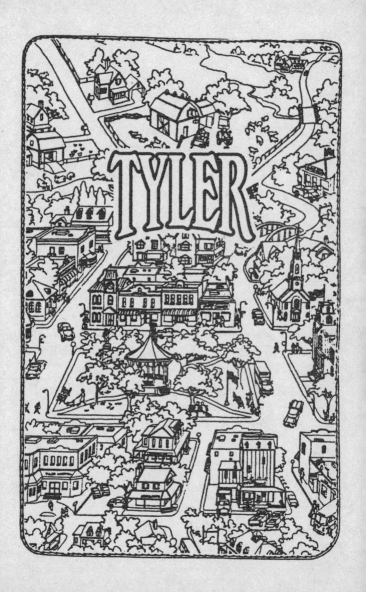

CHAPTER ONE

ELISE FERGUSON BRUSHED her fingertips through her short pale hair, smoothing it at the same time as she tried to fluff it. The perm she had gotten a few months ago was already loosening and she knew that soon she would have to get another. But right now she just didn't have the time to think about it.

She leaned forward, peering closely into the mirror at the fine lines that seemed to have appeared from nowhere over the past few years. Then she moved back, checking whether the hurried makeup job had been sufficient. From a distance, it worked. She didn't look substantially worse for wear than any other fifty-three-year-old who had just spent a morning in hell. And with the donning of her dress-for-success, reserved-for-meetings suit, she gave the illusion of complete competency. No one would believe that a scant half hour before, dampened through and through, she had raced into the bathroom, streaked with dirt from head to toe, her baby-fine hair sticking out at odd angles and her dress a shambles.

Elise's stomach gave a nervous rumble. She knew she probably should eat something, but there wasn't time for that, either. She had to be back at the library in—she checked her watch—five minutes. *Five minutes!* Impossible!

She reached for a bottle of her favorite scent and misted a light bouquet of spring flowers over herself. Then, grabbing a pair of tiny gold studs, she slipped them into her ears as she hurried down the stairs.

"Elise!" Her sister's voice held a petulant edge. "*Elise!* I need you to do something for me!"

Elise veered into the living room, where her older sister, Bea, sat before the television set, their fat yellow cat, Buttercup, in her lap.

Bea's gaze revealed her disapproval. "I asked before you went upstairs, but you didn't hear me, I suppose. I'd like my wrap! It's cool in the house today. You left too many windows open."

It was summer; the temperature outside was in the mid-eighties. Still, Elise didn't protest. "Would you like me to close them?" she asked.

Bea frowned grumpily. "No, just get my wrap. And the mail. I heard the postman come about an hour ago."

Elise hurried onto the porch, checked the mailbox and withdrew some bills and a magazine. Bea's doll collectors' magazine. That would make her happy. She hurried back inside and delivered the magazine before moving into the kitchen. "I'm just going to warm up leftovers today, Bea," she called into the next room. "I have a meeting I'm already late for."

Her sister mumbled something that Elise didn't understand, but she didn't ask her to repeat it. Elise popped a bowl of yesterday's shepherd's pie into the microwave, arranged a small salad, buttered a piece of wheat bread and sweetened a glass of iced tea. All this she balanced on a serving tray and brought to her sister.

Bea shifted the cat from her lap, all the while grumbling beneath her breath. Finally, she said clearly, "I'm *still* cool!"

Elise groaned and glanced at her watch. Then she hurried into the bedroom just off the living room to find the wrap. "Here," she said, spreading the soft material over her sister's shoulders. "Is there anything else?"

At one time Bea had been beautiful, with silver-blond hair flowing softly to the middle of her back, bright blue eyes that flashed with anticipation and a delicacy of features and build that the two sisters still shared. Now, Bea pulled her hair into an unbecoming knot at the base of her neck, discontent had faded the color of her eyes and bitterness contorted the fragility of her features.

Adjusting her wheelchair to a more comfortable position at the side table, Bea said dismissingly, "No, I wouldn't dream of asking for anything else. I wouldn't want to keep you from your meeting."

Elise suffered a pang of guilt. "It's with the architect, Bea. The professor who's going to see if he can help us build the new library. I'd forgotten all about it what with the water leak and everything. Remember when I first came in, I told you that a number of books had gotten wet and that people from all over Tyler had come to help?"

Her sister fixed her with a cool gaze. "You said something, but I didn't understand. I thought you'd fallen into a mud puddle."

Elise sighed and rubbed a hand across her brow, a telling gesture that she was unaware of using. "I'll explain everything this evening, all right? Right now I really have to..."

"Go. I know. You *always* have to go."

Elise wanted to scream. She wanted to yell at her sister that she couldn't help it if she had to hurry off to her job. That if she hadn't done so for these past thirty years they wouldn't have eaten very well. There would be no house, no television, no leisurely outings, no subscriptions to doll collectors' magazines, no vast collection of dolls.... But she kept her tongue, just as she had for all these years, knowing that Bea had reason to be bitter. "Yes, I do," she agreed. "I'll try to be home by six-thirty, but if I can't, I'll get Josephine to come make your dinner. I'll let you know."

Bea picked at the pie with her fork and didn't say anything, a point Elise didn't regret as she finally left the house. She was already nervous enough about her meeting with the architectural professor. The stakes were high—as in whether Tyler would continue to have a library and she herself a job!

Elise dashed for her car, a moderately old, tan Ford Escort, and quickly backed out of the drive. In her mind she rehearsed an apology for being late, one she hoped she would be able to deliver with a modicum of dignity.

THE ALBERTA INGALLS Memorial Library was housed in a spacious home built around the turn of the century. A series of narrow, vertical windows showcased the second-floor exterior, while a large wraparound porch with strong white columns gave character to the first. Over the years, Elise had planned the landscaping herself, encouraging the growth of rich evergreen shrubs along the base of the porch and seasonal flowers in the accompanying wide beds. The grass had a lush green cast, with shade provided by both oak and maple trees.

Normally the scene was placid, inviting patrons to come inside for a leisurely browse, but that was not the image presented today. Elise was forced to bypass the jammed parking spaces in front of the building and add her car to the numerous others crowded end to end along both sides of the street.

The library was a hive of activity. People moved busily inside and out. The front porch, usually reserved for quiet reading, was congested with folding tables. They in turn bore the weight of numerous books that were being set on end and fanned open so that they could begin to dry, even as more books continued to be removed from the water-damaged room within.

Elise gathered her purse from the passenger seat and hurried toward the scene. She was grateful to all the people who had turned out. It seemed as if everyone in town who could help had come when told about the emergency.

As Elise stepped onto the porch, Delia Mayhew, one of the library's two part-time aids, rushed to greet her. "We've gotten almost all the books out now, Elise. We're down to the *V*s on the last shelf!" Delia's dusky cheeks were flushed a becoming shade of pink and her dark eyes were shining. She had just turned twenty-one and had seldom, if ever, traveled farther than a two-hundred-mile radius from her home. For her, the accident that morning was a cause for genuine excitement.

Alyssa Baron looked up from her work with the wettest books. Elegant, blond and regal of bearing, Alyssa could always be counted upon in times of trouble. As the only daughter of the town's most influential man, she seemed to feel service to the people of Tyler was her duty. She and her very pregnant daughter, Liza Forrester, were carefully placing sections of paper toweling between individual pages to act as blotting agents. "It's a good thing the accident happened in the Biography Room," Alyssa murmured wryly after hearing Delia's somewhat oddly worded description. "Otherwise we'd have a hard time telling exactly where we were."

Grinning at her mother's wry jest, Liza agreed, "Oh, definitely. The Dewey Decimal classification 973.629A just doesn't have the same ring to it as a V, does it?"

Cliff Forrester, Liza's husband, came up beside them. "What's this about V?" he asked, watching as his wife tore off another section of paper towel and placed it between two pages. "You're not planning names for the baby, are you? What starts with a V? Let's see: Virgil, Venus..."

Liza tilted her head and gave a devilish smile. "What would you do if I wanted to name our child Venus?"

Cliff smiled slowly and surprised Elise by winking at her. Normally, he was so quiet and self-contained. "Why, I'd agree," he said. "What else?"

Johnny Kelsey dropped an armload of books onto a table behind Elise. "I've talked with Pastor Schoff," he announced, causing Elise to turn toward him. "We can have the church hall any time we want it. When I get off work this evening, I'll bring some of the men from the F and M and we can shift all this again." He motioned to the tables and books scattered along the porch. "That's still what you want, isn't it? To get this lot moved inside somewhere?"

Elise met the deep-set gray eyes of the man she'd known since childhood. "If you could do that, Johnny, it would be wonderful. Do I need to speak with Pastor Schoff myself?"

Anna Kelsey arrived just in time to hear Elise's question. She, too, was delivering an armload of damp books. "Probably should," she said. "I'm sure he could arrange fresh volunteers for tonight if you ask him."

"I'll call right away. *Oh!*" Elise suddenly looked stricken. Once again she had gotten carried away by the immediate problem and forgotten the more looming threat. "Has anyone seen Professor Fairmont?"

There was a series of shrugs and head shakes. "Not since earlier," Alyssa said.

"What about Renata?" Elise asked. "She said she'd watch out for him."

Again Alyssa shook her head.

Elise's stomach tightened. Robert Fairmont's reputation was impressive. As a practicing architect, he had won numerous design awards, and his track record as a teacher was impressive, too. A growing number of his former students were beginning to make names for themselves, with many attributing much of their success to him. Had he been insulted that she was late for their appointment, and so had decided to leave?

"Where's Pauline?" she tried yet again, starting to feel more than a little desperate. Delia pointed to a group of people at the far end of the porch. With a soft murmur, Elise excused herself.

Pauline Martin, the library's only full-time aid, was a plump woman in her early forties with short, light brown hair and a perpetual expression of amused good cheer. An earth-mother type, she loved working with the children who came to the library, and along with Elise had developed a program that several libraries in other small towns now emulated.

When she saw Elise, Pauline broke into a beaming smile. "You look perfect! Don't touch a thing! Otherwise you'll get all dirty again. Have you heard? We can use the hall at Fellowship Lutheran. Pastor Schoff didn't understand at first why we couldn't just put the books in another part of the library, but when Johnny told him about the dampness spreading to the rest of the collection, he agreed right away. Just like Johnny understood when you told him earlier. He—"

Elise broke into the ongoing stream. If Pauline were turned loose, they could be standing there for hours. "Pauline, Professor Fairmont—have you seen him?"

Pauline frowned. "Why, yes. Just a little while ago. He was . . . somewhere." She scanned the people on the porch. "The last time I saw him, he was by the front steps."

"Was he leaving?" Elise couldn't help the note of alarm in her voice.

Pauline frowned in puzzlement. "Why would he leave when he's come all the way from Milwaukee?"

"I'll check inside." Elise hurried through the open double doors that led into the library proper.

A steady stream of people was moving up and down the hall that led to a room at the rear of the library. There, a buildup of water from a leaking pipe had caused a portion of the ceiling to give way. Some people exiting from the hall were heading to the porch with damp volumes. Others had been assigned the task of stacking the numerous books that had managed to remain dry in an area off to one side of the circulation desk.

Elise shivered, remembering the horror of the moment when water had first sprayed everywhere. For a short space of time, her emotions had given way as well as she had tried frantically to rescue the books nearest the disaster.

At the Biography Room's door, the tall young man next in line stood aside to let Elise enter. He was Ricky Travis, a recent graduate of Tyler High School. "Miss Ferguson," Ricky said respectfully.

A glimmer of a smile touched Elise's lips. Ricky was a person it was sometimes hard to like. A typical teenager, he'd had his share of ups and downs over the past year. In particular, he'd had difficulties on the high school football team. Some in town thought him cocky, but Elise knew another side of him. She remembered the little boy who had devoured books on dinosaurs the way other little boys eat cake. The fiercer the dinosaur, the better. Ricky had been able to rattle even the most complicated scientific names off his tongue. Next, he had progressed to adventure tales and finally to science fiction—his current favorite. "Ricky," she acknowledged softly. She included a couple of Ricky's friends in her smile and stepped into the chaos of the room.

Even though they had finally managed to cut off the water supply to the library, occasional drops still fell from the raw open wound on the ceiling. Bits of soggy plaster clung to the gaping edges of the hole, while other pieces cluttered the wet floor, mixing with dirt that had collected in the lathing for nearly a hundred years. Elise had tried to clear away the worst of the muck before she went home, sweeping it to one side, but numerous feet trampling through to rescue books hadn't helped the situation. Several thick cotton towels had been spread as doormats into the hall, in an attempt to keep tracking to a minimum, but their success was debatable.

Josephine Mackie, principal of Tyler High School, waved to Elise from across the room. Elise lifted a hand and started to make her way toward her, all the while murmuring encouragement to those in the process of removing the last of the books as well as those taking down the free-standing shelves.

Several people in the rescue force Elise didn't recognize, but she was grateful for their willingness to help even if she didn't know them personally. One man in particular seemed to be enjoying himself. With his sleeves rolled up to his elbows and smudges of dirt on what once had been a pristine white shirt, he braced one of the metal shelf units so that Patrick Kelsey, Johnny and Anna's oldest, could loosen the bolts that held it to the next section. Grinning, he said something that made Patrick laugh.

He was an attractive man, probably somewhere in his mid to late fifties, with wavy black hair sprinkled lightly with silver, an olive complexion that made him look as if he had a year-round tan, a capable, active-looking body and a rather rugged set to his features. He glanced up as Elise continued to watch him, and she was struck by the fact that his eyes were a curious shade of yellow and brown. But it was not so much their unusual color as their expression that unsettled her. Confident, vital and knowingly amused, they lent him the air of a man who could all too easily perceive the foibles and fantasies of the people around him.

Illogically, Elise averted her gaze, afraid that he might see inside of her. A moment later, after castigating herself for being fanciful, she looked back, only to find that his attention had returned to Patrick Kelsey.

Continuing on to Josephine's side, Elise was perplexed that her heart rate had quickened. It was this horrible day, she told herself firmly. Nothing more than too much stress. She had passed her recent physical exam with flying colors; the only caveat the doctor had given her was to lighten up and not work so hard. *Her? Lighten up?* With one library literally falling down around her head and a new one whose construction, because of fiscal problems, had ground to a halt with only the foundation work complete? And to top it off, she had now lost the visiting professor, the only person who could help them solve their problem!

Josephine Mackie was almost seven years Elise's senior, closer to Bea's age than her own. But that illusionary difference had evaporated over time, and they'd been best friends for more years than either of them cared to think about.

A slender, gray-haired woman with a long thin nose, and pale gray eyes that hid behind round, rimless glasses, Josephine had presided over the high school with an iron hand for almost as many years as Elise had been Tyler's chief librarian. She demanded that students and teachers alike do their best, holding them to strict guidelines. But she also ruled with fairness and maintained an open-door policy to anyone who had troubles. She had seen a lot and helped a lot, and the sharpness of her expression concealed a tender heart. As head of Tyler's Friends of the Library organization, she frequently worked with Elise on various projects.

"Don't look so panicked," Josephine rebuked her fondly, taking a guess at the cause of Elise's worried expression. "Everything is under control. The plumber's on his way, the pipe will be fixed in no time, and then we can get the water turned back on and begin the cleanup."

"It's not that," Elise replied, looking around anxiously. Her gaze skimmed over the man at the shelves before moving on to the other strangers in the room. None of them fit her idea of how a professor of architecture should look. "I've really messed things up, Josephine. He's not here. I think he's gone home . . . gone back to Milwaukee. He'll probably never agree to meet with me again. I'll have to go to the town council and tell them that I—"

"Elise," Josephine interrupted her pleasantly. "He's over there."

"What? Where?" Elise's head swung round, trying to follow the direction her friend pointed.

"At the shelves, with Patrick Kelsey. I saw you looking at him just now. I thought you knew."

Elise closed her eyes. That man was Professor Fairmont, and he had been roped into helping. A man of his stature. "No," she said weakly. "I didn't know."

Josephine rubbed her grimy hands on the rag she had been using to wipe down the shelves. "He's really quite nice," she said mildly. "He impressed me. He arrived early for your appointment, saw the mess and didn't hesitate. He just took off his jacket and dug right in."

"Oh, God," Elise breathed.

Josephine looked at her. "What's the matter? Should I have stopped him?"

Elise shrugged guiltily. "Oh, no. I didn't mean that. It's just..."

"Elise." Josephine gave her one of the patented principal looks she had been honing on recalcitrant students for years. "Go talk to the man. Apologize. Thank him for helping. It's all you can do."

Patrick had succeeded in releasing the final bolt that held the first shelving unit to the next, and as a result, the unit swung free. Immediately, a strong pair of hands compensated for the release of tension, balancing the unit until Ricky and his friends could come forward to relieve the holder of its weight. Then the unit itself was spirited out of the room.

Elise's nerves fluttered. She'd known what she was going to have to do even before Josephine told her. She drew a deep breath and, after a quick, heartening glance at her friend, closed the distance between herself and the professor.

Robert Fairmont concentrated on his work, watching as Patrick bent to release the initial bolts holding the next unit. Elise stopped just in front of him. The neat crispness of her reserved-for-meetings suit seemed so out of place in the circumstances, her makeup too carefully applied. She was the only person in the library who wasn't working, who wasn't sullied.

"Professor Fairmont?" she asked, her voice strained. He looked up and again she was struck by the uniqueness of his eyes. She smiled to cover her nervousness and thrust out a welcoming hand. "I'm Elise Ferguson, the chief librarian here. I'm sorry I wasn't available to greet you earlier, but as you can see, we've had a little accident."

"This whole place is an accident, if you ask me," Patrick Kelsey declared, straightening. "When Mom called to tell Pam and me what had happened, we thought it was the roof. Another bad storm and the whole thing could blow off. I'd hate to think of the cleanup then!"

"So would I," Elise murmured.

Robert Fairmont started to take her hand but paused first to wipe his own along the side of his dark slacks. His touch, when it came, was warm, sure. "This is enough of a calamity, I should think," he said.

His voice set off a series of alarms along Elise's already disturbed nerve endings. It was low and soft, the voice of a man who didn't have to shout to be heard because people automatically listened.

Patrick motioned for someone else to assist him, then said to Elise, "We can take care of this if you two need to talk. I was just telling Robert here how badly we need the new library, then I found out who he was. Sure hope you two can work something out."

Robert Fairmont's smile was assured. "We'll do our best."

Elise was conscious that he followed closely behind her as she walked out of the room. At a quiet corner in the hall, she turned to face him. "I'm sorry about all of this," she said. "It couldn't have come at a worse time. Would you like to talk in my office? It's just down the hall. It's dry," she added as an extra incentive.

An array of lines crinkled the corners of his eyes and the creases in his cheeks deepened when he smiled. His was a strong face, weathered by life and tempered by experience. "Dry has a definite appeal today," he agreed.

Elise turned away, unsure if he was laughing at her. She decided to take his reply at face value.

"Are the books salvageable?" he asked as he fell into step at her side.

"Hopefully most will be. Even the wettest. Our worst enemy is mold, not water. That's why we had to get them into circulating air so quickly, so they could start the process of drying. We couldn't afford to wait. Only the books with coated pages will have to be sent away to a vacuum chamber to be dried—they'll fuse into hard blocks otherwise. Again, hopefully, there won't be many of those, because the procedure can be expensive . . . something we just don't need right now."

She unlocked the door to her office and ushered him inside. The room was cramped, as were most of the other rooms in the library, both in the public and staff areas. Boxes were stacked on the floor; books and catalogs rested on every available flat surface. Notes fluttered from her small bulletin board. The town had outgrown the facility a number of years ago, far longer than the past two or so years that they had spent planning the new building. Not even continued weeding of books and materials could create enough space for everything and everyone.

Elise made no apology for the condition of the room. It was something she just couldn't help. She took a seat behind her work station and nodded toward the empty chair. "Our ability to make coffee is hampered, of course," she said. "But if you'd care to have some, I'm sure we can find someone who wouldn't mind..."

"No need," he said, folding his length into the proffered chair. His gaze once again searched the room before alighting on Elise. "Actually, I have a proposition to put to you. Why don't we postpone this meeting for a day or two? Possibly even longer than that. You have your hands full now and I'm in no great hurry. I can wait."

Elise had managed to school her face of all emotion, but at his suggestion, she jerked forward, her expression intent. "But we can't do that!" she cried. "The new library can't wait! You've seen how bad the situation is here. You've heard about the roof... and that's not all! I love this old house. I've loved it all the years I've worked here and even before, when I came as a child to use it. But we've reached the point where we just can't stay any longer—not with everything like it is. We *have* to build the new library. Either that or we make the necessary repairs, and I'm afraid that after all the money the town's already spent on plans and contracts and fees, there won't be enough money left to... Then we'll lose everything—buildings, books..."

She stopped, her throat tightening. He didn't need to know all that. She didn't need to tell him.

After a moment he said, "A day or two won't matter at this stage. Relax a bit. You can't build a new library all on your own. That's why I'm here. To see if I can help."

"But..."

Robert Fairmont, professor of architecture at the University of Wisconsin, Milwaukee, leaned forward to still the fingers that worked against each other on top of her desk. His smile flashed reassurance. "Relax," he repeated softly. "In a few days we can talk. Say, on Friday. In the meantime, you can get things under control here, and I'll go over the plans I have from the firm in greater detail. The time won't be wasted."

As she listened to him speak, Elise felt the tension she had been carrying all day melt away, as if his certainty could protect her. It was a nice feeling; her burdens had somehow been lifted. But the magic didn't last. The difficulties both she and the town faced could not be ignored for long. She pulled her hands away, severing their connection. Still, what he said about delaying the consultation made sense. With all the people working nearby, she would be divided in her allegiance. She would want to be in both places at once. "All right," she agreed tightly. "We'll meet again on Friday."

"Good," he said, smiling. Then he stood up.

Elise remained in her chair. She continued to stare at him, completely unaware, for the moment, of what she was doing. Then she, too, got quickly to her feet, her cheeks flushing with embarrassment. She was a competent woman. People trusted her to do the right thing. They trusted her with the growing minds of their children. She was responsible for every program and every book that came into or went out of the library. She was responsible for budget planning, for equipment purchases, for not indulging in gossip when she was in the perfect job for it. She knew everyone's tastes, everyone's interests, and sometimes, it seemed, everyone's problems. Yet at this moment she felt like a little girl again, off center, off balance. It *had* to be the day, she told herself. It had to be.

She led him back to the Biography Room, but just outside the door, she paused to say stiltedly, "Don't feel you have to help any longer. You shouldn't have been pressed into service in the first place. We have enough people now. There's no need for you to stay."

He met her look levelly. "I helped because I wanted to. I love books and old houses. I think I'll stay a little longer... that is, if it's all right with you."

Elise shrugged, trying to maintain some kind of cool facade. "As you wish, Mr.... Professor..."

"Robert," he suggested. "Just call me Robert. And I'll call you Elise."

Elise's heart jumped when he said her name, a fact that startled her. What was *wrong* with her? Maybe she should go see Dr. Baron and have another checkup.

"All right," she murmured, and walking into the damaged room, she headed directly for the safe harbor that was Josephine.

She tried not to notice Robert Fairmont as he worked—that after checking to see if Patrick had further need of him, he started to shift the fallen debris, carrying out the larger pieces of plaster Elise had pushed to one side and disposing of the rest with a dustpan, broom and mop.

Then she tried desperately not to notice that she *had* noticed.

CHAPTER TWO

ELISE GUIDED her Escort into the garage, the long day having finally taken its toll. At the moment she felt every bit of her fifty-three years. In fact, she felt a hundred and fifty-three! Her head ached, her back ached, her feet ached. She had been too exhausted to do more than pick at her food earlier when someone was kind enough to bring dinner to the volunteers at the church hall. But at least they had gotten the job done. Most of the books were now resting jauntily on end, their pages fanned open, continuing the process of drying. And the books that needed to be sent away and were valuable enough for the library to justify the costly procedure of reclaiming them had been frozen as procedure dictated. In all, only a small number would likely be lost. Considering everything, they had gotten off lightly. If the leak had been larger, or if it had occurred somewhere else—say, over the Tyler Collection that she had spent years gathering and that contained archival papers of the town's history as well as old photographs that couldn't be replaced... Elise shuddered at the thought. The day would have been a catastrophe. Now the only difficulty was the worrisome fact that such a catastrophe could still occur. If the pipes in one section of the library were in such poor condition, it stood to reason that pipes elsewhere could be the same. Not to mention the condition of the roof. Elise shook her head in quick denial. She didn't want to think about the condition of the roof!

After gathering her purse and jacket, she let herself out of the car. Where once her suit had been crisp and smart, the skirt and blouse now looked to be in almost as wretched a condition as her dress had earlier. She hadn't bothered to go home again to change into clothes suitable for the book rescue work. She hadn't wanted to take the time. So she'd just removed her jacket and set to work. And after an afternoon spent wiping down shelves and walls and floors, and an evening supervising the transfer of water-damaged books, her clothes might never be the same.

Elise fitted her key into the back door lock and stepped inside the house that she and Bea had lived in for most of their adult lives. The design was perfect for Bea's needs, and what wasn't had been altered. Their parents had bought and refitted the house just a few years before their deaths.

Distinctive theme music from a popular television drama spilled out of the living room, alerting Elise to the presence of the others. She knew Josephine was there because her car was parked at the end of the sidewalk.

Both women looked up when Elise entered the room. The cat made the first move toward greeting, stirring her slightly pudgy body to get up, and then stretching her back into a high arch before starting a slow, regal walk toward the person who fed her. Tiny noises of pleasure sounded deep in her throat.

"It's certainly about time," Bea pronounced shortly. "We'd just about given you up for dead!"

Ignoring Bea's remark, Josephine said, "You look exhausted. Were you able to finish?"

Elise crouched to stroke the cat, who was rubbing against her legs in an ecstatic show of goodwill. "Buttercup... hello. My goodness, did you miss me?" She laughed lightly when Buttercup purred a response. Scooping the cat into her arms, she straightened and answered Josephine's question. "Yes, thank goodness. At least, with this part. Of course, tomorrow the insurance people will come and we'll have to see about getting the ceiling repaired. Not to mention arranging things with the vacuum-chamber people and continuing to work with the books at the church. Then we have to do something with all the books that didn't get damp but had to be moved anyway. They're just stacked haphazardly about. Then..." Buttercup grew restless and twisted to be set free. Elise released her, then claimed a seat on the couch for herself.

"I'm sorry I asked," Josephine murmured dryly, gazing at Elise with compassion.

"So that means tomorrow is going to be another repeat of today," Bea said tightly, not showing any compassion. "You'll be away again all day and half the night."

"No, Bea," Elise answered levelly. "Today was unusual because of the accident."

"I was going to give you five more minutes and then go to bed," Bea snapped. "If you want to stay out all night, well, that's up to you. But there are those of us who have to sleep!"

"I'm home now, Bea," Elise defended herself tiredly.

"I told you to go to bed, Bea," Josephine said, taking up Elise's cause. "I told you I'd brush your hair."

"No." Bea shook her head. "It's the least Elise can do after being away each day for so long. And especially the way she abandoned me today."

Elise closed her eyes. Right now she didn't think she had strength left to lift the brush.

"Let me do it for you tonight," Josephine urged. "Just this once."

Bea gathered her possessions onto her lap, adjusting the wheelchair as needed. She collected her magazine, her sewing, her tissues, her wrap. "Elise can do as she wants," she replied primly. "If she doesn't want to brush my hair, she certainly doesn't have to." She then made a production of pushing herself across the room, making it seem difficult, hard to accomplish.

Elise started to get up but Josephine stopped her. "At least let me help you to your room, Bea. Elise is tired. She needs to rest."

"I can take care of it myself!" Bea snapped. "I don't need help from you!"

"Bea!" Elise protested.

Bea turned. She lifted her chin. Her body seemed delicate in the chair, but when she chose, her angry spirit could dominate even the most determined soul. "I can't say it's been nice, because it hasn't. Today has been an absolute *nightmare!* Josephine, there's no need for you to come over tomorrow. I'll be fine. I can do without a meal or two. It won't hurt me."

"Bea!" Josephine chastised her in turn.

Bea threw their visitor a superior look before her eyes moved on to her sister. Once they were settled upon Elise, though, her expression became harder to define.

Tears of exhaustion sprang into Elise's eyes. She had to blink rapidly to keep them from falling.

A tiny, satisfied smile feathered the side of Bea's mouth. Then she turned away and rolled resolutely out of the room.

The television blared into a newsbreak but no one seemed to notice. At the closing click of Bea's door, Josephine switched off the set. Silence permeated the room.

A moment later Elise said softly, "I suppose today has been difficult for her."

Josephine's jaw was tight. "I don't see why. Between the two of us we've done everything we possibly could for her. She takes advantage of you, Elise, you know that. Anyone else would tell her to take her dictatorial ways and jump into the nearest—"

Elise sat forward, interrupting her. "Tomorrow really shouldn't be as bad as today. There'll be a lot to do, but at least I know what to expect. I can't tell you how horrible it was this morning to look into that room and see that gigantic bubble hanging from the ceiling. Then to be standing almost under it when it broke!" Elise started to laugh, a release from tension. "I was grabbing books, trying to get them out of harm's way, then, whoosh! We had our own indoor monsoon!"

"How did you get along with Professor Fairmont?" Josephine asked. "Does he think he can do anything to help with the new library?"

Elise's laughter stopped. She had been successful in keeping the man out of her thoughts from shortly after she saw him leave late in the afternoon to this moment. She shrugged. "We didn't really have time to talk. He's coming back on Friday. We'll discuss it then."

Josephine nodded. "I told you before that he impressed me. I like the way he looks you straight in the eye and doesn't bother to hide what he thinks. You know where you stand with someone like that. Not that he can't charm the birds from the trees when he wants— you can see that at first glance, too. But there's something underneath. A fine, strong character."

Buttercup leaped gracefully onto the couch and started to purr as Elise absently stroked her silky head. "I felt like he could see too much," she mused.

"What do you mean?" Josephine asked, frowning.

Elise shook her head, then was forced to cover a huge yawn.

Smiling good-naturedly, Josephine stood up. "The best favor you can do for yourself right now is get into bed and not worry about a thing. I've taken care of the kitchen. All the dishes are washed and put away. I also made some of Bea's favorite breakfast rolls for tomorrow morning, so that should keep her happy, at least for a while." Josephine took a moment to examine her friend closely. "It probably won't do any good," she said, "but I'm going to say it anyway. You're taking too much onto yourself, Elise. Wearing yourself too thin. You can't handle all the burdens of this town as well as those of your family. One person can carry only so much!"

Elise returned the woman's gaze with tolerant amusement. "I'll remember to give you the same speech the beginning of next semester when you're single-handedly trying to drag the high school along in your wake. We've known each other for too long, Josephine."

Josephine grimaced. "You're probably right. Sometimes I think I'll retire early. Go off on one of those world cruises, the kind that only single people can get a ticket on. Meet some nice man and settle down. Want to come along?"

"What? And shock everyone in Tyler? We're going to keep doing what we're doing forever, remember? Our lives can't change. Town institutions don't just get up and waltz away from their duties."

Josephine located her purse. "Maybe one day we'll surprise them all. The head of the library waltzes off, the head of the high school waltzes off...."

"I'll just be happy to have the new library."

Josephine nodded in resignation. "Me, too. One small step. Then maybe the school can build a new science lab. We're not asking for that much, are we?"

Elise saw her friend to the door and gave her a warm hug. "Thanks for all you did today. At the library. Here."

"Anytime. Well, no. I didn't mean it that way. We certainly don't want another accident."

Elise waved as Josephine drove away, then she closed the door and secured it. The house was quiet when she turned. Quiet and somehow empty. Bea was in her room, waiting to have her hair brushed. The marmalade cat was fast asleep on the couch. Echoes of their parents still could be felt in the decor that had changed little since their deaths so many years before. Yet there were times when it just wasn't enough.

Elise drew a soft breath, braced her weary shoulders and went to tap on Bea's door. The call for entry came without hesitation.

Bea was sitting up in bed, the wheelchair off at an angle nearby. Elise moved it in order to get the brush out of the bedside table drawer. Bea had already taken her hair down, the long, pale threads her last remaining pride. Wordlessly, Elise perched on the edge of the mattress and began the ritual that ended each sister's day.

As usual, Bea relaxed when the long strokes with the brush began, and as usual, Elise's mind wandered. Tonight her thoughts flew to a certain time in the day when she had sat at her desk directly opposite a vital, attractive man, and he had placed his hand over hers and told her not to worry. And for a few enchanted seconds, she *hadn't* worried. All her cares had lifted as she became lost in the certainty of his voice and the look in his unusual yellow-brown eyes.

Bea moved impatiently. "Have you gone to sleep?" she demanded. "You've stopped brushing!"

Elise immediately shook the memory away, glad that her sister couldn't see the warm flush that had crept into her cheeks.

AMID THE FAMILIAR surroundings of his apartment in Milwaukee, Robert Fairmont sat at his drafting table and contemplated the set of blueprints for the Tyler library. He frowned in concentration as he moved from

sheet to sheet and finally to the specifications at the end.
It was a good job, nothing less than he expected from
Fred Dupont—which was exactly what he'd decided
after reviewing the project the day before. Fred had
been a good student and now he was a good practicing
architect in the firm with which Robert himself was af-
filiated. But Robert could see where civic pride and a
good artist's instincts had eventually led to a clash with
today's fiscal reality.

He checked the papers that constituted the history of
the project. First contact with the firm had come nearly
three years before, at a time when matching funds from
state and federal sources were much easier for small
towns like Tyler to access. As those sources dried up,
any number of civic projects all over the state had been
put on hold.

He returned to the specifications. Yes, it truly was a
beautiful job. The library would have been a building
all involved could be proud of. Only now it faced the
same threats as had the courthouse in Johnstown Corners and the new administration building in Benning-
ton Falls before he had found a way to save them. Could
he help the people of Tyler in the same way?

He smiled slightly to himself. The simplest solution
would be to lop off the top floor of the two-story Greek
Revival structure, but he doubted that the chief librarian would sit still for that. And he couldn't blame her.
Space was so cramped in the building that presently
housed the library. What would be the sense of con-
structing a new building that gave them very little additional room? The collection wouldn't get wet, but that
was about all he could promise.

Robert moved away from the drawing board to stand at the series of wide windows that overlooked Lake Michigan. Lights were starting to twinkle along the shore as the setting sun rapidly plunged the area into night. He leaned against the thick plate glass, his shoulder registering its solidness as well as its coolness as he hummed softly in accompaniment to the delicate strains of the Mozart piano concerto that reverberated throughout the apartment. There was no one to complain if he was slightly off-key or to protest that he hummed too loudly; no one to criticize his choice of music. His features relaxed into contentment. A short time later, when the movement drew to a close, he sighed, and with reluctance allowed his thoughts to return to the events of the day.

His time in Tyler had been far different from what he'd expected. He had planned to pass a couple of hours in consultation about the library, then be on his way back to Milwaukee, about an hour's drive away. As it turned out, most of the day had been spent in hard physical labor! Row upon row of books had needed to be moved, shelves had to be taken down, the room where the leak had occurred had had to be emptied so that repairs could be made and all surfaces properly cleaned. There hadn't been time to do much consulting—at least, not with the chief librarian. But he had been able to pick up on the feelings of a number of his fellow workers. It seemed that the old house that had served as Tyler's library for the past forty years had reached the point of no return. Everyone agreed it was in terrible condition and might fall down at any given moment—an exaggeration, Robert knew, but one that expressed the townspeople's feelings succinctly. All seemed to want the new library to be built, but no one had a good idea of how to replace the funding that had been lost. Their attempts to raise additional money had barely scratched the surface of what was needed, which made their frustration easy to understand. So, too, was the desperation of the librarian, who pretended to be calm and collected in the midst of disaster, but who in reality was in a near-explosive state of worry.

Robert pushed away from the window and moved restlessly about the apartment. He was glad he had a project to think about, something to keep his mind occupied for the dog days of summer. Unlike past summers, when he had traveled, this one he had decided to spend at home. And he could already tell that his decision had been a mistake.

He moved back to the drawing table and continued to hum, both lightly and on-key, as he exchanged the plans of the Tyler library for a set of yellow tracing sheets on which he had been sketching his version of a modern-day cathedral. After securing it in place, he sat down to work. It was his whimsy that one day one of his renderings would rival the best that Europe had to offer in style, grace and innovative grandeur.

The German poet Goethe had once likened architecture to "frozen music." That was the way Robert thought of his craft. It appealed both to the artist in him and to the engineer. The challenge was everything.

ELISE HURRIED downstairs, aware that once again she was late. For a person who prided herself on being punctual, the past few days had been a trial. There had been problems with the insurance company, with arranging an appointment for the vacuum chamber, even with the hall at Fellowship Lutheran. Somehow someone had overlooked the fact that the church hall was scheduled for use that weekend, and it had taken a number of calls, plus Elise's own pleading intervention, to make arrangements for the planned awards dinner to be held instead at the hall belonging to the Episcopal Church of the Good Shepherd.

Once Elise got behind in her schedule, she seemed to stay behind. She had thought to have most things under control by this morning, only to discover that Joe Santori could come three days early to repair the ceiling of the Biography Room. And she wasn't about to tell him not to come. The way things were progressing, a refusal could equal several weeks' delay. So she had stayed at the library longer than planned, which made her late arriving home to prepare Bea's lunch, which accordingly had delayed her preparation for her second meeting with Robert Fairmont.

A light film of perspiration glazed her body, the result of a too-hot shower, a too-warm house and heightened tension. She wore another suit, a backup reserved-for-meetings suit that was the same pale blue color as her eyes. It didn't quite manage the psychological boost of the red suit she'd donned three days before, but it was close. Fired with determination, she felt in control, competent and businesslike.

She had thought about everything that had happened when she met the professor the first time and decided that her reaction had been magnified all out of proportion. None of it had been real. When she saw him today he would prove to be an ordinary human being with eyes that saw nothing beyond the commonplace and a voice that held no particular power. He would come, they would talk, and hopefully Tyler would be able to build its new library. Afterward, she would go on just as she had always gone on, with one day following another.

Bea made no demand as Elise came downstairs. Giving in to curiosity, Elise peeked around the doorway into the family room. As usual, Bea was sitting in front of the television set, but instead of watching the broadcast game show, she had fallen asleep.

Elise paused, not wanting to wake her. But when Buttercup gave a meow of welcome and with feline grace jumped from the couch to the floor without disturbing Bea, Elise was drawn farther into the room. Chances to observe her sister unnoticed were extremely rare.

Bea's blond head had no brace. She slept sitting upright, her slender body fragile in the dull-colored, shapeless dress. In repose, her features were soft, almost beautiful again. The ravages of bitterness and self-pity might never have been.

Elise studied her, then as shadows of the past began to dance before her eyes, she became very still. She saw Bea as she once had been: happy, smiling, unhampered...a flirt at seventeen. And she saw herself at eleven: half child, half budding young woman, who doubted herself even as she thought her sister one of the most magnificent beings in the world. Then had come a fateful Wisconsin winter, a snowfall, the gradual formation of ice....

A primitive cry sounded deep in Elise's throat as her features twisted with pain. She tried to thrust the terrible memory away. It hurt too much! She loved her sister. She didn't want anything bad to have happened to her. She didn't want to remember!

Bea's eyes opened with startling suddenness. In them, there was no question as to where she was or what was taking place. She looked directly at Elise and said, "You look like you've seen a ghost!"

Elise tried to control the trembling of her limbs. She tried to act as if nothing was wrong. But she knew that Bea could see through her performance. "No, I just— You were sleeping and I thought—"

Bea had perfected a certain smile over the years, a smile that combined innocence and raw power. It was a smile that instantly plunged Elise into distress without her being fully aware of the cause. Bea used it now. "I wasn't sleeping," she said.

"But your eyes were closed!" Elise wanted to run from the room. She always felt so exposed at these moments.

"I was resting, that's all. Are you leaving again?"

Elise rubbed a hand across her brow. Her hard-won poise had disappeared as if in a puff of smoke. The meeting was going to be a disaster. Robert Fairmont would arrive in Tyler and all her worst nightmares would come true. He would tell her that cutting costs would be impossible. That she should stay in the old library and be jolly well glad that she had it...even if the town council did dig in their heels and refuse to spend any more money on it for needed repairs. Then he would look penetratingly at her and see everything that she kept hidden inside, see her deepest thoughts and desires. See her for the fraud that she truly was! "Uh...yes," she stammered. "I have a meeting."

"With that professor?" Bea lifted an eyebrow in speculation. "The way Josephine described him, he sounds a little too hoity-toity for my taste. He must think quite a lot of himself."

"I wouldn't know," Elise murmured, glancing at the door and escape.

Bea saw the look and dismissed her angrily. "Oh, go on. Leave! You're not exactly a scintillating conversationalist anyway. Just get me a pitcher of lemonade before you go. The house is on the warm side today."

"Would you like me to switch on the air-conditioning?"

"What? And have me freeze? No, I should certainly say not. Just get me the lemonade."

Elise wished that she had never stopped to glance into the room. If Bea was quiet, she should have taken advantage of the moment and slipped silently out of the house.

While mixing her sister's refreshment, she tried to repair the damage that had been done to her assurance. But she knew the job remained only half-finished when, upon her return, Bea's sniff of disapproval still caused her pain.

ELISE SWUNG her car into the rear parking area of the library that was usually reserved for the staff. This afternoon, however, a truck was parked close to the back entrance and the whine of an electric saw could be heard coming from deep within the building. Joe Santori and his young assistant, Lars Travis, were still hard at work.

Elise set the emergency brake and stepped outside. Under the guise of adjusting the shoulder strap of her purse, she closed her eyes and took a deep breath. Then, strengthening her spine, she set off, seemingly ready for anything.

The interior of the library was divided into individual rooms, just as it had been during its occupation by the Friedrichs, the family who had once lived there. The floors were oak, buffed to a well-worn luster by the custodian, Jimmy Randolph, and in what once must have been an expensive touch, prodigious amounts of geometrically carved moldings decorated the walls, the doorways, the windows and even the bookcases that had been built into the home's private library.

Changes had been made to convert the building to public use, but most of the changes involved running electrical conduits along the floor to various work stations for the staff and filling almost all the rooms with shelves. No walls had been taken down and only a few added.

Elise hesitated in the doorway of the large front room that had served the Friedrichs as a combination living and dining room and that now served as the library's main circulation area. Her gaze swept over staff and patrons. From the calm that had descended over the facility, no one would have believed that only a short time ago the area had been involved in such chaos. Delia Mayhew was at the circulation desk checking out books, Pauline was on her way to the Children's Room, where the regularly scheduled preschool story time was due to start, and Rebecca Sinclair, new to Tyler but already a treasure as a volunteer, was wheeling a cart loaded with books to be reshelved. Several people were standing at the long card catalog, searching through the alphabetized indexes, while others sat at nearby tables with narrow catalog drawers at their elbows as they hastily jotted down information they needed.

A light frown touched Elise's brow. She had already stopped by her office, expecting to find Robert Fairmont there. Before leaving for home, she had asked the staff to keep an eye out for him, to show him into her office when he arrived and then to offer him coffee or tea or whatever else it took to keep him entertained until she returned. But he wasn't there. Her office was as empty as when she left it.

She caught Delia's eye and lifted her eyebrows in puzzlement. Delia immediately glanced toward the card catalog, causing Elise to examine that area again. And sure enough, there he was, standing beside the massive file, gazing back at her with such knowing amusement that Elise felt her whole body burn with embarrassment. Had he been there all along? How had she missed him? His smile grew, as if he were privy to those thoughts as well!

Elise struggled to control her reaction. She had to deal with this man, talk with him intelligently. She couldn't afford to let him see that he unsettled her so badly. It was all in her mind, she told herself. Only in her mind!

He came toward her and stopped a short pace away. "Elise," he said. His voice was simultaneously honey and fire.

Elise glanced at Delia for help, but Delia was talking to two of Britt Hansen's children as she began the process of checking out their books. Elise's gaze was drawn back to the professor.

He was dressed impeccably in light gray pants and a charcoal blazer with a stylish tie brightening his white shirt. His hair was brushed perfectly into place, full and thick and wavy, the threads of silver shining splendidly among the dark. His skin was still nicely tanned, the lines on his face lending a distinguished aura of wisdom and experience.

She smiled tightly. "I'm—I'm sorry I'm late again. Things are still, well . . ."

"I stopped by the room with the leak earlier. It looks as if everything is coming along nicely there at least."

Elise was glad to have something to talk about. "Ahead of schedule, actually. The men weren't supposed to come until next week."

"Surely that's good news."

"Oh, yes! Definitely! At the moment I'll take anything that looks like good news. It's been such a..." She could hear herself continue to blather on about the problems she had faced over the past few days. Her words seemed to go on and on, and she couldn't make them stop.

When there was the slightest pause in her monologue, he broke in . . . which only heightened Elise's embarrassment at her behavior. She never talked endlessly like that! If there was one person in Tyler in control of her tongue, she was it! Still, he'd almost had to physically restrain her in order to insert a word.

"I think we can do it," he said simply, delivering his verdict without aggrandizement.

Elise blinked. At first her mind didn't register what he'd said. "Do what?" she asked.

His smile returned. "The library. It's going to take some work. We'll have to go over everything to see exactly what you need and what you don't need. See where we can cut corners. But I don't see why it can't be done."

For the moment Elise forgot everything but her joy at his words. Happiness lighted her eyes and her face, making them glow. "You're willing to try?" she exclaimed.

"If you are," he agreed.

She would put in as many hours as were needed. Exist on two hours of sleep each night. Do whatever was necessary to...

"Elise?" The voice calling her name was different. Male, but definitely not belonging to Robert Fairmont.

Elise turned to see Joe Santori standing beside them, dust from the gypsum board he had been using to repair the ceiling clinging to his skin and clothing even though it was evident he'd tried to brush himself off. Elise felt as if she had been shaken from a dream again, only this time a good one. "Yes, Joe?" she asked. "Is there a problem?"

Joe shifted uncomfortably from foot to foot. He was a large man, well-built, with curly black hair and a quiet pride in his work. "Well, yes. We've hit a little snag." He hesitated. "Water's starting to show up again. Not much," he was quick to add when he saw Elise blanch, "just a few drops. But the quicker we get Mike McNamara back out here, the better it will be. We sure can't close her up as it is."

Elise stood very still, then she felt herself start to sway. The soft background noises in the library receded into a hollow hum and Joe's face blurred. Over a sudden tightness in her throat, she managed to say, "Would—would you mind calling him, Joe? Right now... I just can't..." Fingers reached out to steady her, pulling her against a solid strength.

Joe stepped forward in concern, guilt flashing over his features.

Elise wanted to tell him that everything was all right, that what was happening wasn't his fault. It wasn't *anyone's* fault, except possibly her own. She had been pushing too hard and not eating properly, and now she was paying the price. Not that she wouldn't mind a temporary respite from her problems. To get completely away, to have a few moments of unadulterated peace... that seemed the most wonderful bliss. Though she felt bad when she saw Joe's worried look. And when she turned to see that it was Robert Fairmont she leaned against so contentedly, she felt even worse.

She longed for unconsciousness, but it never came... which in a rather pathetic sort of way was funny. She was too responsible even to faint properly!

With her thoughts still slightly fuzzy, she met the gaze of the architect. In his eyes she saw concern, but also something else: his recognition that a part of her wanted to laugh! Surprise made him blink, then answering amusement sparked in his unusual eyes.

A smile tugged at Elise's lips and, unable to help herself, she started to giggle, which caused Joe to completely misread the situation. Thinking that she was crying, he called out to Delia, who, when she saw that Elise looked near to collapse, abandoned the circulation desk and came running toward them. A few patrons rushed over as well.

"Does she need a doctor?" someone asked.

"Is it a heart attack?" someone else queried.

"Oh, my God!" Delia cried.

"Water started to drip from the ceiling again," Joe explained to the audience at large. "I *had* to tell her."

Elise choked. "Joe, it's okay. I just forgot to eat lunch, that's all." Then her face crumpled into laughter again, which the crowd mistook for pain. The whole situation was just too much! One misunderstanding followed another.

A hand came out to shield her face, turning it in to the fine woolen material of a blazer. "I think she just needs some time alone," Robert Fairmont said quietly but with dignified authority.

Pauline rushed up, called away from the children by someone who had witnessed the scene. Her round face was pallid, full of fear. "What's happened?" she demanded. "What's wrong? Elise?"

Robert swept Elise fully into his arms. She kept her face buried against his shoulder. Suddenly she wanted to cry. Laughter had evolved into tears.

"I'm taking her home. She needs to rest," he said. He turned to Joe Santori. "Why don't you call her later this afternoon to let her know what the plumber says. I'm sure she'll want to know." Joe nodded agreement.

Elise took a series of unsteady breaths as she felt herself being transported through the front door and onto the porch, then along the sidewalk to the line of parking slots that angled off the street. She peeked around the architect's shoulder and saw that the little group of concerned people had followed them onto the porch. They watched as he placed her feet on the ground and dug in his pocket for the keys to a dark blue Mercedes.

He opened the door and bent to lift her inside, but she stopped him.

"I can get in myself," she said.

He pulled back to look at her. "Are you sure?" he asked.

She nodded wordlessly.

He stood back, ready to lend assistance if needed. But it wasn't needed . . . not this time. While crossing to the driver's side, he waved to the small crowd and called out something, something she didn't understand.

She watched as he slid behind the wheel, secured her seat belt and his own, then brought the engine to life. The car smelled of leather and a good men's cologne, and its engine purred with understated power and efficiency.

Certainly this wasn't the way she had expected to leave the library today!

CHAPTER THREE

"WHAT DID YOU SAY to them?" she asked.

"I told them you were better. There's no use in them continuing to worry."

"Thank you," she said simply.

He shifted position. Obviously his intention was to look over his shoulder and reverse out of the parking slot, but he stopped short to look at her. The shiny buttons of his blazer had been set free and the material spread to show that no spare flesh hung over his belt when he sat down. The belt itself was of high-quality leather, black, matching his shoes. The creases in his slacks were precise, disappearing only along the hard muscles of his thighs.

Elise's gaze whipped away. She wasn't accustomed to examining men so closely. Particularly men whose masculinity vibrated forcefully in the air around them.

"You are, aren't you?" he asked.

Elise had to search for his meaning. Finally she connected it to his earlier assurance to the crowd. She nodded tightly. "Oh, yes. I'm fine." Yet her hands twisted in her lap and her body was as taut as an overstrung bow. He continued to watch her. Unable to stand it any longer, she at last demanded, "What is it? Why are we still sitting here? I thought you said you were going to take me home."

She knew she sounded the exact stereotype of a spinster librarian who found herself in close confines with an attractive, eligible male. Instinctively, her gaze shot to his left hand. He wore no ring, but that didn't signify anything. Any number of married men didn't wear rings anymore.

He smiled and she twitched uncomfortably in her seat. Had he seen her quick glance at his hand? Elise wanted to leap out of the car, but her legs felt like twin weights. They didn't want to move.

"Well, I was," he explained drolly, "but I don't know where 'home' is. Would you like to direct me?"

Elise bit her bottom lip. "Go down this street to the right. Turn left, then left again after the fourth stop sign."

"It's all right, you know," he said calmly, not having moved.

"What is?" she asked. She didn't want to look at him anymore or talk to him. She just wanted to go home, go upstairs and stretch out in her bed. Maybe she *had* pushed herself a bit too far.

"To laugh when everything seems darkest. Sometimes it's the only thing a person can do to protect his sanity." He shifted the car into reverse and backed into the street.

There was a great difference between riding in a Mercedes and riding in her Escort. Bumps in the road were barely noticeable. Trees and grass and houses seemed to glide by in a haze of comfort. He took the first turn smoothly, effortlessly. But instead of relaxing, Elise grew more tense. Ultimately she burst out, "I shouldn't be doing this! I'm needed at the library. And my car! What am I going to do about my car? I'll need it later."

"Can't someone at the library drop it off for you?" he asked.

"I can't ask anyone to do that! No, this is silly. Take me back, please."

He glanced at her. "They won't be happy to see you return so soon. They were ready to call an ambulance."

"But you know I wasn't that bad!"

"I do, yes. But they don't. If you go back now, they'll worry. They'll watch you, dissect your every move. Is that what you want?" When she didn't answer, he continued, "Tell you what. Why don't you take off a couple of hours. Get some rest. Satisfy everyone. Then I'll take you back to the library myself."

"I still don't think . . ."

"It won't fall down without you, you know. Contrary to popular belief, the building looks fairly sturdy. And even if you were there and it did fall down, would you be able to hold it up all by yourself?"

"You're making fun of me!" she accused.

He glanced away from the street. "Not really."

The Mercedes slid to a halt at the final stop sign before making the next left. Elise wanted to continue to argue, but held her tongue as she reluctantly admitted that what he said was true. Everyone *would* watch her, waiting to see if she might weaken again. And she would hate that, even if it was done in the name of caring. Also, there was the concept of living to fight another day. Maybe, just this once, she should take a little time to gather her strength so that she could deal with all the difficulties that were to follow...which included her meetings with this architect! It was apparent that she was going to need every bit of energy she could muster.

"TURN RIGHT at the next corner," Elise said, continuing her instructions.

Her voice held a musical quality even as she perched stiffly on the seat next to him. Robert did as she requested, steering the car onto a street of houses that looked to have been built sometime between the two great wars. None contained any unique architectural features; they were purely utilitarian, built for growing families. Wide yards, aged trees, sidewalks that could use some repair. Upkeep on most houses was ongoing. A few needed work.

"It's the first house on the left," she said.

Robert turned into the narrow driveway. He cut the engine and turned slightly toward her. He still wasn't completely sure she was as all right as she claimed. She was so thin...fragile looking. He could easily encompass her wrist between his middle finger and thumb with room to spare! Her short hair, lightly curling, changed from blond to silver depending upon the angle and degree of light. Her naturally pale skin held the lightest trace of a summer tan. Carved, delicate features, a long, graceful neck, a narrow waist.... He could only guess at her age, but he'd estimate late forties, early fifties. Her face had a quality that youth didn't know...of numerous challenges won and lost and, as well, a haunting shadow of pain deeply held.

"Thank you for bringing me home," she murmured, remaining stiff and formal in her manner even as she reached for the door handle.

"I'll see you inside," he offered.

"That's not necessary." She threw him a look from pale blue eyes that exactly matched the suit she wore. The look bade him not to press. But it also showed him her uncertainty. She didn't know what to do with him! Twice they'd arranged to meet to discuss the new library and twice some outside event had gotten in the way. She couldn't ask him into the house to work because she knew he wouldn't agree to do so. Also, she was irritated with him because he had advised her to rest . . . something she obviously didn't do a great deal. But she couldn't just dismiss him. She needed him. So there she was, in a quandary. He tried to ease the situation for her. She'd already been through enough.

"I have friends who live on Lake Geneva. They've told me to stop by any time I'm in the area. Why don't I go visit them for a couple of hours, then I'll swing back by here and take you to the library. We can talk after that. It shouldn't take long today. Just a few preliminaries."

He'd wanted to do a lot more than that. He'd wanted to dig right in and feel out where she stood on a number of necessary changes. He already had a few proposals in mind. But looking into that pale face and seeing the edge of tiredness she couldn't disguise made him willing to wait.

"Why just a few preliminaries?" she questioned, latching on to the key word. "I'd rather get on with this, wouldn't you? Progress as far as we can."

"Well, because . . ."

"I'm perfectly all right!" she insisted. "I simply forgot to eat lunch, that's all. Then when Joe said what he did . . . I had a perfect right to be upset! Joe knew it. That's why he didn't want to tell me."

"Do you faint every time you get upset?"

"I didn't faint!"

"You came close to it."

"But I didn't actually faint!" Her denial was low and surprisingly fierce. She took a breath. "You've said you think we can make this new library work. I'm going to hold you to that, Mr. Fairmont. I'm willing to put in whatever amount of time it takes. You should be, too."

"That's what an architect does, Miss—"

"Good. Now, you go visit your friends. I think that's an excellent idea. Then come back and we'll get started on the plans."

Robert continued to look at her, a smile pulling at his lips. She might appear to be fragile, but he could see that she was a force to be reckoned with when she spoke on behalf of the library. It might have been her child, a living, breathing entity she would give her all to protect. Attack it and you attacked her.

"Whatever you say," he murmured dryly.

Her cheeks took on a rosy hue and she quickly let herself out of the car. He watched as she walked, her back straight, to the tiny porch that fronted the house, then she disappeared inside.

Robert's gaze stayed on the door for a moment before moving away. Her house was one of the more neatly kept homes on the block. The white paint was fresh, the shrubs trimmed and numerous flowers bloomed in their beds. The look was pleasing to the eye.

He restarted the car. If he was going to stop in on Harry and June, he needed to find a telephone. Not that he wouldn't enjoy a simple ride in the country if they weren't at home. But he felt he should give them ample warning. He backed out of the drive, and after another glance at the unprepossessing house Elise lived in, accelerated down the street.

ROBERT TURNED AWAY from the pay phone at the service station. His friends were at home and had begged him to visit. It was months since they'd heard from him, they'd complained. And they were right. During term, there was always so much to do in the design studio, working with his students, challenging them to grow and to see beyond what was expected. Students of architecture, particularly during the last weeks of a semester, were some of the most overworked scholars on campus. Some practically lived in the studio in order to meet their deadlines. Accordingly, their teachers devoted long hours to the subject as well—a fact that Robert wouldn't change. He loved working with his students, conveying knowledge and receiving in turn intellectual stimulation.

Yet between his work at the university and his work with the firm, little time was left to keep up social obligations. Friends sometimes became lost in the shuffle. Which was one of the reasons why he had never married. He didn't feel his life-style would be fair to a wife. He had heeded perhaps a little too well the advice of an admired professor—that an architect should never encumber himself prematurely with outside obligations. Translated, that meant a wife, children and a mortgage. Not if the architect intended to travel extensively or to immerse himself in all the work involved in starting his own practice. It was advice he himself had given students over the years, advice that he still believed. Only sometimes did he wonder if he might have carried it a little too far.

Robert shrugged the thought away. He paid for the gasoline that had been pumped into his car and set off along the highway that would take him to Lake Geneva. But instead of looking forward to the enjoyment he would soon experience upon seeing his old friends, he found his thoughts returning to the Tyler library. Not the new one. The old one.

Robert had loved old buildings all his life, particularly old homes. To him, they were the key to another age—an age that in many ways was much more graceful than the present. As a child, he had lived in just such a house, creating fantasy worlds from basement to attic. He had always dreamed of owning one himself, but as the years passed, his dream faded. Still, he loved to look at such structures and to poke around in them when given the chance.

His business in Tyler afforded just such an opportunity. The old library, though decried by its users, was interesting to him. His guess was that it had been built at or near the turn of the century, and judging from the exterior and interior style, influenced by the revolution in architecture that had taken place around that time. It was the period when fellow Wisconsinite Frank Lloyd

Wright had begun to evolve the personal style that so greatly influenced twentieth-century architecture.

Robert's two short investigations of the building had whetted his appetite to see more. Both times he'd been distracted by other things: the water damage to the books, his second appointment with the librarian. He wanted more time to look around. And he saw no reason why, as he worked closely with Elise Ferguson, he couldn't take it.

THE DOORBELL RANG and Elise went to answer it. Butterflies were aflight in her stomach. The fluttering increased when she saw that Robert Fairmont stood on the porch. She'd known all along it would be him, but reality seemed more potent than her thoughts.

"Hello," she said, striving to keep her voice circum-spect.

"Hello," he returned, a smile both in his eyes and on his lips.

She stepped back, wordlessly inviting him inside. He moved past her into the formal front room. She saw his gaze quickly take in his surroundings—the heavy furniture and curtains, the ornate rug. Repeatedly over the years since their parents' death Elise had wanted to redecorate, but Bea had stayed her hand. Bea didn't welcome change. She wanted everything to remain as it was, no matter how out-of-date or ungainly.

Elise cleared her throat. "You, uh, saw your friends?"

"Yes. You look . . . rested."

Elise shifted uneasily. She wanted to tell him about the numerous telephone calls she'd received from people who wanted to know how she felt. They'd come from patrons who had been at the library, from the library staff, from people who hadn't been there but who had heard the news through Tyler's lightning-quick grapevine. In fact, she'd spent more time on the phone reassuring everyone than she had doing anything else. But she couldn't make herself tell him. Having him inside her home completely unnerved her. Turned her into the equivalent of a tongue-tied sixteen-year-old.

"Elise! Elise!" Bea's irritated repetition of her name came just before she wheeled into the room. When she saw Robert Fairmont, she came to an abrupt stop. "Who are you?" she demanded, looking him up and down. She didn't seem particularly pleased with what she saw.

Elise hurried into speech. "Bea, this is Robert Fairmont, the architect who's going to help us with the library. I've told you about him, remember?" She hated to think what her sister might say. With Bea, you never knew. "Professor Fairmont...my sister, Bea."

Robert Fairmont moved closer to Bea and held out his hand. "Call me Robert," he offered.

Bea looked at his hand as if it contained poison. "Yes," she said tartly. "I know who you are."

Robert let his hand fall slowly back to his side.

An awkward moment passed before Bea turned her attention to Elise. "Elise, I want you to take that darned telephone off the hook! It's rung every few minutes all afternoon. I can't rest, I can't think. If it rings again, it's going to drive me mad!"

To emphasize her point, the telephone rang that very moment. Bea groaned while Elise dashed to answer it.

Only a part of Elise's attention was devoted to the caller, however, as she continued to listen to the conversation that took place between her sister and Robert Fairmont.

"Elise gave everyone a fright today," she heard him say. "People are concerned about her."

"I don't see why," Bea replied grumpily. "She's as strong as an ox."

"It seems she's been under a lot of strain recently."

Bea cocked her head to one side. "Are you trying to tell me you know my sister better than I do? You may be a fine-and-fancy architect in the town you come from, but I guarantee that you don't know a thing about..."

Elise hurriedly broke off with the caller, saying, "I'm perfectly fine, really. In fact, I'm going back to the library this afternoon. Listen, Annabelle, I really do have to go. Do you mind if I...?" She murmured a couple of polite yeses and hung up. Then she moved quickly back across the room. "That was Annabelle," she said to Bea, hoping to break the tension that existed between her sister and Robert Fairmont. She knew all the signals for when Bea didn't like someone, and those flags were flying at full mast. "Our postmistress," she explained to Robert. "She just wanted to see how I was." The words she had been unable to find earlier now rushed out of her in a whirl. "She heard it from someone who came into the post office. They'd heard it from someone who heard it from someone else who had been in the library. It's truly amazing. I think I've had a call from almost everyone in town!"

Robert's gaze traveled from Bea to her. Elise couldn't tell what he thought. Then a smile slowly lightened his features. "You're a very lucky woman," he said, "to have so many people care about you."

Elise surrendered to the charm of his smile, but Bea seemed totally immune. She harrumphed crossly, "They're all a bunch of silly people who don't have anything better to do with their time."

Elise was embarrassed by Bea's hateful demeanor. The inhabitants of Tyler knew her; they were accustomed to her sharp tongue. But Robert Fairmont was a guest in their town, in their home. He wouldn't understand. "Maybe we should go back to the library," she suggested. "I truly would like to show everyone that I'm—"

"It was my understanding that you were home for the day!" Bea snapped, interrupting her.

"No, Bea," Elise explained. "I told you I was going back."

"Because of *him?*" Bea glanced spitefully at the professor.

"No, because I have to. I have work to do, Bea. You know that."

"But you almost fainted. What if you do it again?"

Elise knew that Bea wasn't voicing concern for her well-being. In her own way her sister loved her, but it wasn't in Bea to think of another person first. Particularly not Elise.

"Then I'll sit down and wait for it to be over!" Elise returned shortly. She took a bracing breath. "I'll be home no later than six-thirty. I promise."

She reached for her purse, glad of her forethought in setting it near the door. Then she turned to Robert. "Are you ready?" she asked with brittle control.

Robert nodded, but before moving away, he addressed Bea. "It was nice to meet you. Maybe next time it will be under better circumstances." He was making an excuse for her ill humor.

Bea snapped. "I don't see any reason why there should *be* a next time."

Pain filled Elise's heart as she wondered what Bea's life, not to mention her own, would have been like if Bea hadn't fallen on the icy steps. Blindly, she walked toward the door. Robert was just behind her and, sensing her need, he reached out to lightly touch her back, guiding her toward the exit.

Gratitude instantly took the place of pain, and not even Bea's acerbic reminder, "Six-thirty, Elise!" could steal away the warmth that temporarily surrounded her being.

BEA SAT ALONE in the house, grumbling to herself. She was always alone, or so it seemed. She should be used to it. But it didn't make the hours pass any faster. In Elise's opinion, as long as she had her television and her books, her magazines and her dolls, she would be all right. Then Elise could go out into the world with a free conscience and not have to think about her. Leave her all alone except for the marmalade cat...who at present wasn't anywhere to be seen.

"Buttercup!" Bea called, snapping her fingers near the floor. "Come to Bea, Buttercup!" she called again, but it did no good. The silly cat was sleeping somewhere, probably somewhere that she shouldn't.

Bea straightened, drawing her hand back into her lap. She sighed and looked at the closed front door. Her eyes narrowed. She didn't like that man. Not one little bit. She knew danger when she saw it, and he was definitely danger! Elise practically quivered every time he looked at her. She might not be completely aware of it herself, but Bea was.

Her mind went back to another man, years before, who had come calling on Elise. Elise had been twenty...no, nineteen. How many years ago was that? Thirty-four. *My God,* Bea thought dully. That meant she'd been in this chair for... Bea let her chin drop. *Forty-two years!*

A moment later she lifted her hands to examine them. The fingers were still long and narrow, tapering to delicate oval nails at the tips. But the skin had lost a great deal of its elasticity and age spots had begun to appear.

Her lips tightened. She was growing old. And what did she have to show for it? Nothing.

With a strength of purpose that would have surprised Elise had she been there, Bea pushed her chair over to the hall mirror, where she arranged herself in the best possible light. What she saw reflected was a drab-looking woman shrunk into an invalid's chair. Dried-up; prune-faced. She tried to smile, but the muscles protested and her effort came off as more of a leer. She moved impatiently away.

No, she didn't like that man, that fancy architecture professor. She didn't like the way he looked at her, or the way he looked at Elise...which were two entirely different matters. Bea would have to be vigilant if she didn't want to be left alone. Would have to watch Elise for any threatening signs.

Buttercup sidled up to the chair and, purring, rubbed her yellow side along the rubber rim of the right wheel.

"Ah! So there you are!" Bea exclaimed. She reached down to scoop the cat onto her lap. Buttercup responded by arching her back. "Yes," Bea said a few moments later, still absently stroking a silky neck. "I must be extremely watchful."

THE MERCEDES DIDN'T SEEM nearly as alien as it had on her previous ride. Still, Elise could not relax. She glanced at Robert Fairmont as he competently negotiated the Tyler streets. He didn't look in the least disturbed, but she was. Bea's rudeness had been unforgivable. She tried to apologize.

"I'm sorry that Bea... She didn't really mean..." Elise took a breath and started over. "Bea can be extremely difficult at times."

Robert glanced at her. "There's no need to apologize."

Elise shook her head. "No, I believe there is. She says things, does things. I understand because I live with her. But she forgets that other people *don't* understand."

"Has she been in a wheelchair long?"

"Most of her life."

Robert was silent. Elise knew that her answer had abolished another excuse. A person unused to physical impairment could be forgiven for lashing out. Bea didn't have that defense.

Elise's hands tightened in her lap. "I can't blame her, though. If it were me..."

How many times over the years had she wished that it *had* been her instead of Bea who had fallen on the steps? Even now she wished that she could trade places with her. Of course, she doubted that Bea would have cared for her in quite the same way. She'd probably be a resident of Worthington House now, possibly even placed in the skilled-care facility. She'd *be* one of the people she brought books to on a weekly basis. There would be no library as she knew it....

A light touch brought Elise from her reverie. She jumped, blinking.

Robert smiled. "You were a thousand miles away," he said, replacing his hand on the steering wheel.

Elise hadn't meant to woolgather. She resumed her apology. "I just wanted you to know that it wasn't anything personal. Bea's just...like that." Yet Elise was afraid that it was very much personal. Bea disliked certain people more than others. Her reasoning was a mystery.

"It didn't bother me," he said firmly.

Elise sighed.

Soon the library came into view. Several cars were parked out front. Robert maneuvered the Mercedes into a slot next to a pickup. When they got out, instead of immediately coming to join Elise on the sidewalk, Robert opened the back door of the car and leaned inside to extract a long tube from the back seat. Elise knew what it contained: the plans for the new library.

He closed the door and walked up to her. Jiggling the tube, he said, "If you're not up to this, say so. And any time you get tired, say so as well."

"I'm perfectly—"

"—All right. I know. But it sounds as if this town tried to kill you with kindness when you were supposed to be resting. You're little better off now than you were earlier. Except maybe you've eaten. You have eaten, haven't you?"

Elise nodded as she fell into step at his side. She was very much aware of him. Aware of how handsome he was, of the lean vitality of his body, of the power of his personality. It felt good to be walking next to him; it felt good that he seemed to care about her well-being.

"I forgot to ask," he said as they started up the library's front steps. "Did you hear anything more about the leak?"

"Joe said the plumber would come right away. Hopefully, he's been and gone. That way Joe can finish. Otherwise, it could take weeks."

"And you need the room."

"We always need the room."

Pauline was the first to see them. She looked up from a stack of returned books and quickly came to take Elise's hand. "Are you sure you should be doing this?" she asked. "I know what you said, but this has been such a hard week . . . for everyone, but for you in particular." She turned to Robert. "Elise is one of our town treasures. We don't quite know how we'd get along without her. The library would collapse—that's a fact!"

"Of course I'm sure," Elise answered brusquely. Pauline made her sound like a monument, like something pigeons sat on! Which wasn't a description she wanted Robert Fairmont to remember when he...if he!...ever thought of her. "How is Joe getting along?" she asked, to deflect any further unfortunate comments. "Have you checked recently?"

Pauline shook her head as Delia rushed over.

"Oh, Elise!" It was obvious Delia had found another cause for excitement. "We were all so worried, even after Pauline called you. We thought about calling Dr. Baron, but we decided not to."

Jeffrey Baron was the only grandson of Judson Ingalls, the most prominent man in Tyler, and the great-grandson of Alberta Ingalls, for whom the library was named. He also happened to be Elise's doctor.

"Thank heaven for that, at least," Elise murmured. She indicated Robert. "Would one of you please show Professor Fairmont to my office? I think I should check with Joe myself. I—I won't be long." The assurance had been directed to Robert, but she didn't look at him.

She felt ridiculous as she hurried off toward the Biography Room. He knew what she was doing, of course. Running away. But she wasn't accustomed to such overpowering attention. Even warned to expect it, she found it hard to take. She had merely come close to passing out, for heaven's sake. She hadn't actually done it. Neither had she expired! Yet from the way everyone behaved, it was as if they expected her to correct that particular oversight at any given moment!

She moved briskly into the work area, not pausing even when she came upon the soft canvas tarps that had been spread over much of the floor and draped over the built-in bookcases along the walls. The hole in the ceiling was larger than ever, but the edges were cut smooth in preparation for repair.

As was his habit, Joe sang snatches of an opera as he worked, but he stopped the instant he saw Elise. From the look of concern that instantly clouded his handsome features, Elise knew he was about to question her precipitate decision to return to work, so she quickly deflected him by saying, "I take it the plumber has already been here?" She held her shoulders straight, her chin high. She wanted to look her usual efficient self. She nodded to Lars, who had pulled off his hat and now held it rather self-consciously in front of his gangly, adolescent body.

Joe blinked and swallowed the words he had been about to say. "Uh—yes. He, uh...he says everything is fine as far as he can tell. It was a leak along the same pipe, at another joint. He replaced that bit and checked the fittings as far as he could. He didn't see any other problems, but he says he can't guarantee a thing. The system's so old."

The plumber had said almost those exact words to Elise when she'd called to thank him for coming out to fix the first leak. Yet she hadn't expected trouble again so quickly. She moved closer to the hole and peered up, then backed away. "Do you think you'll be finished today?" she asked.

"Sure thing," Joe said. "Except for the paint. I'll stop by tomorrow and take care of that."

Elise frowned. "Don't you normally take Saturdays off? I'm sure I remember Susannah saying that you and she and Gina were going to do something special."

He grinned. "This won't take half an hour. Then it will be done and you won't have to worry anymore."

Confronted with Joe's noble effort to ease her way, Elise could not show misgivings. She smiled brightly, just as he wanted her to. But as she left the room to return to her office, her cheerful smile crumbled. It would take a great deal more than a half hour's worth of paint to fix everything she had to worry about.

CHAPTER FOUR

"THERE ARE TWO WAYS to cut costs," Robert said as he and Elise studied the plans. "We can make the library smaller, reduce the overall size. Or we can downscale the quality of the materials we use. I recommend we try a combination of the two." He had thrown his jacket over the arm of her chair, his only concession to comfort.

The set of blueprints unrolled on Elise's cleared desk was an exact copy of the set the town council had on file. Elise knew almost every line by heart from her work with the other architect for the better part of three years.

She tilted her head, frowning. "I'm not sure what you mean by 'downscale the quality.' How? What do you mean?"

Robert grinned. "It's the difference between a gold toilet seat and a brass one. Does it really make any difference to the user?"

Elise stared at him, then she, too, started to grin.

He continued. "I'm exaggerating, but you see what I mean. Your town council went first class on this structure...which is fine. People want to be proud of their public buildings, which they think reflect the community. Chambers of Commerce love this atti-tude. They put pictures of first-class buildings in all their brochures to get people to visit here, to move here. *Look! See what a progressive place Tyler is? Look at the new library we've built ourselves. Gold toilet seats!"*

Elise started to giggle.

Robert's eyes twinkled. "There are *degrees* of quality. My job is to help you decide just exactly how much quality you want and can afford and where you want to put it." He turned to a booklet of photocopied specifications. "For example, these windows. This particular brand costs a small fortune. There's no reason why something less expensive can't work equally as well. And these crown moldings. Same thing. I know where we can find something just as good for a lot less. Then we get to the library plan itself...." He looked at her. "See what I mean?"

Elise nodded.

He went on, "There's a lot of space here that's wasted. I know!" He raised a hand as if to ward off attack. "But there is. When you have lots of money, space is wonderful. When you don't..."

Elise saw herself sitting in a brand-new library with barely enough room to turn around. She protested, "But we have to have space. Patrons need to feel they have room to breathe, not to mention the staff! And the books...do you know books need air, too?"

Robert nodded. "As a matter of fact, I do. I also know you followed all the standards for library design, and I'm not talking about cutting anything there. I'm talking about the extras." He flipped back through the plan until he arrived at the page he wanted. "Exactly how important is this atrium?"

Elise had loved the idea of bringing the out-of-doors inside. Wide sheets of glass would seal any moisture away from the book collection, so that patrons and staff alike could be treated to more than just the odd pot plant stationed forlornly on the circulation and reference desks. Looking forward to tending the area herself, she had already started to research which plants would be better suited. She shook her head. "Not important enough to keep us from building the library."

Robert agreed. "Now, consider the curved stairway. What if, instead of having it where it is, taking up so much space...what if we move it to one side and straighten it out a bit...." While he talked, he began to make a quick succession of strokes with a red pen.

Fascinated, Elise watched as Robert's ideas were transformed into a picture. With relatively little effort, he captured the feel of the main circulation area, deleting the atrium and shifting the stairway. Then with a few additional strokes, he sketched in the work areas, the new computerized cataloging system, even a few people, one of whom was sitting at a terminal and scratching his head at the mysteries of advanced technology. The people weren't really people in the traditional sense of the word. But with a few practiced squiggles and swirls, Robert had given them life and form.

He looked up at her, his eyes dancing at his joke.

Elise didn't try to resist his charm. She was awed by both his ability and his magnetism.

"You understand that this is just one suggestion," he said. "Something to think about. Along with a few other changes, it would allow us to reduce the overall size of the building, which in turn would save money. Then, with careful downscaling..."

"Is this what you did in the other towns?" she asked. "When you helped them save their buildings?"

"It is."

Elise said slowly, "I got the impression from your associate that we couldn't spend enough money. Mr. Dupont wanted to do things even the council thought were a little..."

"An architect's job is to spend his client's money. He's an artist. He—or she—has a vision of what the structure *can* be."

"Why are you different? You have a vision, too, don't you?"

"I like to see people get what they need, what they've planned for. I like the challenge of trying to give it to them without..." He stopped.

"Without what?" she asked, interested.

Robert shrugged. "Without sacrificing either real quality or innovation." He continued, "Anyway, it's a new era now from when you started planning the library. If Fred were designing it today, the outcome would be different."

"It's too bad he's so busy these days," Elise said, keeping her gaze lowered to the plan and not meaning at all what she said. "How does he feel about you changing his work?"

Robert chuckled. "He was once a student of mine. He's used to my questioning his ideas."

There was a knock on the door and Pauline poked her head in. "Elise," she said. "The representative from

Arrow Publishing is here. She says she has an appointment."

Elise's gaze flickered to Robert. They had been having a nice conversation. She didn't want it to end.

"Do you want me to tell her to come back another day?" Pauline asked, sensing Elise's hesitation.

Elise sighed. "No. Tell her I'll be with her in..." She glanced at her watch.

Robert cut in, "We've accomplished all we can reasonably expect to today. I'll play around with this idea some more and try to work up a few others, then maybe I can come back to Tyler tomorrow to see what you think. That is, if you're free."

Besides Sunday, when the library was closed, Elise and Pauline, the library's two full-time staff members, had decided between themselves which other day they wanted free. Pauline had chosen Monday, when her husband had his regular day off from his job. Elise had reserved Saturday. That was when she did all her household shopping, cleaning and gardening. But since Joe was going to finish the repairs to the Biography Room tomorrow she could easily stop by the library for an hour or so, both to thank Joe and to meet with Robert. Bea wouldn't miss her; Saturday was the day she usually went out with friends to shop and have lunch. Friends who were also friends of Elise and knew that both sisters needed a break.

"Does eleven o'clock sound good to you?" she asked.

Robert Fairmont nodded.

Elise continued to look at him. Then something seemed to shift and she found that she couldn't look away. The two of them just stood there, gazing into each other's eyes....

Pauline cleared her throat.

Elise jumped. When she saw that Pauline was still waiting, her face flamed. What in heaven's name was happening to her? She was dependable, steady, *spinsterish* Elise! She couldn't afford to go gaga over a man, no matter how personable he was, or how good-looking!

Elise started to leave, but Robert stopped her by saying, "I was wondering. Old homes are something of a hobby of mine. Would you have any objections if I just...looked around?"

Color still tinged Elise's cheeks as her gaze slid self-consciously over him. "No, why should I? Feel free to look all you want." Then she made as dignified an exit as she could.

She was breathless once she reached the hall, which caused Pauline to view her with renewed concern. "Are you all right, Elise? You're not feeling faint again, are you? I *knew* we should have called Dr. Baron. Why don't you go see him tomorrow? Tell him what happened. Tell him that you—"

Elise broke into the cautionary advice. "The rep from Arrow. You said she was here?"

"Over there," Pauline said, pointing to a nicely groomed woman waiting near the reference desk.

Elise tried to put the past few minutes out of her mind as she went to greet the book publishing representative. Normally, she hated to spend much time with reps, who habitually thought every book on their list was desperately needed by the library and who often grew petu-

lant when she agreed to buy only a few or none at all.
At the moment, though, Elise was perfectly happy to
have the woman to talk to. Listening to a sales pitch was
immensely preferable to the painful process of examining her own motivations.

ROBERT WAS FREE to explore the old house and he did
so with enthusiasm. By dint of a well-trained eye, he
was able to ignore the changes that had been incorpo-
rated to make the structure into the town's library. He
didn't consider the shelves that filled almost every
room, the myriad posters and wall hangings. He dis-
counted the accompanying tables and chairs, the file
cabinets, the desks, the map cases, the bulletin boards.
His interest was in the structure itself. The design.

It was easy to understand why the townspeople
wanted a new building. Apart from problems with the
plumbing, the roof, out-of-date wiring and a lack of
adequate space—all complaints he had heard from the
townspeople firsthand—the interior of the building had
suffered hard times. What once must have been a
beautiful expanse of wood flooring was now worn almost bare of finish. Though evidently cleaned and
buffed with religious fervor, it no longer gleamed in
harmony with the intricately carved wooden panels and
moldings that set it off. The baseboards had also suffered over the years, from age and from a vast array of
nicks and scratches. Most walls were in desperate need
of a fresh coat of paint, while numerous old patches to
the plaster were glaringly evident. And that was just
downstairs.

Leading to the second floor, the stairway treads were badly worn and the painted banister chipped. In the upstairs hall a section of flooring bore deep scars, as if something heavy had been dragged along its surface. Doors were missing from every room, the hardware nakedly exposed on each jamb, and in several places the ceiling was discolored by water spots from recent and not so recent storms.

Yet none of this dampened Robert's growing excitement about the place. Because beneath the obvious signs of overuse, he saw—or thought he saw—something else.

Near the turn of the century, a very talented young architect from Chicago had been lucky enough to work with two of the giants of his time—initially with Louis Sullivan, the inventor of the first modern architectural style in America, and later with Frank Lloyd Wright, whose genius fired a revolution in architectural philosophy and design. After serving an apprenticeship with each master, Stephen deVille struck out on his own. His designs had proved to be highly popular, and if his life had not been cut tragically short, he might have found a place among the luminaries of American architecture. As it was, he had a small yet devoted following among modern architects who appreciated his own special brand of genius. And it was evidence of this genius that Robert thought he saw in the old Tyler library.

The distinctive vertical massing of forms within and without the structure, the openness of its interior plan, the extensive use of wood with complicated geometric patterns, the innovative application of brick and stucco—all pointed to the school of design that Stephen deVille was a part of. In particular, though, it was the small, almost whimsical touches that cried out his name. The dumbwaiter, which originally brought meals and supplies from the first level of the house to the second and which the library staff now used to transport books upstairs, was a complicated design of brass filigree that at first sight looked to be a cluster of flowers and hovering bees, and on second viewing proved to be wood nymphs dancing beneath the leering faces of satyrs. And the porcelain sink fittings in the kitchen, which were remarkably well-preserved. The cold side bore the facial likeness of a Grecian woman captured in a crescent moon, while the hot side sported the face of a bearded man within the confines of a fully rayed sun.

Robert's excitement mounted as his discoveries increased. In challenge to his theory, though, was his recognition that the house could merely be the work of an imitator. Popular artists always had imitators, and architects were no exception. A unique design idea spread upon acceptance and was repeated over and over, its reuse more an accolade to the original architect than a rip-off. A second challenge to his theory was the paucity of his knowledge. Robert knew enough about Stephen deVille to *suspect* that the house might have been his design, but he didn't know enough to be sure.

He made another sweep of the rooms, committing to a small notepad all the details he could manage. As soon as he got back to Milwaukee, he would hit the books at the university to fill in the gaps of his education.

Several times he saw people he had met during the book rescue, and he took a moment to speak with them.

Passing the room undergoing repair, he waved to Joe Santori and his helper. Then, reentering the main checkout area, he saw that Elise was still sitting at the same out-of-the-way table as she had been earlier, with the same smartly dressed woman. For a second Robert considered interrupting them, to ask Elise if she knew the name of the architect who had designed the house. Also, she looked as if she could use rescuing.

Elise looked up. Catching her eye, Robert smiled. Even though he had known her for only a short time, he could tell she wasn't interested in what the woman had to say. There was a glazed look on her face that he had frequently seen etched on the faces of students who didn't last six weeks in the architectural studies program. The subject either bored them or was too much for them.

Elise gave a mild start upon registering his gaze, then she smiled slightly in return. But it wasn't a smile of invitation. She sat very tall and straight, her slender body at forced attention. She was doing her job.

Robert decided not to intervene. One of the fruits of growing up in a household where the women were all well ahead of their time in their belief of male/female equality was that without them being fully aware of it, he and his brother had learned to negotiate the mine field of feminine thought. His sisters, his aunts, his mother... not one would sit still for any form of masculine condescension. As a result, in his adult life Robert enjoyed women; he respected them and treated them as thinking beings. He supposed that was why he got on so well with his female students. His brother managed equally well in his chosen field of gynecology.

He watched as Elise refocused her attention on her visitor. He knew it wasn't easy for her to balance all she did; the library, her home, her sister. Robert frowned. Bea . . . yes, that was her name. Talk about two completely contradictory individuals! Elise had a softness just beneath the surface of her brisk demeanor. But Bea—Bea was angry with everyone, including her sister, and she didn't mind where, when or at whom she struck out.

Robert had always prided himself on getting a quick read on people. It was an attribute that helped him in his work, both at the firm and in the studio. His reading of Bea made him feel nothing but compassion for Elise.

She looked up again and caught him still watching her. This time it was Robert who started. He hadn't realized that he'd continued to study her. He gave her a salute and turned away, anxious to be on his way. He had a lot of work to do that evening and he was more than ready to get started.

ELISE LEFT the library shortly after five-thirty, releasing it to the capable hands of her staff. She had one thing left to do before returning home—she had to stop by the church hall to check how the book drying was getting on. As Anna Kelsey had prophesied, on the evening of the book transfer Pastor Schoff had managed to obtain numerous volunteers to set up the tables and spread out the books. Some of them had even committed themselves to return several times each day for the next week to ten days, to systematically refan the dampened pages. Without their assistance, Elise and the staff would have had to handle the time-consuming chore on their own.

The low hum of a dehumidifier blended with the excited whir of numerous fans as both types of appliances worked to keep moisture-free air circulating among the books, which ranged from slightly damp along the edges to wet through and through. Each book was sitting on end, its pages spread open, allowing the paper to dry.

Two women were at the far end of the room, laboriously picking up books and riffling pages before putting them back into place. One was Anna Kelsey, the other Marie Innes, a teacher at one of Tyler's elementary schools. Both women looked up as she approached.

The warmth of Anna's smile went a long way toward lightening Elise's spirit. With her kinetic blue eyes, burnished hair and can-do attitude, Anna never let a problem linger long. In her opinion, the difficulties one encountered along life's journey were put there for the express purpose of being overcome, and she cheerfully set out to overcome them. She had been that way for as long as Elise had known her, and that had been for most of their lives.

"I should know better than to not take you at your word." Anna greeted her with a hug. "You said you were fine and here you are, looking like you meant it." An incurable romantic, she also added, "I've heard who took you home—Professor Fairmont. My, my, my! I'd faint, too, if I could be sure that he was standing nearby. *And* if I could be sure that Johnny would never hear about it." Her eyes twinkled. "On second thought, maybe I'd chance it even then!"

Marie Innes giggled. Anna turned to her. "Did you see him the other day, Marie? No? Oh, you weren't there, were you? You didn't come until later. Well, he—"

"He thinks we can save the library," Elise interrupted, hoping to stop Anna's good-natured teasing.

Her attempt was successful. Anna immediately dropped her jocular tone, her expression becoming serious. "He said that? Does he mean it?"

Elise nodded. "We started work this afternoon. He's going to expand a cost-cutting idea we discussed and bring it back tomorrow. It's going to take a bit of work to decide what we need and what we don't need, but he says it can be done."

Marie moved farther away, starting to work on another table.

"What kind of cost cutting?" Anna asked, frowning.

"Well, the atrium will probably have to go."

"Oh, Elise, no!" Anna looked at her with regret. She knew how much Elise had wanted it.

Elise shrugged. "I'd rather have a new library than flowers and plants."

"True," Anna agreed. She looked at all the drying books. "These poor babies certainly need a new home. What's the use of going to all this trouble if they're just going to get wet again?" She looked at Elise. "What did the town council say? Did Alyssa scream? She wanted that atrium almost as much as you did."

Elise grimaced. "I haven't told her yet. I thought I'd call tonight."

"Oh..." Anna sounded hesitant.

"What is it?" Elise asked, sensing that something was wrong.

"Well, it's just..." Anna glanced at Marie and lowered her voice. "All this publicity around her mother's body is upsetting her. She tries to act as if it doesn't, but it *has* to! I mean, she wouldn't be human if it didn't. I've tried to talk with her, but she just won't listen. And with all this gossip!" Anna lowered her voice even more. "Brick thinks it won't be long before the State Medical Examiner's office issues a finding about cause of death. Finally! They've certainly taken their own sweet time, even if they are understaffed and underfunded, like they claim. All these months. I ask you!"

A nephew well placed in the Tyler police department sometimes had its advantages. Brick must have leaned toward law enforcement all his life, Elise realized. As a young boy he had devoured every installment of the Hardy Boys mysteries and sometimes, secretly, a Nancy Drew or two.

"From what I hear, Judson is devastated. Poor man," Anna sighed.

Immersed in her own troubles, Elise had not paid as much attention to what was going on in town as she might have. She'd heard about the skeletal remains found on the grounds at Timberlake Lodge, and about the body having been identified as Margaret Ingalls's through her dental records. She'd also heard snatches of speculation concerning Judson's possible involvement with his wife's death. The passage of forty years had done little to erase the memories of Margaret's wanton behavior, for the stories were passed on from one generation to the next. But Elise had not taken into account the widespread repercussions in a town the size of Tyler.

She reconsidered her earlier decision. "Maybe I should wait to talk to Alyssa then. See if the atrium really has to be eliminated before I say anything. I wouldn't want to upset her even more."

Anna shook her head sadly. "I'm afraid there's not going to be a way for her to avoid being hurt."

Elise looked at her companion. Did Anna know something she wasn't saying? Or was it a feeling she had absorbed from Brick? Elise didn't ask. She had a strong suspicion that whatever the outcome, it was something she was going to hear a lot more about whether she wanted to or not. And from a number of different sources.

She glanced at her watch again and saw that the minutes had flown by. If she didn't hurry she would be late, and then Bea would be the one upset!

She broke away from the two women as quickly as she could, telling them how grateful she was for their help and how glad she was that Tyler folk knew how to pull together.

But like other small towns the world over, she thought as she raced off, Tyler enjoyed a periodic wallow in the mud. Especially when the topic of conversation was about someone who was normally beyond reproach. A pillar of the community.

Like Judson Ingalls.

Or the chief librarian . . . a woman who at fifty-three really *should* know better than to respond to the charms of a sweet-talking man.

CHAPTER FIVE

As soon as Elise turned the key in the lock, Bea was on her.

"You're late!" she accused. She was waiting in the kitchen beside the back door.

"Only five minutes," Elise defended.

"You said six-thirty!"

"It's barely that now."

Bea wheeled her chair to one side of the room, then back again. All the while she bobbed her head, as if preparing for battle. Sometimes when she acted that way she reminded Elise of an enraged parrot pacing back and forth on her perch. Elise turned to put her purse on the counter.

"Were you with him?" Bea demanded. "Is that why you're late? I saw the way you looked at him earlier. Don't think I didn't! It was just the same as when that Kenneth Faraday used to come around. And look what happened with him!"

Any guilt Elise might have felt at the possible meanness of her thoughts disappeared with Bea's words. She whirled back around, her expression wounded.

"Exactly the same!" Bea continued, seeming impervious to the pain she had caused. "You two got all lovey-dovey and then he walked out on you. Treated you like you were some kind of soiled baggage that he didn't want to be bothered with anymore. I tried to tell you, remember? But you wouldn't listen to me. Oh, no! You said you *loved* him." She harrumphed. "You should have listened to me. I could have saved you a whole lot of heartache."

Elise's face felt tight as she asked, "Why are you doing this, Bea?"

Her sister glared at her. "To keep you from acting the fool again! That man is trouble, Elise. Big trouble. I have a bad feeling about him. He'll use you, just like Kenneth Faraday did, only this time it will be worse. You're not as young as you were the first time. People won't be as compassionate. They'll think you should have known what you were getting yourself into and not done it!"

"I barely know him," Elise whispered.

"Good. Keep it that way. Nip it in the bud. That's the safest way."

It hurt Elise to be reminded about Kenneth, to remember the emotional devastation she'd experienced upon finding his note. Her world had collapsed. "I'm going to change now," she said levelly. "Then I'll come down and make dinner. If you're hungrier than usual, there's some fresh cantaloupe in the refrigerator. Would you like me to get a slice for you?"

Bea shook her head and Elise turned away. As she started to leave the kitchen, Bea called after her, "He's the same kind of man, Elise. A user! He'll get on your good side, get what he wants, and then he'll walk away. Mark my words. This time, listen to me!"

Elise's steps faltered but she managed to go on. Clinging to a modicum of dignity, she didn't stop until she was in the safety of her room upstairs. Then her shoulders slumped and her hands came up to cover her face, and the tears that had wanted to fall before had free command of the moment.

THE NEXT MORNING Bea acted as if nothing had happened, as if she hadn't said what she had to Elise the previous night, bringing up past hurts and warning of future disasters. And Elise let her get away with it. Sometimes that was easier than confrontation.

Elise saw her sister off with their friends for a day of shopping, then finished getting ready herself. If she paid more attention to her grooming than usual, if the dress she wore was one of her favorites because the color and style was becoming to her, if she was more selective in her choice of scent . . . it wasn't because she was going to meet Robert Fairmont.

And if you believe that, I have a bridge I'd like to sell you! she thought dryly as she looked at herself in the mirror. Bright excitement showed in her eyes and her skin was lightly flushed. On a young girl, the look was endearing. But on someone her age . . . ?

She turned away from the reflection. Bea was right. If she continued to go on the way she was going, she would surely make a fool of herself. Nip it in the bud, that was what Bea had said. And that was exactly what she'd do. Purely as a form of self-protection.

Her resolve lasted for all of thirty minutes . . . or until, shortly after entering the library, she caught sight of

Robert Fairmont coming into the building through the main doors.

For a moment he stood still and looked around. Today he had exchanged blazer and slacks for a more casual attire, tan pants pleated fashionably at the waist and a navy shirt made of some kind of soft-looking material. Contrasting white buttons ran up the front of the shirt, and sleeves rolled to the elbow completed the look.

When he spotted her at the circulation desk, he smiled and started to walk toward her, which caused Elise's heart to jump. He looked so handsome, so assured, so... dependable.

She finished what she was doing with unsteady fingers. When he stopped across from her, she looked up.

"Good morning," he said.

"Good morning," she responded.

His gaze moved over her and Elise could hardly breathe. She was aware of her every inadequacy.

"You look very nice this morning," he said, obviously not seeing what she did. "Are you ready to go to work?"

"Certainly." She came around from behind the desk. As she did, she said to Diane Conrad, one of the library's part-time aids, "Professor Fairmont and I will be in my office if anyone needs me."

Diane, a sturdy blonde, was such a fitness freak that her idea of a good time was climbing a mountain with nothing more than a good pair of shoes and her bare fingertips. That was what she had been doing at the time of the Biography Room disaster. This was her first day back on the job.

Diane nodded, her gaze flickering over Robert. He smiled, meeting her look with such open friendliness that Diane forgot what she was doing. It took the piping voice of a disgruntled ten-year-old to bring her back to the business at hand. With cheeks coloring, she took the book the boy wanted to check out.

Elise gave her helper a sympathetic glance. She knew exactly how she felt. Sparing Diane further embarrassment, she turned to lead the way to her office.

"Did Joe finish his work?" Robert asked, catching up to her.

"Would you like to see?" she asked in return.

At his nod she veered toward the Biography Room, and after entering it, stood back so that he could inspect the results.

Robert moved about the cleared area, where only the bare shelves attached to the walls gave witness to the fact that the room was part of a library. His attention was on the freshly painted ceiling. "Very nice," he complimented. "Your Joe Santori is a good workman."

Elise was proud of the results. "If you haven't seen Timberlake Lodge yet, you should take the time during one of your trips to Tyler. Joe was the contractor in charge of the lodge's renovation. He did a beautiful job there, too."

"Timberlake Lodge?"

"It's on the lake just outside of town . . . one of the Addison chain. It's really quite nice."

Robert murmured, "They usually are."

By mutual agreement they continued to her office. Elise had already cleared her desk and Robert wordlessly covered it with a set of papers. "I took into account everything that we talked about yesterday," he said, jumping right in. "And I've come up with a more formal plan, just to see how it works. We can save ourselves a lot of money if we follow this idea along with the cost cuts we talked about."

Elise leaned forward, frowning slightly as she examined the top sheet. He had transformed his off-the-cuff sketch into a more polished rendering. Only this time there were no people displayed humorously on the page.

"I promised other ideas as well," he said, drawing out the lower sheets. "But I still believe the first layout is best."

Elise studied each of the other sheets. In one, all the rooms had been reduced in size, which spread the sacrifice around but resulted in all quarters being much too cramped. In another, the staff work area had been consolidated with shipping and receiving, the book-storage space reduced but the atrium retained. In the last, the entire second floor had been removed and though the ground level had been expanded to about a quarter more than the original size, it still resulted in an overall reduction of space.

"If we concentrate only on size reduction," Robert explained, "you're not going to like the results."

"Yes, I see what you mean," Elise said quietly. "The first plan is definitely better. But what about the foundation we already have? What will we do with it? This is smaller. Will we have to start over?"

"Foundations can be modified. It's done all the time."

Elise stood back. "We'll have to talk to the town council. Get their approval."

"I was told that you're the real person to please."

"They still have to see it," she repeated stubbornly.

Robert smiled. "Fine. I agree. Only before we do, let's see what we can do with our cost modifications. Then we can give them a clear picture of what's involved and also an estimate of the bottom line."

She tilted her head. "Speaking of bottom lines . . . I was told something about you, too. Nora Forrester said that you've refused to accept a fee. That you'll only take money for your expenses. Is that true?"

"It is."

Elise's frown deepened. "Why? Why would you do something like that? I'm sure someone as successful as you could command an astronomical fee. Why are you willing to go to all this trouble for nothing?"

Robert busied himself by rolling up the set of papers. Her questions seemed to embarrass him. "Civic duty, I suppose."

Elise wouldn't let him off the hook. "Most people today don't give a fig for civic duty. The bottom line—*their* bottom line—is what counts. What makes you so different?"

His glance showed his irritation. "Probably the same thing that makes you different! How many people are willing to devote so much of themselves to a place like this? I've seen the way people here treat you. I'm surprised they haven't commissioned a statue to be placed in your honor in front of the new library!"

"Well, maybe they should put up two!" she retorted just as smartly. "One of you and one of me. *If* the place ever gets built, that is!"

Robert's expression mirrored his surprise. Then he burst out laughing. And after a moment, Elise joined in.

Finally, still laughing, Robert assured her, "Oh, it will get built, all right. But I don't think the statues are such a good idea. Do you know what a good sculptor costs these days?"

"I couldn't begin to guess," Elise replied. "But if it's more than fifty cents, it's too much. We can't afford it!"

They shared laughter once again, then Robert said, "You, uh...suggested that I take time to see the lodge near here. How would you feel about showing it to me? We could have lunch."

The smile froze on Elise's lips even as she tried not to let that fact show. This was where she should nip any buds. But once again her determination deserted her. "That would be lovely," she heard herself say. "I'd like that very much."

Then she had to suffer the warmth of his approving smile.

TIMBERLAKE LODGE HAD once been used as a private retreat by Judson Ingalls and his family to entertain friends and business acquaintances. Set in beautiful wooded seclusion on the crest of a small hill, it claimed a spectacular view of Timber Lake. As Elise explained to Robert, it recently had been renovated before its purchase by the Addison Hotel chain.

A large wooden structure with a veranda across the whole front, it both fit into and stood out from its surroundings. On the inside, the rustic flavor continued with an abundance of wood paneling, antiques and chintzes. It seemed a world apart from the ordinary struggles of life and had proved to be a popular destination for out-of-town guests, both nowadays and in the past.

As Elise and Robert were seated in the dining room, Elise saw no familiar faces at the nearby tables. Of the twenty or so people present for lunch, all must have been either tourists or business travelers.

"Enjoy your meal, Ms. Ferguson," Timmy Smith said as he held out a chair for her. "You, too sir. Your waitress is Shirleen. She'll be with you in a moment."

The young man didn't live in Tyler but in a nearby town. Elise knew him from a high school project he had worked on, taking advantage of the Tyler library's fine collection of local histories.

Robert's gaze was amused as he looked at her. "Is there anyone in this town you *don't* know?" he asked.

Elise glanced at Timmy's retreating back. "Well, most of the guests here, actually. I don't recognize anyone."

"I didn't mean tourists."

"Well..." Elise sat tensely on the edge of her chair. "I do know almost everyone in Tyler. But it's only natural. I've lived here practically all my life. Tourists come and go, but the rest of the population remains pretty constant. People tend to stay in Tyler. We're all...very close."

"As in everyone knows what everyone else is doing? Isn't that a bit hard to live with?"

Elise shook her head. "Not really. It has its other side, too. If you're in trouble, people help. Think of all the folks who came to help out at the library. I'm sure they had other plans for the day, but they dropped them when they heard about the books."

Robert leaned back. "And how are the books coming along? Are they drying out?"

Elise nodded. "Some can be brought back to the library in the next few days. Others will take longer. We're really very lucky. None of them was submerged, just sprayed. Some more than others, of course." She frowned. "I'm still a bit worried about a few of the rarer books with coated pages, though. They're among the group we're sending to Madison—that's where the vacuum facility is located. I'm not sure if they can be saved. And it would be such a shame if we lost them. They're very old."

"The idea seems to hurt you physically."

"I love books," she answered simply.

Robert took a sip of water. "Is that what made you want to become a librarian?"

Elise's smile was dry. "I never really wanted to *be* anything. It just sort of happened. I worked at the library, first as a volunteer, then as an assistant. Then, when the chief librarian retired, everyone just assumed that I'd continue in her place. And I did. Along the way I took a lot of courses to learn more about what I was doing, and eventually earned my degrees. I still attend courses, actually. There's a lot to know about running a library."

"How long have you done this?" he asked.

Elise glanced away uncomfortably. Her answer would make her seem so old. A man like Robert Fairmont must be accustomed to sharing meals with women half her age. Beautiful women. Young and vital, with their whole lives still ahead of them. She said, "Thirty years. Twenty-five as chief librarian."

"That's a long time," he murmured.

Elise flushed lightly. "Yes."

"No wonder they all think so highly of you. The place probably *would* fall down without you."

Elise welcomed the arrival of their waitress. Robert asked if she would like a glass of wine, then refused wine himself when she replied in the negative. Under the best of conditions, Elise didn't have a good head for spirits. As giddy as she felt without the aid of alcohol, she'd probably do something completely horrific to humiliate herself if she took even a few sips.

After ordering their meal, they waited. The soft sound of conversation floated around them. For the life of her, Elise herself could think of nothing to say. Bea had warned her that she'd be playing a dangerous game if she succumbed to Robert Fairmont's charm. And here she was, succumbing. She could think of no place she'd rather be at this moment than here, with him. He wasn't the type of man Bea thought. Anyway, what did Bea know? She had barely spoken more than three sentences to him, and those had been ill-tempered.

Elise made a decision. From that moment on she would completely ignore anything that Bea had to say in regard to Robert Fairmont. She, Elise, was well into adulthood; she could make decisions for herself. She liked the visiting architectural professor and she wasn't going to shut him out just because Bea wanted her to. And if she got hurt…well, she got hurt. Still, she didn't expect the relationship between them to move beyond the scope of their work together. This lunch was just a getting-to-know-you type lunch. It meant nothing.

To him.

ROBERT WATCHED HER from across the table. She was as tightly strung as a fine violin. Her hands fidgeted first with the silverware, then with each other—long, slender, graceful fingers that ended with delicate oval nails enameled in the palest pink. The line of her fingers was a perfect match for the rest of her, which was long and slender like a delicately stemmed flower. Only she probably would resent his making such a comparison. A thread of steel ran under the deceptive fragility of her appearance. The steel of determination.

She wasn't young, but sometimes she acted young, as young as some of his students at the university. It must be because she saw the world through uncomplicated eyes. At times shy, at times courageous, she was an intriguing mix.

Robert shifted in his seat. He had told himself that he'd asked her to lunch because he wanted to question her further about the old house. But now he wasn't completely sure if that was true. Certainly, he wanted to know more about the place. Especially after his investigations in the university's library last night had made him more convinced than ever that the house had been designed by Stephen deVille. Looking at her, though— witnessing the slightly nervous way she glanced at him, the coltishness of her actions, the fine blond hair curling lightly around her face, the clearness of her cornflower-blue eyes—he just wasn't sure anymore.

He cleared his throat. "You were right. The lodge is beautiful. Joe Santori did all this himself?"

Elise seemed relieved to have something to talk about. She nodded. "He and his men. And Liza. Liza Forrester...Alyssa Baron's younger daughter and Judson Ingalls's granddaughter." She smiled faintly. "I know all the relationships must sound extremely complicated to an outsider, but it's really quite simple. The Ingalls family is one of Tyler's oldest. They were among our first settlers. And it was Judson Ingalls's mother who was responsible for Tyler having a library. She talked her son into buying the old Friedrich place and deeding it over to the town. It's named after her. She fancied herself a poet and she got tired of having to go all the way to Sugar Creek, the county seat, every time she wanted to check out a book. Anyway, Liza is married to Cliff Forrester—you probably met him at the library. A tall, dark-haired man in his late thirties, very quiet. Liza is a decorator. She did all this." Elise indicated the room around them and beyond.

"Tyler seems to have a lot of talented people."

"We do, actually. Have you heard of Renata Meyer? She's an artist who just recently moved back to Tyler from Milwaukee. She's really quite good. She's the person who thought to call Alyssa the day of the flood, when all I could do was run in circles, trying to rescue as many books as I could on my own."

"That name is familiar," Robert agreed.

"When you want something done in Tyler, you call one of the Ingalls. Judson owns Ingalls Farm and Machinery—the largest business in town. Jeffrey, Alyssa's son, is a doctor, and her other daughter, Amanda, is a lawyer. They both practice here."

"They certainly are an influential family."

Elise nodded, her expression growing serious. "They've had their share of troubles recently, though. Something that started here, actually. At the lodge."

Robert noticed that as she talked about the town and its inhabitants, she seemed to relax. She wasn't nearly as tense.

She looked back over her shoulder toward the lake, then continued. "Last fall, when Judson started renovations—before he decided to sell the place—one of Joe's men was using a backhoe to check the condition of a plumbing line out toward the lake... and he unearthed a body. I know! It sounds like a TV soap opera or a movie, but it happened. It was a skeleton, actually. The discovery made all the newspapers. I know I saw it in both the *Milwaukee Journal* and the *Milwaukee Sentinel.* I keep a file on current events in Tyler that will eventually go into the Tyler Room as part of our history. I'm sure I clipped the story from the *Sentinel.*"

"I never saw it."

"Well, it wasn't a big story... then. It grew bigger, though, when the remains were identified as those of Margaret Ingalls, Judson's wife. She disappeared about forty years ago, not long after Bea's accident. Everyone thought that she'd just run off. Things weren't exactly easy in the marriage. I remember hearing something about that myself, even though the grown-ups hushed up when any children were about. There were all kinds of rumors about Margaret and her parties. She used to have them right here, in the lodge."

"Was she murdered?" Robert asked.

"Well, she had to have been. Otherwise, how would she—"

"End up in the ground. That was a stupid question," Robert admitted wryly.

Elise barely noticed his interruption. "No one knows how it happened or why. But again, there are a lot of rumors. Some people think that Judson may have—" Abruptly, she stopped talking.

Robert prompted her. "Go on." He was caught up in her telling of the story.

She shook her head. "No. I don't believe it for a moment. I think it's more likely that Margaret was having one of her famous parties, someone got her alone and went berserk. Stranger things have happened. And all along poor Judson thought that she'd abandoned him. Alyssa was only seven at the time. She grew up thinking she'd been abandoned, too. It's no wonder that she—" Again Elise stopped short.

Robert looked at her curiously. "That she...what?"

Elise shook her head again. "I don't like gossip. I think it hurts everyone it touches."

"You weren't gossiping," he said.

Blue eyes met his fiercely. "I know what I was doing. It's one thing to tell a story that's part of the public record. But it's not right to speculate."

"To speculate is human."

"Please don't make excuses."

At that moment the waitress arrived with their meal. The young woman arranged their plates in front of them and withdrew. Elise didn't make a move for her napkin or silverware and Robert sought to ease her conscience.

Casually flicking his napkin onto his lap, he said, "What happened here has an odd similarity to something that happened not too far away. Only in this instance it was readily apparent 'who done it.' It was at Taliesin, Frank Lloyd Wright's encampment at Spring Green. Have you ever been there?" he asked.

"No."

"Well, it's a huge place. A country estate. There's a house and a design workshop, kept just the way the great man left it. Wright originally built it for himself and his mistress shortly after the turn of the century...after he abandoned his wife of twenty years and his six children in Chicago, and the mistress left her husband for him as well. A few years later, while Wright was away at a construction site, a madman killed his mistress and her two children, along with several other people, and then set fire to Taliesin. Burned down the house—it had to be rebuilt.

"Possibly there's a moral somewhere to unite the two cases," Robert continued. "Like in that film about marital infidelity a few years ago... the one where the other woman becomes completely unhinged because she doesn't want the affair to end. Maybe it's that it just doesn't pay to play around on your spouse."

Elise was silent. Then she asked baldly, "What about you? Are you married?"

Robert's smile was slow. "No. So you don't have to worry about an enraged mate stalking up to the table. What about you?"

She seemed surprised that he asked. "No," she said. Then she put an end to further questioning by shaking open her napkin and starting to eat.

Somewhere between their main course of trout amandine and their dessert—he chose a slice of cheesecake, and she settled on a bowl of fresh strawberries covered with light cream—Robert broached the subject that he had held in abeyance all morning.

"I've already explained that old houses are a hobby of mine. I like to look at them and wonder about the people who owned them, the people who built them." He paused. "What can you tell me about the house the library is using right now? You mentioned some people named Friedrich. Were they the original owners?"

Elise nodded, stirring a teaspoon of sugar into her coffee. "Willem Friedrich was an entrepreneur in Chicago from the late 1800s to about 1916. His company did a booming business in wagons and carriages. He even manufactured gun carriages for the military. Then, after the Great War, everything changed. People didn't want wagons and carriages anymore. They wanted automobiles. So Willem's business went bust almost overnight. Willem was born in Tyler and he'd had a home built here, so it was to Tyler that he returned, bringing his family with him."

Elise carefully placed the spoon on the saucer and took a sip of coffee. "The family had a lavish life-style in Chicago, so I doubt that any of them were ever truly happy here. Tyler never has been what could be termed scintillating, unless you count the times when Margaret Ingalls tried to liven up the place. Anyway, Willem had managed to hold on to some of his private funds, and he invested them in another venture that also went bust because demand dried up."

She smiled wryly. "I suppose you could say that poor Willem wasn't much of a visionary. He lost everything. His daughters made bad marriages and came home to live. His wife kept to herself and eventually died. Then Willem died, too. The daughters kept the house—and I use that term loosely. You should have seen the state of the place when Judson bought it! Let's just say it had seen better days. He had to make a number of repairs before the town could even begin to bring books into it."

"What happened to the daughters?" Robert asked curiously.

"One married again to someone out of state, and the other just moved away. Her two children had resettled near their father in the Upper Peninsula of Michigan and she went to live near them."

"How do you know all this?" Robert asked. "You sound like the town's curator."

Elise fiddled with the cup handle. "I suppose that's because in a way I am. History was always my favorite subject in school, and I've tried very hard to collect everything I could about the area's past, especially Tyler's."

"I've heard a lot of talk about the Tyler Room. Everyone seems very proud of it."

"Did you go inside and look at it yesterday?"

"Actually, I wasn't paying much attention to what the rooms contained," Robert had to admit.

She smiled. "I'll give you a guided tour when we get back."

"I'd like that," he said. And he was surprised at how much warmth he felt at the invitation. He had other questions to ask, many of them. But he decided not to ruin the moment by pressing too hard.

Instead, he took his first taste of cheesecake and was surprised by that as well. It was delicious!

CHAPTER SIX

ELISE FELT SATED, both in spirit and appetite. After settling down a bit, she had enjoyed her lunch with Robert Fairmont. He was an interesting person to be with, to talk to. He listened when she spoke and seemed to value what she said.

Immediately upon their return to the library, she took him upstairs to the Tyler Room. No water stains marked the ceiling of this area. If any had appeared, Elise would have spent whatever was necessary to repair that particular section of the roof, even if it had meant using her own sparse funds.

Most of the collection in this room could not be duplicated. It consisted of photographs dating back to the Civil War, diaries, archival papers and keepsakes, old civic records, spoken histories.... And even then Elise had not stopped. To her, history was an ongoing thing. For the people of tomorrow, *today* would be history. As she had told Robert earlier, she maintained a record of current events, and had been doing so for almost as long as she'd been chief librarian. Plus every book she could get her hands on that sketched the history of Wisconsin—especially southeastern Wisconsin—had a place on these shelves.

She watched as Robert examined the contents of a glass display case, where she'd put photographs of early Tyler, along with letters and business papers from some of the town's earliest pioneers. One such letter had been written by Jackie Kelsey, the Kelsey family's first ancestor in Wisconsin. It spoke of his indebtedness to Gunther Ingalls, Judson's grandfather, for all that he had done for him and his family, but went on to reiterate his determination to set off for the California gold fields where so many people were striking it rich. The letter also served as a receipt for one hundred dollars, a fortune in that day, for Jackie's half interest in the Tyler Mercantile and Feed Store, the forerunner of Ingalls F and M. That Jackie Kelsey had failed to find his fortune and had returned to Tyler a broken, bitter man was not documented there. It was common knowledge in the history of the community, but there was no proof of his failure except for his recorded presence some years later and the ever-expanding line of Kelseys that helped populate Tyler today. Another letter detailed the difficulties of a family named Kerner, long since lost to Tyler, but interesting to today's residents because Mr. Kerner had been Tyler's first teacher.

Robert studied each article, giving them his undivided attention. Then he looked up. "Amazing," he said softly.

"I change the exhibit each month to keep it fresh."

Robert nodded. He moved to the shelves that contained books on the area's history. "So, anything a person cares to know about Tyler is in this room."

"Well, not everything," Elise admitted. "There was a fire in the town hall in the 1920s, and we lost a number of records up to that point. After I started the Tyler Room, the town council decided to move the remaining early records here, thinking that this would be the best place to preserve them. They kept a copy, of course, and Sugar Creek has a record. But we have the originals."

Robert looked at her. "Actually, I was wondering who built this house. You wouldn't happen to know, would you?"

Elise was at a loss. "I wouldn't have the slightest idea," she said.

"Ah, well," he murmured.

She saw his disappointment and ventured, "Possibly you could look it up. As I said before, not all the records were lost. Is it important?"

Robert shook his head. "Not really. I was just... curious."

Elise motioned for him to follow her across the room to a tall filing cabinet, which she unlocked. "Actually, most people use the copies at the town hall whenever they have a need, but if there's a question because the copy is unclear, they come here." She brought out several large books and ledgers and placed them on a table. She opened one to expose the flowery, almost illegible script on a faintly lined page. "I don't know if there's a record of that kind of thing. The property records—recordings of deeds, changes of title—might be here, but as to who actually built the house..." She shrugged. "If you need to look further, we do have more records. They're in the other drawers, but they're not organized. Just let one of us know when you want to use them."

"You wouldn't mind if I looked for a clue?"

"Not at all. That's what a library is for."

His response was a whimsical smile. Then he surprised her by saying, "Someday I'll have to show you my world. I wonder if you'd like it?"

As he continued to look at her, Elise's giddiness returned. She knew she was probably hallucinating, making much more of the moment than was actually there, but that didn't stop her from savoring her fantasy. She didn't even try to break their locked gazes.

His smile slowly faded and the light in his unusual eyes changed, became more serious. He took a short step toward her, reaching out. But they were interrupted by the shrill laughter of two small children at play in the hallway. Robert's hand immediately fell away and Elise's resulting gasp for breath was clearly audible.

The children continued their chase until their mother caught up with them in the doorway of the Tyler Room. After issuing an admonition, she looked at Elise and apologized. "I'm so sorry, Miss Ferguson. Sometimes the twins are just too much for me. I turned my back for a second and they were gone!"

Elise could see the confusion in Miranda Sheppard's eyes. The young mother sensed that she and her children had interrupted something, but she didn't know what. Elise forced a stiff smile. "It's perfectly all right, Miranda. They didn't harm anything." After another apology, the little family moved away, the mother with a firm hold on each child's hand.

Elise busied herself by collecting the books and ledgers. She replaced them in the file drawer. "You, uh...should feel free to look at this any time you want," she said levelly. "And to explore the library as well. We—we in Tyler are going to owe a great deal to you, Professor... Robert..." She stopped. She didn't sound comfortable calling him by either name.

Robert didn't respond for a moment, then he said quietly, "I don't do what I do to make people feel indebted to me, or to gain favors. I do it because I want to, because it makes me feel good." He paused. "Elise...look at me."

The key had been in the lock for several seconds. Elise finally turned it and replaced it in her pocket. After that, she lifted her gaze.

Robert smiled, and once again she was warmed by his easy charm. "It's going to be difficult to work together if we're on edge all the time. I like you, Elise. I'll freely admit that. And I think you like me. Do you think we could agree to be friends?"

The terms *like* and *friends* could have any number of meanings. "I—I don't see why not," she said softly.

His smile broadened. "Why don't we start over?" He playfully thrust out his hand. "You call me Robert and I'll call you Elise, and we won't stand on any formalities."

Elise placed her hand shyly in his. He gave it a light squeeze and released it. Then he glanced at his watch. "I didn't mean to keep you this long. I know you're busy. But I believe it's important for people who are going to work closely together to have a chance to get to know each other first. It makes everything easier in the end." He paused. "When would be a good time for us to get together again? Do you have any free time to-morrow?''

"Tomorrow's Sunday."

"I know."

Elise thought of how she usually spent her Sundays, keeping Bea company, doing a little gardening, catching up on her reading and correspondence. Not exactly wild excitement. She'd much rather spend the day with him. "Well, the library is closed."

"I know that, too. I saw the sign out front."

Elise frowned. "But what about you? I don't want to take up all your time with work. Don't you have any previous . . . commitments?"

"Nope, not a one."

Slowly she said, "Then why don't you let me pay you back? You treated me to lunch today, I'll treat you to dinner tomorrow. Come to our house about . . ." She stopped. Bea wouldn't like having Robert to dinner. "About two o'clock," she continued, disregarding what her sister would or wouldn't like. If Bea was hateful, she and Robert would come to the library to work after they ate. Which meant that they would probably end up here.

"Two o'clock," he said. "I'll be there. Is there any-thing I can bring?"

"Only yourself . . . and the plans, of course."

Elise wondered if he saw through her subterfuge. But he was the one who had brought up the idea of working together tomorrow. All she was doing was offering the courtesy of a meal.

She glanced at her watch as well. Time had gone by much faster than she thought. Bea would be home by now, and she didn't want to keep her waiting. Bea's shopping and lunch trips usually left her in a good mood for the rest of the afternoon. Elise didn't want to do anything to set her off. Not when tomorrow was likely to prove a difficult day.

"Tomorrow then," Elise murmured.

When she started to pull away, Robert held back. "I think I'll stay here a bit longer. Look around," he murmured vaguely.

"Do you want the file unlocked?" Elise asked.

He shook his head. "Not this time. I'll just…explore some more on my own."

He looked so appealing standing there that Elise wished she could stay. But she knew she would be with him again tomorrow. She didn't care that some people might think she was rushing things. There would probably be some talk in town as soon as it was known that she had invited him to dinner. She didn't care about that, either. In her life, opportunities to bask in the attention of eligible males hadn't exactly been thick on the tree, and she wasn't going to let this one chance slip away. No matter what.

ROBERT WATCHED her leave and he wondered at the slight tug of regret that he felt. He had enjoyed being with her, enjoyed listening as she told him about the town and its people. It was obvious that she loved the place. But he didn't let himself dwell long on the matter. Almost before she had time to start down the staircase, he moved to examine the old fireplace that at some period had been closed up.

Because it was partially blocked from view by the tall filing cabinet, he had missed it during his previous foray into the house's design. Also, he had been excited about his dumbwaiter find and might have given this room short shrift. At any rate, he decided to rectify the problem straight away, because there was something about the fireplace that had caught his interest.

Located in what once must have served as the master bedroom for the Friedrich home, the fireplace was constructed of tawny Roman pressed brick laid in bands of regularly projecting and receding courses that created a powerful horizontal effect. The crowning touch was a Romanesque arch of the same narrow brick, fanned on end to give the illusion of the rays of the setting sun.

Robert backed away, frowning. The deep raking of the horizontal joints between bricks in combination with the near invisibility of the vertical joints pointed a finger in an unexpected direction.

With a new suspicion forming in his mind, Robert hurried downstairs and across the open room to the fireplace that dominated the far wall. He didn't notice the people who stepped out of his way or looked at him oddly. He walked straight to the structure and began to study it.

From the excellent craftsmanship of its broad brick hearth to the strength of the weight-bearing lintel, the fireplace magnified the knot of excitement that had taken hold in Robert's stomach. Then he found an inscription cut into the lintel's flat sandstone surface. It had been covered over with plaster or putty, but if he looked at it from just the proper angle, he could read the words:

The reality of the house is order.
The glory of the house is hospitality.

Robert actually began to tremble. Even though he wasn't an expert on the works of Frank Lloyd Wright, he knew that those words were part of an inscription the great man had cut on a lintel in another house near Chicago, one that he had designed himself. Which meant that Wright must have had a hand in the design of *this* house. At least as far as the two fireplaces were concerned. And who knew how much more? In his research, Robert had discovered that Stephen deVille had been a favorite student of Wright's. What if this house was an early Stephen deVille, built right at the time when he struck out on his own? And what if Wright, wishing his protégé well, had lent a little of the magic of his name to one of deVille's first projects?

Robert had to stop himself from shouting. Everything hinged on an entire series of "what if's," but "what if" it were true? It would be an amazing find!

Robert looked around for Elise. He wanted to tell her what he'd found . . . what he suspected. But she was nowhere in sight, and when he asked a startled library assistant if she had already left, the woman answered, wide-eyed, that Elise had gone home.

Struggling to contain his exhilaration, Robert left the library, too. His mind raced as he drove back to Milwaukee. All his suspicions would do no good if he couldn't confirm them. And he knew the one man to ask: his friend, Max Prescot, who lived in Chicago and was an expert in the work of both Frank Lloyd Wright and Stephen deVille. He would call him as soon as he got to his apartment.

ELISE MET TWO PEOPLE she was compelled to stop and talk to before she finally managed to arrive home that evening. The first was Josephine.

She met her after she'd decided to make a quick stop at Olsen's Supermarket to pick up what she needed for tomorrow's meal. After they exchanged the prerequisite round of hello-how-are-you's and commiserated that they had very little time to chat, Josephine took stock of Elise and said, "Have you been taking mega-doses of vitamins since I saw you last? You look positively blooming."

"I do?" Elise replied, surprised.

Josephine nodded. "You do. It wouldn't have anything to do with Professor Fairmont, would it? Someone told me they saw you having lunch with him at the lodge today. Normally, I wouldn't have listened, but when they said your name, my ears pricked up."

"Who was it?" Elise asked quickly. The answer would tell her how quickly word would spread through town.

"Annabelle Scanlon, actually. Sorry."

"What was *she* doing there?" Elise asked.

"Personally delivering a letter...? I don't know. But she saw you."

Elise shook her head in exasperation. Annabelle was probably the worst gossip Tyler could claim. And as postmistress, she had the widest scope.

"Well?" Josephine prompted her. "Are you going to tell me about it?"

Elise shrugged, and seeing that the nearest checkout stand was suddenly free, she made a quick sprint for the spot. "It wasn't anything," she said as she started to unload her basket. "I'll tell you about it another time, okay? It really wasn't anything."

Josephine looked as if she believed her about as much as she believed a six-foot-three, two-hundred-and-twenty-pound high school fullback when he told her he hadn't hoisted the opposing team's fiberglass mascot onto the bank's marquee, when she had the bank manager in the next office who said he had seen the fullback do it! But good friend that she was, Josephine let Elise escape with a dryly worded "You do that," before she hurried off to complete her own shopping.

The second person Elise met was her doctor. She had decided to make one more quick stop, at the florist's, and Dr. Baron was coming out of the shop just as she was heading in.

A tall, handsome man just out of his twenties, with thick chestnut hair and dark blue eyes, he was Tyler's most eligible bachelor. He was also a very good and dedicated doctor. At the moment he carried a bouquet of bright flowers wrapped in green paper and cellophane.

"They're for Mom," he explained when he saw Elise glance at them. "I thought she could use some cheering up."

Elise remembered what Anna Kelsey had told her about Alyssa and murmured agreement.

Jeff looked at her closely. "I heard you needed a little cheering up yourself yesterday. Actually, a little picking up. Maybe you should stop by the office, let me take another look. But then, seeing you now, you look pretty good. There's color in your cheeks, a spark in your eye."

"I tried to tell everyone there wasn't anything wrong. All I needed was a meal."

"Still, maybe you should—"

The beeper that Jeffrey Baron wore attached to his belt sounded. He reached immediately to shut it off, then shifted it so that he could read the brief message. Elise saw him frown and his lips tighten.

When he looked back at her, it was apparent he had forgotten what they had been talking about. "Sorry, Elise. I have to go. I've got to . . ."

Elise backed out of his way. "No problem," she murmured. "I hope it's nothing serious."

"Me, too!" Jeff called over his shoulder as he hurried toward his car.

Elise continued into the florist's shop, glad in a way that she had been saved the trouble of refusing an office call, but concerned about who might be the cause of Dr. Baron's worried look.

ROBERT LET the telephone receiver slide back onto its base. Max Prescot was out of town and was not expected back for two weeks. Robert had given his name and number and had left a message for Max to call him as soon as he returned, but he still felt there should be something more that he could do. Excitement continued to burn hot in his belly and in his mind. A house by Stephen deVille was important. But a house built by Stephen deVille with touches by Frank Lloyd Wright. . .

The place was in terrible shape. A lot of work would need to be done in order to restore it. The venture would take huge amounts of cash, but it could be done.

He walked to the plate-glass window that overlooked the lakeshore. Ah, what he wouldn't give to be able to restore it himself! It would mean that a long-held dream of his would at last come true.

Robert sipped the freshly squeezed orange juice he had carried with him to the window. The flavor was sweet with a tart edge . . . just as was life. He had decided that long ago. This moment was more proof. If he was correct in what he surmised, he had found something truly special. Also, if he was proved correct, the selling price of the house—even in its advanced state of disrepair—would be greatly inflated, and when added to the cost of restoration, would force him completely out of the market. Through years of hard work he had managed to position himself in what could be termed comfortable means. But he was nowhere near what could be thought of as wealthy.

Robert continued to stare out the window. Elise had said she loved history. What would she think when she discovered that she had been working in a building with such a claim to history all those years and hadn't known it?

It was slightly puzzling to him why he'd wanted to tell her right away. Search her out, give her the news. But since it was going to be a while before he could gain certification for his find, perhaps it was best that she didn't know. He'd hate to raise her expectations and then disappoint her. He could easily be wrong. Everything that excited him about the house could still be the work of a grand copier.

Robert tilted his glass and swallowed the rest of the juice with determination. If he had two weeks to wait, he would make good use of them. Elise had offered the records in the Tyler Room...and he was prepared to look through each and every one.

ELISE CAREFULLY PLACED the flowers she'd purchased into one of the bags of groceries she had collected from the store. Some people might think it silly that she, who loved to garden, would even consider buying flowers from a shop. But she didn't like to denude her beds. She liked the wild display the flowers gave and reciprocated by allowing their blooms to remain in place throughout their life cycle.

She glanced at the house. She knew Bea was waiting. Should she tell her today, or should she wait until tomorrow morning? If told now, Bea would brood all evening and make life extremely difficult. If told tomorrow, she would brood all morning and be even more caustic to Robert when he came.

Elise decided to tell her as soon as she got inside. She'd rather take the brunt of Bea's ill humor herself than inflict it on their guest.

Picking up the two bags, Elise braced her shoulders and walked to the back door.

CHAPTER SEVEN

BEA WATCHED her sister's flurried movements with angry eyes. If Elise thought for one moment that she was going to be nice to this . . . this *intruder,* then she could just think again! The house had practically been turned upside down since yesterday evening. Everything had been scrubbed and vacuumed and polished. And now Elise had been cooking for what seemed hours. And for what? To entertain that man! Elise had even tried to get Bea to wear one of the outfits Anna Kelsey had long ago given her, bought from Gates Department Store, but she wouldn't do it. She didn't feel like wearing periwinkle blue. She was much happier in her usual drab gray dress and definitely more comfortable with its loose construction.

Bea sniffed her anger, but Elise didn't seem to notice. She was too busy humming to herself in the kitchen as she basted the chickens she had stuffed earlier that morning and looked to the vegetables she was going to serve with them. At least they would have a good meal, Bea decided, but she doubted that she would eat more than just a little. She didn't want to give Elise the satisfaction.

The doorbell rang and Elise started. Her head automatically swiveled to Bea, as if she might ask her to answer it. But when Bea sat stolidly in place, Elise put down the spoon she had been using and, after lowering the flame beneath each pot, went to answer it herself. The only deviation from her course was when she paused to plead, "Be pleasant to him, Bea. He's really a very nice man." Which was exactly the wrong thing to say, and Bea could see that Elise became aware of her mistake when her eyes clouded and her bottom lip caught nervously between her teeth.

Bea listened as her sister greeted her guest. Her words were brittle, tense...as if she expected a bomb to go off at any moment. Bea smiled at her accomplishment.

He came into the room where Bea was sitting, the large room at the rear of the house where she and Elise spent most of their time together. He wore dark pants and a cream-colored shirt that was open at the neck. Without hesitation he walked straight to Bea and extended a hand. "It's good to see you again," he said.

Bea sniffed and ignored him.

This time he was ready for such a reaction. Unfazed, he turned immediately to Elise, and with a smile offered the bottle of wine that he carried. "I wasn't sure what we were having," he said, "so I played it safe. Chardonnay should go well with anything."

"Oh, I'm sorry. I should have told you." Elise was quick to apologize.

"Not at all," Robert denied. "I like surprises."

Bea rolled her eyes. They were just being too, too sweet! She decided to intervene. "Wine has sulfates!" she announced condemningly. "They're very dangerous."

Elise darted her a panicky look. "Only if a person is allergic. You're not allergic, Bea. Neither am I."

"And I don't want to be, either," Bea declared grumpily. "I'll pass on the fancy stuff. Just give me water."

Again Elise bit her bottom lip, unaware that by showing her uncertainty she only increased Bea's satisfaction.

Bea sensed the weight of someone's gaze hard upon her, and she looked up to find Robert Fairmont studying her. For the space of one freewheeling second, Bea felt as if he knew everything about her: what she felt, what she thought, the resentment she had for being forced to spend her life in this chair...even the person she blamed for her accident! But as quickly as the next second followed the first, Bea managed to regain her hateful confidence. She met his appraisal look for look, and silently warned him not to take advantage.

He seemed not in the least unsettled by her warning, a fact that Bea didn't like. Possibly that was what she had perceived about him from the beginning—he was not awed by her anger or by the ferocity of her ill humor.

"Water isn't always the best bet in the world today, either," he said mildly. "Especially water from the tap."

Bea tilted her chin. She had been challenged. "I'll have you know Tyler's water is some of the best in the state!"

He smiled. "Then possibly I'll join you. On your recommendation, of course."

Bea didn't know what to say. Had she just been bested in her own game? She started to speak, stopped, started once again and then retreated into sullen silence.

Elise looked at Bea in some concern, but Robert Fairmont smoothed the moment by saying, "Whatever you're cooking smells absolutely delicious. Thank you, Elise, for asking me. You, too, Bea."

Elise seemed more unsure about what was happening than Bea was. Her smile came and went as she waited for her sister to make some caustic remark. When she didn't, Elise was relieved, yet she remained confused. "I've stuffed two hens," she murmured. "It's not difficult to—"

Bea broke into the unnecessary explanation. "I'm going to my room. Don't bother to call me when dinner is ready. I'm not at all hungry." She started to push away, once again making the task seem almost more than she could accomplish.

Strong hands caught hold of the grips on the back of her chair and her forward motion increased accordingly. Bea looked back across the room. Elise remained in the same spot she'd occupied earlier. Only Robert Fairmont had moved. Bea's gaze swept over her shoulder, and she blinked in surprise to see him so close. He smiled and her head whipped back around. "No.." she protested, but he didn't stop pushing.

"In here?" he asked when they neared her door "This looks to be the direction you were headed."

"I can do it myself!" Bea claimed.

He immediately let go. Rattled, Bea continued the journey. Again to her surprise, he accompanied her into her room. Now it was Bea who was tense, not knowing what to expect. She wheeled around to face him and imperiously directed, "Please. This is my room."

He had spotted her display of dolls, which took up the length of one wall. He moved from one shelf to another, examining them.

Bea had started her collection even before the accident. Her parents had given her the first doll for her thirteenth birthday and it had gone on from there. Christmases, birthdays... Each new boyfriend quickly learned that in order to get on Bea's good side he was required to offer her a special gift. After the accident, people gave her dolls out of guilt. Elise was the first.

Bea had dolls from different countries, clothed in their native dress. She had dolls that belonged to special collector's series, dolls that were old, dolls that were rare, dolls that cost very little. Baby dolls, adult dolls, celebrity dolls. No one was allowed to touch them except herself... and Elise, when she dusted. Each had a name.

He turned, his yellow-brown eyes alight with prying interest. "That's quite a collection," he said, stating the obvious.

"I'd like you to leave," Bea said frostily.

"One of my sisters collects dolls, too, but not on as grand a scale. She has a Wendy Lawton that she's quite proud of. I see you have one."

"What I have and what I don't have is none of your business!"

He shrugged regret. "All right. I'll leave. But before I do, there's something I'd like you to understand. I know you don't like me. I know you'd rather that I just magically disappear. But it isn't going to work that way.

Elise and I have a lot to accomplish. And we're going to accomplish it, whether you approve or not. This town needs a new library, and together we can be sure that they'll get it. Now, I'll try to stay out of your way as much as I can. But you have to agree to something yourself. You have to agree not to make things hard for Elise. You can start with dinner. She's gone to a lot of trouble preparing it. I think you should change your mind and eat with us. What do you say?''

Bea stared at him. She couldn't believe that he had confronted her so directly. The boldness of his action almost took her breath away. She tossed her head, readying a pithy reply. But again he circumvented her plan.

''I'll tell Elise you changed your mind,'' he said in a wholly friendly manner. As if what he'd just told her couldn't possibly have offended her. As if she would acquiesce as meekly as a lamb.

Bea started to sputter in determined resistance, but he merely smiled and left the room in as easy and as confident a manner as he had entered it.

ELISE WAITED anxiously in place. She'd made a move to follow Robert and Bea into the other room, but Robert had signaled her not to. Through the open door she heard their voices, but she couldn't make out what they were saying. When he reappeared, he was smiling quietly to himself. His smile brightened when he saw her. Not even the slam of Bea's door behind him caused his expression to falter.

''She's changed her mind,'' he said softly. ''She'll eat dinner with us.''

Elise looked uncertainly at the door. "She will?"

Suddenly Elise remembered her cooking vegetables. With a cry of dismay she hurried into the kitchen. Luckily, nothing had burned. As she stirred each pot, she realized that Robert had come into the room with her.

"Is there anything I can do?" he asked.

When told no, he leaned nonchalantly against the most distant counter, obviously not wanting to get in her way. She felt his eyes move about the room. He noted the lowered sections of counter and sink, and the cutout space that allowed the wheelchair to maneuver close. The knobs on the stove were all on the front, and the extralong faucet handles made reaching them easier.

"Does Bea do a great deal of her own cooking?" he asked.

"Well, none actually. I had hoped that she would, but—"

"So she relies on you for almost everything."

Elise paid undue attention to the pot she was stirring. "I don't mind."

Robert stuffed his hands into his pockets. "Maybe you should," he said quietly. When she didn't say anything, he sighed. "Never mind. It's none of my business." Then he laughed shortly. "You two are certainly nothing alike. Bea would have told me that I was sticking my nose in where it didn't belong."

Elise looked up. "You sound as if you approve of that kind of behavior. I consider it rude. I'd never—"

"Again, maybe you should."

Elise carefully put down the spoon. His mild censure hurt her. She did the best she could under trying circumstances. He couldn't possibly know what it was like to live with someone as difficult as Bea. Only a person who lived in the midst of a deserted mine field could even begin to understand.

"I didn't mean to upset you," he said after a moment. "It's just that I know someone who is, as they say now, physically challenged. A friend of mine, a colleague. The friend I visited at Lake Geneva. The suddenness of his disability wasn't easy for him, but it was just as hard for his wife. She almost worked herself to death trying to make everything perfect for him, trying to do for him things that he should have done himself. And without meaning to, she took away his pride. It almost broke apart their marriage."

"Bea and I aren't married. The situation is completely different."

"She still resents you."

Elise turned away stiffly. "Her resentment has nothing to do with the care I give her. Now, please, could we talk about something else? Bea and I have been managing for almost thirty years, and hopefully, we'll continue to manage for another thirty."

"That means you don't foresee any changes in your life."

"Should I?" Elise challenged. She was beginning to resent his interference. She hadn't asked for his thoughts. Why was he so intent upon giving them?

He smiled slightly at her flash of spirit. "Do you know that when you're near your sister your personality undergoes a complete change? You become submissive."

"I am not submissive! How can you say that?"

"Why does she resent you?" he asked, suddenly going back to his previous thought.

Elise shook her head, her eyes darkening with remembered hurt.

He watched her for a long moment before he came to encircle her with his arms. Elise stiffened; then, as the warmth of his embrace began to ease the pain, she relaxed enough to let her forehead rest against his shoulder. Finally she whispered, "I am *not* submissive!" with such fierceness that it revealed just how deeply the idea disturbed her.

He stroked her hair. He was about to say something more when Elise jerked away. "I forgot the chicken!" she cried.

Both turned to the rescue; both reached for the oven door. He pulled back, letting her open it.

Elise knew he continued to watch her. She was very much aware of him—aware that she had just been in his arms. Aware that she very much wanted to return there.

She turned, to tell him that the main course was safe, to tell him that she hadn't meant to get so upset—later, she was never sure which. Without her knowledge he had moved, and she found herself back in his arms. Only this time he wasn't content merely to hold her.

A riot of emotions flooded through Elise as his lips covered hers. Shocked surprise was the least important. Her body came alive in a way it never had before, enough to frighten her, to caution her to pull away. But the sensual draw of his body pressing against her, the headiness of being held so tightly in his embrace, the erotic need engendered by his mouth moving intimately over hers... all prevented her from doing anything except respond in kind.

Slowly the kiss ended, but not the magic. Her heart still thumped wildly, her lips felt bruised, her body was on fire. With huge eyes she looked at him. Blinked. Blinked again. Nothing changed.

He cleared his throat. A muscle pulled along his jaw. He seemed to be having nearly as much trouble coming back to reality as she was. Stepping back, he ran a hand along the side of his head, smoothing his hair when it wasn't needed. "I—I didn't mean..." he said unevenly.

Elise turned away.

Fingers curled around her arm, urging her to face him. When she resisted, he said, "But I'm *not* sorry."

A wave of embarrassment washed over Elise when she remembered the abandonment of her response. She hadn't cared for anything at that moment except him, her and what they were doing. The rest of the world could have drifted away, never to return. Not *ever* to return!

When still she wouldn't budge, he moved in front of her and lifted her chin, keeping his fingers there so that she couldn't look away.

"I'll apologize if you want me to," he said softly, "but I won't mean it."

She tried not to lift her gaze. She actively fought against doing it. But she couldn't prevent herself. He was so close!

His oddly colored eyes were vital and warm, his touch so gentle and caring. "I enjoyed kissing you, Elise. And I'd like to do it again. In fact..."

Before Elise could even blink, he was doing it again. He was kissing her! But this kiss was quieter, shorter, almost teasing. His gaze danced as he pulled away. "There," he said. "Not quite as good as the first, but not bad."

Elise knew she couldn't continue to stand there like a hardened clump of clay. "Are you into rating kisses?" she asked, attempting to go along with his banter.

He appreciated her effort. "Well, that last was barely a *one*. But the other... the other was at least a *six*."

"Only a *six*?"

"Which means we'll have to practice."

Elise felt ridiculously near to tears, a signal that she was reaching an emotional overload. It was impossible that she was standing so close to him, discussing the rating of a kiss. A kiss that they had shared! He was Robert Fairmont, renowned architect and teacher, and she was Elise Ferguson, small-town librarian! He was dashing and sophisticated; she was quiet and sometimes shy. She was also well beyond what could be termed in the vernacular a sweet young thing.

"But not right now," she broke in hurriedly, just in case he might mistake her hesitation for agreement.

"No," he said with amused forbearance. "Not right now."

JUST AS Robert had promised, Bea joined them at the table for their meal. She wasn't pleased, but she didn't make any nasty comments. At least, not right away. She

wheeled to the dinner table in stony silence and satisfied herself by giving Robert a glance of pure dislike.
Yet she watched them both with the alertness of a hawk,
watched as stimuli both apparent and hidden swirled in
the currents of conversation between them. She was
suspicious of their laughter, of their silences.

It was not until they came to the end of the meal that
Bea at last spoke. She said, "I understand that Judson
Ingalls had a bad turn yesterday afternoon, and Alyssa
had to call Jeffrey home to see to him. She was afraid
it was his heart."

Elise remembered when Dr. Baron had rushed away
from the florist's shop. Instantly concerned, she asked,
"*Was* it his heart?"

"I don't believe so. Annabelle said Jeffrey wanted to
run a few tests, but Judson refused. Silly man, and at
his age." She glanced slyly at Robert. "You men have
to be so careful when you get older . . . to not get over-
excited."

Elise grew flustered for more than one reason. *Annabelle!* Had Annabelle told Bea about seeing her with
Robert at the lodge? She herself hadn't said a word.
Then there was Bea's referral to overexcitement. What
did she know? Had she guessed that something physical had occurred between them in the kitchen? Bea had
always been good at seeing things other people wanted
kept hidden. And she wasn't hesitant about using her
knowledge against them.

Grasping at any straw, Elise said, "Judson is almost
eighty, Bea. Robert is . . ." She stopped. She had no idea
how old Robert was.

"Fifty-seven and in excellent health," he supplied. "Excitement keeps a person young, Bea. You should try it sometime."

Bea glared at him.

Elise tried to smooth over the rift. "Judson should be careful. This hasn't been an easy time for him."

Bea sniffed. "Annabelle thinks that Judson somehow got advance word from the State Medical Examiner's Office and it wasn't something he wanted to hear, which was why he had a bad turn."

"Annabelle *thinks!* Once in a while I wish people would wait to get the story straight. All this talk and innuendo . . . it's just terrible!"

Bea snorted. "Half the town thinks he killed her. I remember how strange it was the way his wife just disappeared. One day she was here, raising hell, and the next day she was gone. And no one seemed to care. Well, they care now, that's for sure."

"Bea! Please! Half the town doesn't think any such thing. And for you and Annabelle Scanlon to spread such rumors is unconscionable."

"All I did was listen."

"That's just as bad!"

"Maybe that's how I get my excitement. It's all I have left, isn't it? And we both know why!"

Elise recoiled as if she'd been hit.

Robert, who until this point had remained a silent observer, reacted quickly. "All right, that's enough!" he said with such quiet authority that Bea's victorious smirk was cut short. When he stood and started to move around the table, she kept a wary eye on him, as if unsure what he planned to do. He stopped at Elise's chair and with gentle firmness drew her to her feet.

"You prepared this wonderful meal," he said. "Bea and I are going to clean up."

"I won't do any such—!" Bea began, shocked.

"Do you want to wash or dry?" Robert broke in.

"But I don't expect—" Elise protested.

Robert dropped a quick kiss on Elise's surprised mouth. Right in front of Bea. *Oh, Lord!* Elise groaned to herself. And yet she was thrilled.

"You relax," he said. "We'll take care of everything."

Elise looked from him to Bea. The light of anger burned brightly in Bea's eyes. She was livid at being told what to do. And yet . . . was Robert right? Would it be good for Bea to do a few things for herself from time to time? She knew she would probably catch hell for this later on, but Elise nodded agreement. Bea's eyes narrowed. Yes, Elise decided, she would definitely catch hell. Still, after giving a tentative smile, she walked from the room.

TO HER SURPRISE, a half hour passed before Bea rolled from the kitchen. Her movements were sharp and jagged, her cheeks stained with a hectic flush. She looked neither right nor left, intent only upon gaining the privacy of her room. Once there, she slammed the door with barely restrained fury.

A moment later Robert appeared in the kitchen doorway and shrugged. "She dried," he said simply.

He came to the couch where Elise rested and claimed a seat beside her. Buttercup, who had decided to put in an appearance, looked at him from Elise's lap. With no hesitation, the cat exchanged people, stepping into Robert's lap as easily as if she had done it every day of her life.

"And where did you come from?" Robert asked, lightly scratching a furry neck. Buttercup loved it. She turned in a tight circle and came back for more.

"She usually hides from strangers. You should feel honored."

Robert continued to rub her neck and Buttercup's purring grew louder, making Elise laugh. Finally the cat jumped down and walked away, but not before giving her tail an independent flick.

"She approves of you," Elise said.

"But only so far. That's what that tail flick said—you have your uses, but *I* know who's boss...me, the cat!"

"She does know her own mind," Elise admitted.

"All cats know their own minds," he returned. "That's why some people think they're plotting to take over the world one day...that they're just waiting for the right time."

"Are you one of them?"

"I made my peace with cats a long time ago. When or if the time comes, I'll have diplomatic immunity. So will everyone who's been nice to them. It's only the people who prefer *dogs* who'll suffer."

Elise laughed softly. Grinning, Robert leaned back and draped an arm comfortably along the back of the couch. His gaze showed appreciation for her amusement.

"You laugh like a little girl," he said.

Elise immediately became conscious of her laughter, of her smile, of everything about herself. In her own eyes, she came up wanting. Her smile faded.

"No," he said, sitting slightly forward. "Don't do that. I didn't mean for you to..."

Elise looked at him and once again found herself caught in the magic. It wasn't something she wanted to do—far from it! It just happened. There was a power about him, the strong power of attraction. She had felt it from the first, and with time she had only fallen deeper under its influence. She wanted to pull her gaze away but couldn't do it.

"I don't know why we're wasting time talking about cats," he murmured.

As he leaned closer, Elise stood. She went to stand at the window. The yard next door looked so ordinary. Children played in the summertime warmth; someone in the distance was mowing grass. People were involved in the intricacies of their own worlds, just as she was involved in hers.

"Are—are we going to work this afternoon?" she asked, still looking out the window.

Robert moved and she waited anxiously to learn what he would do. Part of her wanted him to come to her; part of her didn't. Then she heard papers being unfurled and she turned to find him unrolling the set of blueprints on the coffee table.

He winked. "There's a certain safety in numbers, don't you think? Accounting numbers. What say we get to it?"

He understood. Without her telling him, he could see that she needed to take things slowly. That she couldn't just jump into a relationship without thought, without knowledge of her feelings.

Grateful for his insight, she accepted his offer.

just jump into a relationship without thinking, without knowledge of her feelings.

Grateful for his insight, she accepted his offer.

CHAPTER EIGHT

ELISE AND ROBERT worked with the specifications for the next two hours, pausing only for a short coffee break. At her home, with no interruptions, they were able to accomplish a great deal. Most of the decisions came about by his outlining possible alternative materials and by her then making a choice. All along, though, she was aware that Robert was guiding her to a finished product that would ultimately achieve their goal of quality at less expense. Finally, when they had done all they could for that day, Robert put the papers away.

"Would you like another cup of coffee?" Elise asked, hoping to delay his departure.

He smiled lazily. "I wouldn't want to outstay my welcome. I'm taking up your entire afternoon."

"I have nothing else to do. Unless you—"

"Coffee sounds good to me. Thank you."

Elise went into the kitchen. Moments later she returned, carrying a tray. Robert helped her to settle it on the coffee table. While she poured, she felt him watching her. Her hands trembled but not enough to give her away.

"Is that a picture of your parents over there?" he asked, motioning to an old black-and-white studio photograph hung on the wall.

Elise nodded. "That was taken shortly after they married. We have others, but I always felt there was something special about that one."

"You look like your mother," he said, showing that he must have examined it closely while she was away.

"Yes. Bea and I both do."

"Your father seems a very strong man."

"He was."

"You use the past tense. Is he dead?"

"They both are. For almost thirty years."

"Any other brothers or sisters?"

"No, just Bea and myself. We're the last of our line. Our father's brother died without children and our mother was an only child."

"That seems sad somehow."

She shrugged. "It happens." She handed him his cup. "What about you?" she asked. "Do you have brothers and sisters?"

Robert chuckled as he stationed his cup on the table in front of him. "Four sisters and one brother, with each one incredibly fertile. My mother and father are the proud grandparents of twenty-six grandchildren and twelve great-grandchildren. At least so far."

"My goodness," she said.

"I'm the only disappointment in the bunch."

"Surely there's still time," she murmured. Then, realizing what she'd said, she made it worse by continuing, "I mean . . . you're not old. You can find someone and start a family of your own. Men can still produce children well into their... Where women..." She bit her tongue to stop herself.

He was amused. "I could, yes. My problem is that I just haven't found the right person yet."

"Don't you want children?" she asked curiously.

"I'm not sure. That's never been important to me. If it were, I suppose I'd be married by now."

Children had once been very important to Elise. She'd longed to have a little girl or a little boy that she could fuss over, take places, do things with. But slowly she had let go of that dream. It just wasn't going to happen to her. She looked down at her hands, folded in her lap. Now it would never happen.

Robert took one of her hands, gently separating it from the other. He entwined his fingers with her own—long, talented fingers, tanned and strong, she noted. "There are other things in life besides children," he said softly, as if divining her private thoughts. "Like trying to make life better for other people, being a good friend to your friends, being kind to animals ... the list is endless."

Elise's throat tightened.

He gave her hand a light squeeze and teased, "Anyway, children can always be borrowed for a day or two. You get to spoil them rotten and then give them back. You don't have to put up with any of the hassles!"

"That sounds like experience talking," she said unevenly. "Have you done that to your brother and sisters?"

He grinned. "All the time. The kids love to come visit me. Their parents cringe. But I think that's what a bachelor uncle is for."

Elise laughed. Her dip into melancholia had receded. She confided, "Some people in Tyler think the library is my husband and the books my children. I actually heard someone say that once."

"They should be taken out and shot!" he declared, a twinkle in his eye.

Elise shook her head. "I wouldn't go that far."

"That's because you're a nice person."

"And you're not?"

"Ask my students toward the end of next semester."

When he released her hand and reached for his coffee, Elise experienced an odd sensation of emptiness. She asked, "You wondered yesterday how I became a librarian...tell me, how did you become a professor?"

He shot her a narrow look. "You really want to know?"

"I asked."

He took a long sip and leaned back. "I enjoy being a practicing architect," he said. "Having the thrill of creating a design and then watching it take shape in the form of a building. But that's nothing compared to the excitement of watching a mind take shape, of helping it to catch fire and grow. There's nothing else like it in the world. Nothing so...expanding."

Thinking of what she'd heard about his students crediting him with much of their later successes, Elise murmured, "You must be a very good teacher."

"I try," he said lightly.

A silence descended between them, one that neither of them seemed able to break. Much had happened that day. And they were at the point where small talk, no matter how revealing, just didn't work anymore.

Robert moved, jerking Elise's attention from her thoughts. He drew her with him as he stood. "I really should go now," he said softly.

Elise made no reply.

He continued to look at her from a slight advantage in height. "It will take a few days to work things up for the town council, but I'd like to come to Tyler tomorrow to do a little research of my own...at the library. Would that be all right with you?"

It was more than all right, it was wonderful! Elise's spirit soared. "Why, of course," she managed to say circumspectly. They were standing so close together. All it would take would be one touch....

His smile made her heart lurch, and gazing into those golden-brown eyes was like being lost in a wonderland of unlimited promise. She wanted him to kiss her again, ached for him to do so. But after a moment he pulled away.

"I'll see you tomorrow then," he said.

"Oh, yes...yes," Elise murmured, shaking herself mentally.

He collected the plans and started for the door. But before leaving he turned to face her. "There's something I'm curious about," he said, his smile transformed into a light frown.

Elise came to lean lightly against the door, ostensibly to see him out, but in reality as an excuse to be close to him again. "What?" she asked brightly, trying not to sound as shameless as she felt.

"Well, it's about the old library. What's going to happen to it after the new one's built?"

Elise might have expected any number of questions to arise, but that wasn't one of them. Their previous conversation had been so personal. She blinked in surprise. "The old library? Well, I—I suppose it will be torn down. It's not much good for anything anymore. It needs so much work."

"Torn down?" he echoed.

"I should think. The land has a certain value. It's in a fairly good spot. Someone will probably want to build on it right away—another house, a business. That area's not restricted. The money will go to the new library, of course. It's not as if we can't use it." She waited for him to say something. When he didn't, she laughed a little nervously and referred back to her previous answer. "I don't know it for a fact, but that's what I suspect. I seem to remember hearing someone say something about it a year or two ago."

Robert stood very still, staring at her.

Her smile faltered. "Is something wrong? Did I say something to upset you?"

"Uh, no. No, I was just...curious. I suppose that would be the logical..." His words trailed away.

Elise glazed at him in confusion. In spite of his denial, she still had the feeling that she had said something he didn't want to hear. "I'm not sure," she repeated. "It's just what I *think* I heard."

Robert's sober expression cracked into a familiar smile. "Don't think another thing about it," he said. "I just wondered, that's all. It seems such a shame."

"I know what you mean, but—" she shrugged "—what can you do about it?" She hadn't meant him personally, but people in general.

Her intent seemed to miss its mark when he murmured, "I'm not sure. I'm not sure at all."

He stared into the front yard, at the slender maple whose leaves fluttered in the breeze, but Elise didn't think he saw it. He seemed to be looking inside himself, at something she couldn't fathom. Then his head swiveled back around and she became the focus of his attention. His gaze softened.

"I'll see you tomorrow?" he asked.

Elise would move heaven and earth if need be. "Tomorrow," she agreed huskily.

He smiled and her world became illuminated once again.

She watched as he walked from the porch to his car and then waved as he drove away. She was immeasurably glad for the support of the front door. She wasn't sure she could have continued to stand there if she hadn't still leaned against its strength. Her body had started a light trembling, a nameless song trilled in her soul…because there was only one word to define what was happening to her now: love. She was falling in love all over again. It didn't matter that she was fifty-three, that she should know better, that she might look a fool. Something of this magnitude was beyond a person's control. It was a bolt of lightning from a storm-free sky. It made her feel young again . . . alive!

"Has he gone?" The acidic words came from close behind her.

Elise's spirit crashed back to earth. She turned to see that Bea had rolled into the hallway, her features harsh, unforgiving.

"He's gone," Elise said, closing the door. At any other time she might have closed the door on her emotions as well, but not now. This newly dawning ember of love was something she would not let Bea extinguish. She would keep it guarded closely in her heart, to protect it.

"Thank heaven for that!" Bea declared. She gave a quick turn and started to push away. But after a moment, the process seemed too much for her and she asked for her sister's help. "Elise?" she said. "Please?"

Elise remained at the door for another moment, then she moved across the space to her sister. As she did, Bea proved that she still had enough energy left for vilification.

"That man has enough nerve for two people!" she complained. "In my own home! He ordered me about like a slave! I thought about calling Chief Schmidt to have him thrown out, but then I remembered Chief Schmidt retired from the police force late last year and I'm not sure about that woman who took his place. A woman police officer... and they put her in charge instead of Brick! Anyway, I doubted that you'd have gone along with it. Not when you look at him with those big cow eyes. Honestly, Elise, you should be more subtle. Throwing yourself at him like that! It's ridiculous. Absolutely ridiculous!"

When Elise had pushed her into the family room, Bea wrested away control of the wheelchair. In her agitation, she couldn't stand to move so slowly. She began her special brand of pacing, rolling back and forth while her neck worked up and down.

Elise sat down on the couch, her face a controlled mask. She made no attempt to defend herself.

Bea, eyes narrowing, struck harder. "Do you think he could truly be interested in someone like you? To give the man his due, he's a handsome devil. Sophisticated, urbane. He probably has a string of women all waiting to do his bidding. *Young* women. *Beautiful* women. Women who are interesting, who've see something of the world. Not someone like you with their foot half in the grave. With wrinkles and liver spots and a flat chest. Why, the only traveling you've done is in the bathtub, when you read those travel catalogs from the library. If you think a man like that would ever be interested in a person like you—"

Elise stood up, her features emotionless. "I'm going out, Bea. I'll be back . . . when I'm back. Don't bother to wait up."

"Where are you going?" Bea demanded, suddenly alarmed. "What are you going to do?"

Elise walked steadily from the room. She didn't answer.

"I'll need help, Elsie! I'll need help! You can't do this to me. You can't just walk out and—"

Elise allowed the back door to close quietly behind her. Still, her sister's harsh words rang through the wall. "Annabelle told me what she saw yesterday! You didn't think I'd find out, but I did. He'll use you, Elise. *He'll use you!*"

Elise walked steadily to the garage, got inside the car and after a moment dropped her head against the steering wheel. Her instinct was to start the car and drive as far away as she possibly could. But she couldn't go anywhere. Not because she didn't want to, but because in her anger, she had forgotten the most important thing: she didn't have her keys.

JOSEPHINE LIVED a half-hour walk across Tyler from the Ferguson house. Elise took almost an hour to accomplish it. At first she stopped frequently to try to erase Bea's viperish attack from her mind. Later, she stopped to tend the gleaming jewel she now kept in the tenderest part of her heart. No matter what Bea did or said, she wouldn't let it interfere with her feelings for Robert. Everything Elise had seen so far pointed to the fact that he was a wonderful, caring man. Generous, thoughtful. He had even tried to do what was best for Bea! To help her. Bea had rejected him, of course, but Elise wouldn't. Not ever. Not even if—

Her thoughts stumbled to a sudden halt. *Did* she love him? Had the situation become so serious that quickly? She tried to remember the way she'd felt for Kenneth and couldn't. Not completely. She had been so young. He had been, too, only one year her senior. Someone had told her that he'd married a woman from Missouri and settled near St. Louis. It was conceivable that he was a grandfather by this time. Elise shook her head in disbelief. Kenneth, a grandfather! The years had melted away. They were far, far too short! In her mind's eye, she was still nineteen. She didn't *feel* middle-aged.

She hurried to Josephine's neatly framed house and knocked on the door. Then she looked over her shoulder, as if something unknown were pursuing her. To her relief, Josephine answered right away.

"Elise?" Josephine said, her pale eyes examining her friend closely from behind rimless glasses. "Is something wrong?"

In front of anyone else, Elise would have pretended. She would have laughed and said, *Oh, no, everything is wonderful!* But Josephine was her best friend. She didn't try to disguise the strain she felt or the revealing look of hurt in her eyes. "May I come in?" she asked.

Due to her surprise, Josephine had forgotten to invite her inside. Instantly she stepped out of the way. "Of course, of course...come in."

Elise passed into the warmth of her friend's home. It was a relief to be away from the heavy somberness of her parents' out-of-date decor. Josephine had no one to please except herself. That, along with a good eye and good taste, made her home a welcoming oasis.

Elise belatedly tried to straighten her hair. She felt uncomfortably flushed. A conflicting voice told her to leave, not to burden someone else with her problems. But by this time Josephine had taken her arm and was drawing her toward the friendly kitchen. Elise gave no resistance.

Josephine seated her, then put on a kettle of water. "Now," she said as she took the opposite chair, "what's happened?"

Tears rushed into Elise's eyes, but she quickly brushed them away. She hoped Josephine hadn't see them. She shook her head, sniffing reflexively.

"Is it Bea?" Josephine asked, leaning forward. "What's she done this time? Honestly, I think that woman glories in upsetting you. And after all you do for her!''

"I didn't come to complain," Elise whispered.

"I know that. You never do. That's why I have to complain for you. Now, tell me. What happened? What's brought you out like this? It must be something serious.''

The teakettle whistled and Josephine tsked at the interruption. Still, she made a pot of tea and bustled about while it steeped, gathering cups and saucers and spoons. Then she poured a cup for each of them.

The pungent aroma of herbs and spices tickled Elise's nose, triggering more moisture in her eyes. She sniffed again in reaction.

Josephine waited for an answer.

Elise finally looked up. Her friend's face was strong and kind, just like her personality. "I think—I think I'm in love," Elise stated baldly.

Josephine stopped stirring sugar into her tea. "You...what?"

Words tumbled from Elise. "I'm not sure yet. It's early on. And I know it's silly. It's probably all in my imagination. I'll come to my senses in a few weeks and wonder what made me think... I *know* how old I am. I know what I look like. I know I'm not very interesting. But that doesn't change a thing! When I'm with him, I—''

"Who's *him?*" Josephine interrupted, looking serious.

Elise took a trembling breath. "Robert Fairmont."

Josephine remained very still, her eyes boring into Elise's.

Elise rushed into speech again. "See? I told you it was silly. Everyone will say that. I've only known the man for less than a week." Her laugh was high-pitched, anxious. "And he...what would he see in someone like me? It's just like Bea said...." She could tell herself that what Bea thought made no difference, but it did, to some degree. It didn't change anything, but it did taint it. "I look ridiculous!"

Josephine's mouth tightened. "What Beatrice has to say doesn't matter. She'd find something wrong with a saint! It's you who counts, what *you* feel. As for you not having anything to offer...why, that's what's ridiculous!" She paused. "I heard he came to your house for dinner today."

Elise blinked. "Already?"

"Annabelle," Josephine explained, not having to go into further detail.

"So the whole town knows."

"Everyone who's at home."

"But they don't know anything else."

Josephine shook her head. "Minor speculation, that's all. He's an attractive man, available. And you're available, too."

Elise fidgeted with the cup handle. Josephine watched her. Finally she asked, "What about him? What does he feel? Do you know?"

Elise flushed lightly as she remembered his kisses, especially the first one in the kitchen. "I think...he likes me," she answered.

"There's a big difference between liking and loving."

"I know."

Josephine frowned. She pushed her cup and saucer away. She tapped her fingers. "Are you coming to me for advice?" she asked at last.

Elise made no reply.

Josephine heaved a sigh. "You know me, Elise. You know I don't like to interfere in other people's lives unless they ask. I'm going to assume you're asking, so here goes: I like the man. From what I saw of him, he's straight up. He meets your eye and doesn't lie. But..." She paused. "Give it a little time. Don't rush in too fast. Otherwise you could get very badly hurt—"

"Again." Elise completed the thought, knowing that her friend didn't want to bring up the past.

"Again," Josephine confirmed.

Elise got jerkily to her feet. She paced across the narrow room. "It's not something I can control, Josephine. The more I tell myself not to think of him, the more I think of him. I know I should be beyond that now, at my age. But it just doesn't happen that way. Every time he comes near me, I..."

"It's glands," Josephine said succinctly. "I should know. The whole high school is a hotbed of over-excited glands."

Elise's cheeks turned pink. "It's that, too. He is very attractive. But it's more than that. It's him, Josephine. *Him*. The man inside."

"Like you said, there hasn't been much time."

"I don't *have* much time!" Elise replied poignantly. "I'm not a young girl just starting out! I don't have many more chances left! I can't afford to worry about whether or not I'll get hurt."

Josephine lapsed into silence, her gaze turned inward on herself. Elise wondered if she had offended her. She hadn't meant anything of the kind. She slipped back into her seat.

Finally, Josephine said, "Do what you have to do, Elise, and anyone else be damned! There was a time...I know, I never told you, but it was before we became such good friends. There was a time when I could have thrown caution to the winds and gone off with someone I thought I loved. I met him at a teachers' conference. He was one of the speakers. But I didn't go with him. I played it safe. I was afraid of what everyone would say when they found out. I'm still not sure if I loved him, so maybe it was a good thing. Still, I shouldn't have let public opinion color my decision. Who knows? I might have been very happy. Then again, I might have regretted it all my life. The point is, I'll never know! Sometimes I think about him at night and I wonder..." She paused, lost in her memories. Then she looked at Elise and a self-conscious smile touched her lips. "Just be careful, okay?"

Elise responded with a tentative smile of her own. "I'll try," she promised. "Anyway, this might all be a tempest in a teapot." She glanced at the teapot on the table and patted its ceramic side. "I'm not really sure how I feel. It's just... When Bea said..." She couldn't go on.

"Most of all, don't listen to Bea," Josephine warned. "She wants what's best for herself, not for you."

"She's my sister. I love her."

"You should cut the strings a little. Not let her take such advantage."

Elise looked away. Robert had said basically the same thing. But it was easier said than done.

Josephine changed the subject, obviously feeling that it was time. "What about the wet books?" she asked. "Have you been by the church to check on them lately?"

"Pauline was to oversee everything this weekend."

"Would you like to drop by yourself? Just to be sure? I feel like a drive. I'll take you. I noticed you didn't bring your car."

Josephine's motive was clear. She wanted to take Elise's mind off her personal troubles by getting her involved in her work. Elise murmured dryly, "Sure, why not? Then you can take me home. There's still some cake left from dinner. You can come in and have a piece."

"I don't need any cake." Josephine patted a thin hip that she mistakenly thought needed trimming.

"It's my special spice cake," Elise tempted her.

"Well, maybe just a bite," Josephine murmured.

Elise chuckled at her friend's concession. She felt much better than she had when she'd first come here. Uncertainty still hovered just beneath the surface of her life, but she didn't feel as afraid.

ROBERT LET HIMSELF into his apartment, then turned and locked the door. For a moment he just stood there, a part of the familiar darkness.

In all likelihood the house in Tyler would be torn down. The idea was appalling! Elise had said it so glibly, so innocently. Robert had felt blood rush through his veins, heard it race through his head.

Someone would probably buy the site just for the land and tear the building down! With the Frank Lloyd Wright fireplaces and the Stephen deVille architectural design. The dumbwaiter, the faucet handles . . .

Robert walked blindly from the door to his leather couch and collapsed into the comfort of its cushions. He leaned back and stared at the ceiling. If only he could be sure! But he *couldn't* be sure, not unless he found the building's construction records or had Max Prescot there to confirm his suspicions.

Then his mind stopped churning. What difference did this latest bit of information make? Nothing had changed. Elise hadn't said that someone was waiting with wrecking ball poised. It was merely a possibility for the future. The town still needed the old building for its library. He had time. He could do his research and wait for Max's return. Then they would see what happened next. The house wouldn't just disappear.

Robert sighed and absorbed the serenity of his surroundings. It was like a return to the womb—secure, safe.

Slowly, unbidden, a memory came to tantalize him. Elise's face, delicately beautiful. Her eyes, trusting and so very blue . . . as blue as the sky on a clear summer day. Her lips, warm and soft and responsive. Her slender body, surprisingly strong, surprisingly willing. The way she smiled, the way she looked at him . . .

Robert sat forward and switched on a lamp, flooding the room with light. He had to think of something else! It was one thing to enjoy her while he was with her and quite another to think of her after they went their separate ways. For all these years he'd been able to distance himself from the women who came into his life. And he saw no reason for the situation to change now.

Still, despite his determination, the sweetness of her face came back to haunt him while he slept.

CHAPTER NINE

ELISE STARTED the morning with puffy eyes and a headache. Sleep had been elusive in the night and she woke up feeling more exhausted than when she went to bed. As she made her way downstairs, she wrapped her robe loosely about her slender frame and tied it at the waist with a matching belt. On her feet were slippers she had purchased years ago—old friends, nicely worn in. To comb her hair, she had merely run her fingers through it several times. When she got to Bea's door, she tapped and received permission to enter.

Bea greeted her from the bed. "Well, you certainly look a sight!"

"Don't start, Bea," Elise said tiredly.

"Now *you're* telling me what to do! That man has had an evil influence on you, Elise." Bea pulled herself higher in the bed. "For you to walk out on me like that. It was rude, wholly insensitive—"

"Would you like me to brush your hair?" Elise cut in. She hadn't forgiven her sister for her behavior yesterday, but part of her difficulty in getting to sleep last night had been the strain that existed between them. No matter the provocation, she shouldn't have left Bea on her own like that. Just because Bea had been cruel didn't mean that she should be cruel as well. She had an advantage over Bea...and she could never forget the reason why.

"No, I would not!" Bea snapped angrily. "It was supposed to be done last night, not this morning. I brushed it myself. You know I can't sleep if I'm not relaxed."

"I know," Elsie murmured. She moved about the room, straightening articles that were out of place and picking up discarded clothing. She felt Bea's eyes steadily upon her. "Would you like to get up now?" she asked, meeting her sister's disapproving gaze.

Bea's answer dripped with sarcasm. "I wouldn't want to put you out."

Elise would not be drawn out. She even managed to smile. "It's no bother," she claimed.

Bea turned the cover back from her withered legs and watched with satisfaction as Elise gave a tiny grimace of pain. That was part of their ritual, too. Each night, the hair brushing; each morning, the useless legs.

Elise helped her into the old-fashioned chair and arranged her feet in a comfortable position on the footpads, more for her own happiness than for Bea's. She knew Bea couldn't tell the difference, but it made her feel better. Then she pushed her into the en suite bathroom, which had been converted beautifully for an invalid, with rails built into strategic places, a lavatory that was easy to use and a roll-in shower and seat so that Bea could have privacy as she performed her toilet.

"Thanks," Bea murmured, dismissing her.

About the time Elise straightened from changing the bedding, Bea rolled back into the room. Again Elise helped arrange her feet and they started off for the kitchen, with Bea riding comfortably as Elise pushed. The times were too numerous to count that friends had tried to get Bea to consent to a motorized chair. She and Elise could afford it; it would have made her life so much easier. But Bea steadfastly refused. She was afraid of a motorized chair, she said. Afraid that she might fall. Anyway, she had Elise....

They talked of nothing in particular over breakfast, their feelings still strained. Only when Elise turned away after washing the dishes to get ready to go to work did Bea reintroduce the subject of Robert.

"Are you seeing him again today?" she asked coldly. There was no need to say who she meant.

Elise stopped at the door. "He's coming to the library, so yes, I probably will."

"Are you going to bring him here?" Bea demanded.

"Not if I can help it," Elise answered tightly.

Bea was quick to pick up on her tone. "There's no need for that kind of attitude. I may be in this chair, but I'm still your older sister! You should show respect!"

A flare of anger flashed through Elise's eyes but was quickly controlled. "I always try to show respect, Bea," she said evenly. Then, before her sister could reply, she added, "But you should show *me* a little respect, too. It works both ways." Bea blinked, and again, before she could respond, Elise said, "Don't forget, this is the morning I take books to Worthington House, so if I'm a little late for lunch, don't worry. I *will* be here."

Forty-five minutes later, Elise opened the library. On Monday mornings it was always deserted, so she felt perfectly comfortable leaving it in the hands of the part-time staff and one or two volunteers. A half hour after that she'd readied the bookmobile, packing it full of the mysteries and romances, science fiction and westerns, political intrigue and travelogues that the residents and patients at Worthington House enjoyed.

She was particularly careful to include audio-cassettes and large-print editions of books that those who were visually impaired needed in order to enjoy the same diversions. She also tucked away a few children's picture books for Freddie Houser, who had recently come to Worthington House to live after the death of her mother. Freddie was forty, but she was still a child mentally. The last item Elise included was the newest quilting book that the library had acquired. It was a beautiful coffee-table display with striking pictures of numerous quilts, the history behind each piece and in-dividual instructions on how to replicate the design. She knew the women in the Quilting Circle, most of whom resided at Worthington House, would enjoy both look-ing through and studying it.

After a quick word with Delia, Elise set off. She had seen nothing of Robert this morning and had been torn as to the wisdom of making this trip. But it was pre-cisely because she wanted to see him so badly that she decided to do it. Possibly what she needed was to take a step back, to draw a deep breath. It would be a way of testing herself . . . and him.

WORTHINGTON HOUSE WAS a huge Victorian-style mansion that supported a home for the aged in front, with a newly constructed skilled-care facility attached to the rear. Located on a street boasting similar man-sions that were used as private residences, its bearing was dignified stateliness. Judson Ingalls's home was nearby, as was the impressive home of Dr. George Phelps, the chief of staff of Tyler General Hospital and a member of the board of directors of Worthington House.

Elise parked the bookmobile, actually a glorified van, in the area around back. On Mondays the staff left a space for her close to the door, a gesture she greatly appreciated. Minutes later she pushed the cart she used for book transport down the van's ramp and then up the wheelchair ramp that led into the building. The electronic doors opened immediately, allowing her inside.

Care had been taken to ensure that the residents of both sections of the facility would not feel institutionalized. There were numerous homey touches in both decor and design. In the residents' common areas, comfortable chairs and couches encouraged social exchange, tasteful curtains graced the windows and various paintings decorated the walls. In the skilled-care area to the rear, the walls were painted with soft pastels and complemented by wallpapers of matching shades. Cheerful pictures hung in the halls and in each room, and the careful use of plants added a feeling of the out-of-doors.

Elise knew she could have taken a list around to all the building's patrons and had them check off the books they wanted, to be delivered the following week. But to do that would narrow their worlds even further. She wanted them to have a choice of books, just as they would have had if they were able to come to the library themselves.

She was a popular person as she pushed the cart in and out several times, relieving the van of its burden. As usual, she first set up service in a corner of the activity room in the residents' hall.

"I have several Dick Francis mysteries," she said to Zachary Phelps, Dr. George Phelps's aged uncle, who had once been the police chief of Tyler. Actually, he had been police chief when Margaret Ingalls disappeared. He and Judson were good friends then and remained so today. "And several of Colin Dexter's," she said. She held up a paperback. "This one, *Last Seen Wearing,* is good. Inspector Morse is truly baffled about the case of a missing schoolgirl. And I particularly liked this Dick Francis tale, *The Edge.* It's about horse racing, of course, but the intrigue takes place on a train trip across Canada."

The old man grinned, took both books and inspected them. Then he handed her his library card. Zachary Phelps didn't live at Worthington House, but he was a regular visitor, particularly on Mondays when he knew the bookmobile would make a scheduled stop. He could easily have come to the library and availed himself of a much wider array of mysteries, but he liked to discuss his choices with friends who lived in the residence section.

Elise let people mill about, answering questions when asked and recommending books upon request. Slowly, as the morning progressed, her headache receded and she felt better.

Freddie Houser shuffled up to Elise. Her short red hair stuck out in all directions and the expression on her face gave mute evidence that she remained childlike. She wore a mint-green smock with white pants, the same uniform as the nursing staff. Hoping to help her adjust after the sudden loss of her mother as well as her unsettling move, the nurses had found a job for Freddie. They allowed her to pass out snacks and water to the other residents, as if she were a volunteer. It helped her to feel needed, accepted. The ploy must have worked; she looked happy.

"Do you have something for me, Miss Ferguson?" Freddie asked in her little-girl voice. "You told me you would. You told me you'd bring me something."

"I certainly do, Freddie," Elise said. "Here, what do you think?"

Freddie accepted the books Elise gave her and immediately sat down at the nearest table. Her concentration was fierce as she traced the simple lettering and sounded out words beneath the childish pictures.

Elise continued to check out books and receive a number back in return.

"Monday is my favorite day," Hilda Atwood told her, clutching a brace of romance novels to her breast. "When you get to be my age, you have to live through these books. I'm eighty-five, you know. Almost eighty-six. But I'm still kicking!"

Elise grinned, just as she did each week when Hilda repeated those same words. Snow-white hair, her shoulders only a little stooped…Hilda had such a spark to her smile that she was impossible to resist.

"The library just received a fresh donation this week, Hilda. Some are the latest in each series. So you're set for another few months at least."

"Wonderful!" Hilda exclaimed and walked away, the hitch in her step a little less noticeable.

A short time later, when everyone who wanted books had chosen them, Elise took everything back to the van and refilled the book cart. This time she relied more heavily on magazines and cassettes, for those in the skilled-care facility. When a person was restricted to bed, it was sometimes difficult to hold a book. Still, she brought a number of them along, because some people preferred them.

Going from room to room, Elise tried her best to spread good cheer. She took a moment to visit with each patient, asking how they were getting on and listening when they told her.

Almost at the end of the last hall, she came upon Amanda Baron, Alyssa's older daughter. At twenty-nine, Amanda was the lawyer of Judson Ingalls's family. Like her older brother, Jeff, she shared the Baron good looks, yet on her they were more true. She was a feminine version of her father—fine features, light chestnut hair with a tendency to curl, blue eyes that were intelligent, interested. She was quick to smile even though she often seem distracted.

"Oh! Elise," Amanda said, slightly taken aback when they met in the doorway of a patient's room.

"Amanda," Elise greeted her.

From the earliest point in Elise's memory of her, Amanda had been well behaved and polite, unlike her younger sister, Liza, who had been something of a hellion. There was no pretense with Amanda. What you saw was exactly what you got. For a time when she was growing up, Amanda had wanted to be a veterinarian.

She had checked out every book she could on the subject, reading voraciously. But as she entered her middle teens, Amanda discovered the law, and from that point on, studying that had taken precedence over everything else.

"I didn't expect to see you here," Amanda said, giving her a quick smile.

"Nor I you," Elise returned.

Amanda glanced back over her shoulder. "Mr. Johanson asked me to come."

In the room behind them, Ben Johanson had fallen asleep, worn out by whatever business he had conducted with his lawyer.

"How is he?" Elise asked softly.

"As well as can be expected, I suppose."

They moved into the hallway. Elise would leave a couple of audio novels for him at the nurses' station. Ben loved westerns, and Louis L'Amour most of all.

Elise said, "I was speaking with your brother when he received an emergency call, then I heard that your grandfather had been taken ill. How is he? I hope it' not anything serious."

Amanda's expression tightened "He's all right," she said. She gave no further explanation.

Appreciating the necessity for defense against gossip as well as Amanda's ability to shut off further inquiry, Elise said, "Well, tell him Bea and I are both thinking of him and that we wish him well."

Amanda speared Elise with a quick, assessing look. A second later, she relented. She must have remembered that Elise didn't gossip and, from that, concluded that her inquiry was based solely upon concern.

"I will," she said. "And he truly is fine. Mother just overreacted."

Elise reached out to give the younger woman's hand a light squeeze and Amanda wordlessly returned the salute. These were difficult days for the entire Ingalls family.

A short time later Elise left Worthington House and directed the van down the street toward her house. She would stop off and see to Bea first before going back to the library. The process of taking books to Worthington House was time-consuming, but Elise thought it highly worthwhile. It made so many people happy, including herself.

The van bounced over a pothole, which for some crazy reason made her think of Robert. But then, making her think of Robert wasn't all that difficult. Had he come to the library yet? Was he there now? What had he thought when he found her absent? Did he miss seeing her? Was it possible that he had already left?

In reaction to the last thought, Elise's foot automatically pressed down on the accelerator. Gone was her pretense that she wanted to pause for a considering breath. She had taken her breath and nothing had changed. She wanted to see him again, now! Not later.

If it weren't for the fact that Bea was at home waiting for lunch, Elise would have gone straight to the library. As it was, if she went to the library—whether Robert was there or not—she could easily become entangled. There were always any number of problems that needed her immediate attention when she returned after being away for the morning. It could be hours before she would be free to go home again. No, it was best to stick to schedule, even if every particle in her being cried out for her to do exactly as she wanted this time and not listen to anything else.

Elise forced herself to slow down.

ROBERT WAS DISCONCERTED by the sense of emptiness he experienced when he learned that Elise was not at the library. On the journey from Milwaukee to Tyler he had thought only of his search through Tyler's early records, concentrated only on what he might find. But upon walking through the front doors and not seeing her, he had asked for her. When he discovered that she was out with the bookmobile for the morning, his spirit plummeted. She was so much a part of this place! It was hard to be inside of it and not be with her.

After a quick regrouping of his thoughts, he asked for assistance opening the file cabinet in the Tyler Room, and with solemn care, Delia Mayhew walked upstairs with him to do so.

"If you need any help, feel free to ask," she advised and then disappeared downstairs again.

Robert settled himself at the worktable. He started with the bound records and found that they covered the 1840s to the late 1880s. Claims were recorded, disputes noted, births listed as well as deaths; contracts had been given for the construction of a jail and the hiring of a peace officer. Bit by bit the town of Tyler grew before his eyes . . . fascinating reading, but it did him no good. It was not the information that he needed.

He moved on to the unbound sheets. Each paper had been meticulously preserved in an archival-quality plastic pocket, but none had been sorted by date or subject. Deeds, loans, lawsuits, letters, maps...the years and dealings were a jumble. Papers from the Civil War era were mixed with those from 1914. He would have to go through each of them one by one.

After a time Robert sat back, his muscles stiffening. He had been clocking in longer hours than usual at the drawing board recently, trying to put together all the modifications that they had decided upon for the new library, plus a preliminary estimate of construction costs. He was also trying to keep as much as he could of the Greek Revival exterior of the original plan, using twin pilasters—relief representations of columns—instead of the more expensive pair of full columns. Along with that, he had added a few design flairs of his own that he thought would add interest but not increase the cost.

Once the plan was approved, he would get assistance from the firm for the massive work involved in the development of the design and construction documents so that the project could be completed as quickly as possible. If everything went well, Robert thought they were looking at about two months until construction could resume. That would put the building contractors back to work in the fall. And with a little more luck, they could get quite a bit accomplished before the harshest portion of winter set in.

Stretching, Robert stood and walked over to the window. Outside, a gentle breeze was ruffling the leaves of the trees, a child was playing on the sidewalk with a stick, and a small group of people—three men and one woman—were milling about in the library's backyard. Robert's attention was caught. He watched as they closed into a loose circle, talked among themselves and gestured to various parts of the yard.

At that moment someone came into the room, and Robert turned to see Delia Mayhew standing hesitantly just inside the doorway. He beckoned her over.

"What's going on?" he asked, indicating the people below.

Delia came to the window and peered outside, a light frown creasing her brow. A second later the frown cleared. "Oh, that's Mr. Kelsey and Ms. Gates—I mean, Mrs. Forrester—and Mr. Olsen and Mr. Smith. Mr. Olsen owns Olsen's Supermarket across town and Mr. Smith is the manager. It's on the grapevine that they're thinking about opening a second store."

"Around here?" Robert asked, instantly alarmed.

"Probably."

They watched as the group broke up, waving to one another in a friendly manner.

Delia turned to Robert. Her skin was the color of cinnamon in the sunlight, her eyes a rich dark brown. "I came to ask if you've found all you needed. Elise told us to watch out for you special. She also told us that we're going to get our new library because of you. I can't tell you how much that means to us. Me, in particular. This is the best job I've ever had. It sure beats flipping burgers. Have you seen the burger place on the highway just outside of town? That's where I used to work when I was younger. And let me tell you . . . don't ever eat there. It's terrible! The things they do . . ."

Her words sounded in his ear, but Robert couldn't have told anyone later what she said. All he could think of was that if Mr. Olsen and his manager were looking for a site for a new store and they were looking at the library grounds, it could mean only one thing—his nightmare of last night was about to come true! If those people wanted to build a supermarket, they certainly would have no use for the old house. They would tear it down without a thought, without a backward glance!

Delia's gaze had grown curious. Robert knew he must have paled. His body felt weak, as if he'd been hit by a savage blow.

"Is something wrong?" she asked.

He shook his head. "No, nothing. I just... I'm going to take a break now, so if you want to lock up..." He left his sentence unfinished. Then, gathering the materials he had used, he replaced them in the drawer and walked from the room. But not without a backward glance at the beautifully crafted fireplace.

He couldn't let it happen! He had no idea what his weapon to stop them with would be, but he had to find something... fast!

ELISE ARRIVED at the library promptly at 2.00 p.m. Delia was ready to leave from her part-time shift and Diane Conrad, early for her shift, was readying a second reading poster to act as a companion to the one already hanging on the wall in the children's section. By method of brightly colored cutouts of the various Teenage Mutant Ninja Turtles, a chart would monitor each child's reading progress over the summer.

"You just missed Professor Fairmont," Delia said, coming around the circulation desk as she reached into her purse for her car keys.

Elise's heart plunged. The closer she had come to the library, the more anxious she was to see him. She wished she hadn't gone to Worthington House this morning! She could have sent someone else! "Oh?" she said, trying not to let her disappointment show.

Delia shrugged. "He's only out to lunch, I think. He acted kind of funny when he left, but I got the feeling he'd be back."

Diane held up a Teenage Mutant Ninja Turtle character and shook her head. "I just don't understand what the kids see in these things. They'd have given me nightmares when I was a child."

Delia laughed as she started to walk away. "They still give me nightmares. My little brother leaves those little plastic replicas all over the house and I'm the one who steps on them. It's a good thing they don't break!"

Rebecca Sinclair stopped by the circulation desk after Delia left. "Would you like me to empty the bookmobile, Elise? I have time." The woman started to move away after Elise had gratefully agreed, but she turned back to say, "A shipment of books came in earlier. They're not ours, though. The shipping label says they are, but the invoice inside doesn't agree. I thought you should know."

The problems Elise knew she would face upon her return to the library had started. She thanked Rebecca again, and after murmuring a quick word to Diane, set off for the staff work area in back. All the while, the frustration she felt at not seeing Robert continued to grow. On the surface she functioned normally—smiling courteously, answering questions, resolving disputes. But underneath, in the private Elise, anger alternated with pain at their continued separation.

Before she had gone very far, though, she was stopped by Mary Phelps who, looking strained, asked to speak privately with her. Mary was once Dr. George Phelps's wife. During the past year, rumors of long-standing difficulties in their marriage had proved to be true, first with their separation and then with their recent divorce. The split was bitter and involved another woman—Marge Peterson, who ran the local diner and whom almost everyone in town liked. Mary didn't enjoy the same affection. Whether from a deep-seated fear of rejection or a need to lord it over others, Mary had clung to the illusions of grandeur her marriage to an influential doctor in the community provided. She tried too hard to keep up her social position. It was the be-all and end-all of her existence, and it alienated people.

An exotic perfume scented the air around the expensively clad woman and her hair was perfectly coiffed. But Elise wouldn't have traded lives with Mary for anything. In fact, she had always felt a little sorry for her.

"I've come to tell you goodbye, Elisa. I'm moving to Chicago. Melissa thinks I'll be happier there." She named her married daughter.

Elise murmured an appropriate reply.

Mary sniffed, her expression brittle. "And I probably will be. At least there I won't have to watch George cavort around with that hussy! I'm leaving this afternoon. Melissa is coming to get me."

"We'll miss you, Mary," Elise said softly.

"No, you won't," Mary snapped. Then she hedged, "Well, maybe a few will. You might. But most won't. Actually, I'm glad to be moving to Chicago. There's so much to do and see. So many people who . . . well, who aren't hicks. I'll drop you a line now and then, Elise, just to let you know what's happening."

Elise gave a sympathetic smile. "That would be wonderful," she murmured.

Mary, her head held high, walked out the door, down the sidewalk and, figuratively, out of Tyler. It was the end of an era for her and hopefully the beginning of a new, much better one.

Elise drew a breath and released it. Then she started to turn away, planning once again to go to the work area. But, as before, something happened to prevent her. When she looked up, it was to see that Robert had entered the library, and upon seeing her, had altered his course and was heading toward her.

As she watched him cross the room, Elise became highly sensitized to light, to sound, to everything that was happening within herself. She was conscious of a happiness she had never felt before—not this strongly, not this acutely. She was also aware of everything about him: how he dressed, how he moved, how his hair was combed, the expression on his face.

It was then she realized that something was wrong. She had no idea what, but it was in his eyes, in his tight smile.

He took her hand and pulled her into an even quieter area of the large room. "Elise," he said somberly, "I may need your help."

Elise frowned. "Of course. What can I do?"

His gaze softened at her spontaneous offer. Then it sobered again. "I understand that the man who owns Olsen's Supermarket is interested in buying the land the library sits on as a site for a new store."

"No one's told me that," Elise said.

"They were looking at it earlier." He paused. "Elise, *I* want to buy it."

Elise stared at him. "You?" she echoed incredulously. "Why?"

He waved a dismissive hand. "I just do. It's always been a dream of mine to own one of these old houses. They'll want to tear it down. I want to restore it. It has such . . . possibilities."

"But the cost. . . ." she protested.

"Damn the cost!" Robert returned, his voice rising.

Elise sensed that a couple of people turned to look at them, but she didn't look back. The force of Robert's personality was mesmerizing. From profound worry, his expression had changed to deep excitement. He was now like an engine at full power, the throttle pressed to the floor. "What can I do?" she asked.

"Tell me who to talk to. The town council? Who on the council? I don't want to take the chance I'll miss out!"

"Johnny Kelsey, Alyssa Baron, Nora Forrester. They're all on the town council."

He pulled her forward and kissed her. Not a short, perfunctory thank-you kiss, but one that had fire in its brevity. He set her back in place. "You're a beautiful woman, Elise Ferguson," he declared. "Thank you."

The wide smile he gave her warmed Elise to her toes...as if his kiss already hadn't! She laughed. "That's always nice to hear."

"Stick around and I'll tell you more often. Which way to the council's office?"

Elise thought of the misshipped books that awaited her attention, the fact that this was Pauline's day off, not to mention all the other details of daily life in the library...and she shrugged them away. "I'll show you," she volunteered. She had the satisfaction of being on the receiving end of another jubilant smile, not to mention the enjoyment of having his arm settle around her shoulders as they fell into step side by side. She didn't think to tell anyone what she was doing, she was so under his spell.

CHAPTER TEN

ROBERT HAD THOUGHT the situation over very carefully, trying to gauge every aspect, and he finally concluded that there was only one thing to do: proof or no proof, he had to strike first. He had to be sure that the house would remain safe. And he could tell no one his reason.

If word spread about his suspicions, a bidding war could erupt and everything would be lost. He would have to stand aside and watch as someone with far greater resources claimed the house as his own. And if his suspicions proved correct? The person who bought the house might decide not to keep it whole. Like plunderers of old, modern-day profiteers roamed the country looking for just such situations. They cared not at all for the history of the structures they bought. They were interested only in the buildings' treasures. And this house was in such poor condition, it would be easy to make the case for dismantlement. Then the valuable pieces could be sorted out and sold, bit by bit—a stained-glass window here, a fireplace lintel there. Frequently those pieces went for amazing sums of money at auction. To some, they were more valuable singly than as part of a whole house.

To a purist like Robert, such an act was a crime. When architects the stature of Frank Lloyd Wright and Stephen deVille designed a house, they conceived it as a complete entity, sometimes down to the placement of the furniture. It should remain that way to preserve the designer's vision, to preserve history.

And if he was wrong about the house's designer? The joke would be on him. He would own a house with beautiful imitations of the work of these great men. It wouldn't be the same, but Robert was willing to take the chance. In its own right the Friedrich house had a certain charm and a dignity of age and construction that could make it the fulfillment of his dream.

All things considered, he had only one course to follow. And if he hesitated, he would lose...if he hadn't lost already. What if Olsen and Smith had struck a deal with the members of the Tyler town council? What if, when he and Elise arrived at the council's office, it was to learn that the deal had been finalized? Robert's hand tightened on the steering wheel. His lips tightened as well. He wanted that house!

His glance was drawn to Elise, riding quietly in the seat next to him. He experienced a pang of guilt at not telling her the complete truth, but for the moment, because of the delicacy of the situation, he couldn't.

The trip to the council chambers was short. Elise led the way down the hall to the proper office, explaining that because council was made up of members who did not work full-time at the job, most days only a secretary was present to channel calls to the proper individuals within the city government. But on the first Monday of every month, the evening the council came together formally to conduct business, one of the council members was available for several hours in the afternoon to field telephone calls and take complaints from people who would be unable to attend the public meeting. Today that council member was Johnny Kelsey.

Elise and Robert could see him from the doorway as he sat at the oversize desk in the room beyond the secretary's office, looking uncomfortable with the telephone cradled to his ear. He didn't see them, and Elise pulled Robert to one side so that she could speak to him.

"Are you truly certain you want to do this?" she asked. Her soft blue eyes were filled with concern. "Have you had time to think it over properly? That house is going to take a small fortune to repair. You know about the roof, you know about the water pipes, but do you know about the wiring? Some of it was put in not long after electricity was discovered! This is an old house, Robert. Old and dilapidated. There's so much wrong with it that—"

He stilled her lips with a finger. "I know," he said. "I've examined it. But I still want to buy it."

Elise shook her head. "I think you're mad."

"It's what I want to do."

Elise continued to look at him, her sweet face still uncertain, her lips slightly parted...and it was all Robert could do not to sweep her into his arms.

Johnny Kelsey moved smartly out the door and was obviously surprised when he saw them. Elise quickly took a step back, her color rising. Robert smiled.

"I was just on my way down the hall for some water," Johnny explained. "Everybody has some kind of problem today. We need more stop signs; there are too many stop signs. One man's threatening to sue because the garbage people picked up a chair his wife had put out on the curb and he didn't know about it. It was his favorite." Johnny took a deep breath and rubbed his neck. "Honestly, sometimes I don't know why I ever took on this job. It's completely thankless. All you hear are people's gripes."

"We don't have a gripe, Johnny," Elise said. "We're here to solve a problem."

"Then you're just the kind of people I like to talk to." Johnny grinned. "Have a seat in the office and I'll be right back."

Elise and Robert went into the small room, which wasn't exactly luxurious. They had just seated themselves when Johnny returned. He moved behind the large desk. "Now, what can I do for you?" he asked, sitting down. "You say you're going to solve a problem?"

Robert spoke up. "I understand that someone might be interested in buying the old library property."

"Martin Olsen," Johnny agreed.

"What would he do with it?" Robert asked.

"Tear it down and build another grocery store. He's had his eye on the place for a couple of years, but he's still not sure if he wants to expand. His one store is doing great business, but he's afraid he might cut into that by opening a second. Not increase his profit enough to justify the expense. So he's still thinking about it."

"Has he made an offer?"

"Nope."

"Then the field is clear."

"As a bell."

"I'd like to make an offer."

Johnny looked at him closely. "*You'd* like to make an offer?"

Robert nodded. At lunch, after making his decision, he had explored the town's public records and had determined what he considered a fair price. He then added a cushion for competition and now voiced the total.

Johnny sat back in his chair. "You realize you'll have to submit a formal offer."

"I'll have my attorney draw something up. I'd like to get the deal settled as soon as possible. If I have him fax the information to you this afternoon, would we be able to get it settled today?"

"You're in a big hurry."

"I've never been accused of letting grass grow under my feet when I want something." Robert's smile worked its charm even on Johnny.

Johnny grinned back, one man appreciating another man's decisiveness. "We have a general council meeting tonight at seven. Now, I'll have to call Martin Olsen, to let him know what's going on. It's something I think we should do out of courtesy, because he was interested in the property first. Do I have your permission to tell him the amount of your offer?"

Robert gave a tight nod. Then he stood up. "I guess I'd better get busy," he said and turned to help Elise to her feet.

Johnny looked from one to the other, but his glance stayed longest on Robert. "Exactly what do you plan to do with the place?" he asked.

"Renovate it."

"Renovate it?" Johnny repeated incredulously. He laughed, until he saw that Robert was serious. Sobering, he turned to Elise. "Didn't you tell him?"

She shrugged. "He says he still wants it."

Johnny shook his head, as if what people did in the world was sometimes amazing. "I'll put you down to speak at the meeting tonight. I'm sure everyone will want to hear what you have to say."

"Put my name down, too, Johnny," Elise said. "I want to speak as well."

Johnny made a couple of notations, then he saw them to the door.

Once outside the tiny room Robert said, "You didn't have to do that."

"I wanted to," Elise answered.

"But you think I'm mad, remember?"

"Everyone is entitled to a little madness. If it's what you want, I'd like to try to help you get it."

They walked to Robert's car and got inside. But before starting the engine, Robert turned to her. "Why? Why do you want to help me?"

Elise looked away.

Robert gently brought her chin back around. "Why?" he repeated softly.

Elise's gaze fluttered to his.

If only he knew her well enough to read the look in her eyes, he thought. As it was, he saw a swirling mix of hesitancy and warmth, fear and passion. Robert felt his throat tighten. "I don't want to take advantage of you, Elise," he said huskily. "I don't want you to do anything that you feel is wrong."

"How could it be wrong?" she whispered, and suddenly he knew they were no longer talking only of his purchase of the old library. They were talking about themselves and the feelings between them that had started to grow.

Robert shook his head, trying to clear it. But when he looked back at her, nothing had changed. "I don't know what's happening, Elise. Where we'll end up. When I came here the first time, I wasn't expecting..."

Emboldened by his words, Elise touched his lips with her finger. "It doesn't matter," she said. "A person can't always play things safe. I have for most of my life and look what I've got to show for it."

Robert kissed her finger, then he worked his way down to her wrist, where his mouth lingered on the tiny pulse. Excitement mounted within him, yet at the same time so did his consideration for her. He was aware of the cars on the street behind them, aware of the people walking along the sidewalk. The view into the car was unimpeded. "You have a whole town that loves you," he offered.

"But not one special person." Her words were tremulous, difficult to say.

She tried to look away, but he wouldn't let her. He kissed the inside of her wrist again. "Could I be that special person, Elise?" he murmured.

He felt her tremble and he wanted badly to do more than caress her wrist. Their gazes locked. She wanted it, too. Robert's first impulse was to start the car. They could go somewhere, find privacy. Then they could begin to explore....

A car pulled into a parking slot next to the Mercedes. A pretty young woman with shoulder-length brown hair and a slim, athletic body bounced out of the driver's seat. A big, shaggy dog quickly followed. After a quick glance into the Mercedes's passenger seat, the woman recognized Elise and tapped lightly on the window.

Elise started. She jerked her hand away from Robert, then rolled the window down partway.

"Hi!" the woman greeted. "I've been meaning to come see you all week, Elise. I wanted to tell you how sorry I was to have to leave early the day the books got wet. But I had an appointment in Sugar Creek that I couldn't break. Patrick told me he'd forward my apologies. I looked all over to tell you myself, but someone said you'd gone home to change clothes. I truly am sorry I couldn't stay longer."

Elise found a smile. "That's perfectly all right, Pam. I understood."

"Still—" The dog barked and the woman laughed, bending down to rub his furry head. "Samson is in a hurry," she explained. "We're going to the pet shop to buy his favorite treat, Puppy Yummies. He doesn't look like much of a puppy, but he thinks he is." She glanced across at Robert. Her blue eyes were friendly and only slightly curious.

"The two of you may have met at the library," Elise said. "But you probably weren't introduced. Pam, this is Robert Fairmont. Robert, Pam Kelsey. She's married to Patrick Kelsey, Johnny and Anna's son. You and Patrick took down shelves together.''

Robert nodded. ''I remember. Hello.''

Pam smiled brightly. ''Oh, I remember you, too! Patrick said that you—'' Her words were cut off by Samson, who leaped to the end of his leash and jerked her arm. Laughing again, she let herself be dragged away. ''We'll have to talk another time. Samson just can't wait anymore!''

Elise rolled up the window. She watched as Pam disappeared inside a shop a short distance down the street. She wished that she could follow her. She couldn't believe what she'd said only a few moments before. She had practically begged Robert to go to bed with her! She was too humiliated to look at him.

Instead she mumbled, ''Pam came to Tyler last fall. She's the high school's football coach, believe it or not. She took over a mediocre team and turned them into—''

''Elise,'' Robert interrupted.

Elise shut up. He waited for her to look at him. Slowly she did.

His features were so dear to her. If she had wondered before if she truly loved him, she was no longer in doubt. A week, a month, a year, a hundred years... her feelings would never change. ''Yes?'' she whispered.

''I'd like to take you to dinner. Not to discuss the new library or the old library, but to discuss us. Something extraordinary happened to me when I came to Tyler. I didn't recognize it at first, but I do now. I want to be with you, Elise. Tomorrow night. On a man-to-woman basis. Will you come?''

Elise caught her breath. The rhythm of her heart increased. ''Yes,'' she agreed softly. ''I'll come.''

Robert smiled and recaptured her hand. Then he gave her wrist another swift kiss, his eyes dancing with happiness.

ELISE SPENT the rest of the afternoon in a euphoric haze. Robert cared for her. He wanted to be with her. She was ''something extraordinary'' that had come into his life.

Not even the event that dominated the afternoon newspaper could dampen her enthusiasm. She heard the murmurs, saw the whispered conversations and the disbelieving shakes of heads when, after much delay, the report from the Wisconsin Medical Examiner's Office was finally released. But in her altered state of being, the grisly news as to the cause of Margaret Ingalls's death just didn't stick in her mind. Possibly her detachment was a form of protection. She didn't *want* to hear anything sad or upsetting. Her hard-won joy was like the sweetest of nectars, a treasure to be nurtured and preserved.

It wasn't until Elise returned home that she was hit with the harshness of reality. Bea, seeing her dreamy state, took pleasure in being as hateful as she could in her accusations against Judson. Her goal seemed to be to hurt Elise more than the patriarch of the Ingalls's family.

''See?'' she demanded. ''What did I tell you? He knew. That's why he got 'sick' so suddenly over the weekend. He knew what they'd say and what everyone in town would say in turn. Did you read it?" she asked. "Where's the newspaper? Did you bring it inside?"

As Elise handed the latest edition of the *Tyler Citizen* to her sister, she felt a little sick inside.

Bea unfolded it. "See?" She thrust the front page headline at her. "'Massive Blunt Trauma to the Head'... But from what Annabelle said, it was a miracle they could tell anything at all. The body was in the ground all those years and all tangled up in tree roots, not to mention what the backhoe did to it. They probably had to piece everything back together like a jigsaw puzzle. Modern science certainly is wonderful, isn't it? But I suppose Judson doesn't think it's so wonderful."

Elise tried to cling to what was left of her happiness, but it was fast receding. As quickly as she could, she gathered the fragments that remained and locked them inside the same section of her soul as the gemstone of her newly discovered love. "I doubt that Judson was worrying about what the town would think. It probably upset him to hear what had happened to her. He did love Margaret once, remember."

Bea snorted. "He was probably glad to be rid of her. I remember the hell she put him through. But I always kind of admired her. She did exactly what she wanted, when she wanted, and she didn't care who might object. She didn't seem to care that she had a husband, either. He must have been wild with jealousy. That's probably the real story. He caught her with someone and whacked her a good one on the head. Then he buried her and pretended that she'd run away. Our Judson is extremely clever when he wants to be."

"Bea! Please! Stop saying things like that!"

Bea thrust out her chin. "I have every right to speak my mind."

"Not when it can cause harm to someone!"

"Why should I be different from everyone else in Tyler?" Bea demanded.

"Annabelle isn't everyone! Most of the people in town feel sorry for Judson. They know he's not capable of doing harm to anyone, particularly not his wife!"

"Don't you know that even nice people can be pushed too far? Haven't you learned that yet, Elise? Has life been so easy for you that you go around in some sort of daze? You should have seen yourself a few minutes ago. I almost thought you'd been drinking!"

Elise understood exactly how nice people could be pushed too far. She was a nice person and she was often pushed close to the breaking point. Like now, for instance. She strove hard to calm herself.

"It's him, isn't it?" Bea demanded, returning to her favorite theme. "Elise, I keep telling you and telling you—"

Elise's control snapped. "Never mind about him!" she cried. "I don't want you talking about him! *Leave Robert out of this!*"

"He's cast some kind of spell on you, hasn't he? You never used to talk to me that way. I'm only thinking of your own good, Elise. I'm only trying to help!"

Elise rubbed a hand across her brow, pushing her hair back with an agitated movement. She felt torn in two. One part of her wanted to assure Bea that everything would be all right. That Robert was a passing fancy and posed no danger to their way of life. The other part of her longed to go with Robert and not be subjected to Bea's harsh words ever again. To love him and be loved by him and to think of nothing else. In a controlled voice she said, "Well, don't try to help so much. I'm not a child, Bea. I'm old enough to know my own mind."

Bea gave a tight little smile. "But I still think of you as a child, Elise. You know that my most vivid memory is when you were eleven . . . the way you used to like to go over to your girlfriend's house to play. You know I could never forget that, even if you can." Her message was unmistakable.

Elise drew a ragged breath. That same incident was etched indelibly in her own mind. How could she ever forget?

She turned away, her shoulders slumped, her head lowered. If Bea had wanted to cripple her emerging spirit, she had just won an important round. No longer did Elise float in a happy daze. Her spirit was as crushed as Judson Ingalls's must have been.

ROBERT HAD OFFERED to pick her up for the council meeting and she agreed. When the time came, though, all Elise wanted to do was hide in her room. Bea had reacted badly when she learned that Elise would be going out again that evening, and the offer to drop her off at a friend's house met with no approval. It was too late to make such arrangements, she'd claimed. She couldn't just push herself off on people, even on a friend, because it would be rude! Which Bea had never let stop her before.

When the doorbell rang Elise hurried to answer it. To save herself more trouble, she pushed her way onto the porch, forcing Robert to back up. Her smile was strained as she explained, "We should get there early. The seats fill up fast."

Robert viewed her excuse quizzically. "Council meetings in Tyler are that popular?"

"There's not a lot to do here on a Monday night."

She set off for the car and he followed.

She knew he would have no problem seeing that she was tense, just from the way she clasped her hands as she perched uncomfortably on the passenger seat. But if she didn't restrain them, they'd tremble. Her argument with Bea had disturbed her more than she thought. She was as upset as she had been the night she walked to Josephine's. But she wasn't with Josephine tonight. She was with Robert and there were just some things she couldn't tell him ... things she couldn't tell anyone. So she continued to sit anxiously and wait for the evening to be over.

ROBERT GLANCED at Elise. He wondered what was wrong. When he had left her earlier in the day, he'd thought they were coming to some kind of agreement. Both were aware of the attraction that had sprung up between them. Both admitted it. She had seemed happy then, almost girlish. Now, she was this beaten woman who looked as if she'd jump through the car roof if he so much as whispered her name. What had happened? Who had...? Bea! It *had* to be her sister. But what could possibly have occurred between them to cause such a change? He wanted to ask her, but he sensed that she wouldn't confide in him.

Then suddenly he wondered if he wasn't the cause. He had made Bea angry the day before, forced her to do something she hadn't wanted to do. Had she as a result taken her anger out on Elise?

Robert felt another pang of guilt. He was keeping what he suspected was the truth about the house from her. And like an unwelcome guest, he had airily created a situation in her home that she might still be paying for. He wanted to reach out to her, to tell her he was sorry, but he knew he couldn't do that without upsetting her more.

To help ease the situation, he switched on the car's sound system, and soon soothing music by Bach filled the air. To his satisfaction, he saw that as the distance from Elise's house to the council chambers decreased, so, too, did some of her tension. By the time they arrived at the low brick-faced building, she had relaxed enough to glance at him. He gave her a reassuring smile. *Everything will be fine,* he tried to wordlessly tell her. *Don't worry.* And he would have sworn that she received the message, because a smile flickered in return. It even managed to reach her eyes.

Inside the meeting room a number of people were already present. They huddled together in small groups, their faces intent as they focused on their discussions. Despite what Elise told him, Robert was surprised by the turnout.

Elise led the way to a row of chairs near the front of the room and sat down. Her body remained stiff, her expression serious. But this time Robert sensed the cause was different. She acknowledged the people who called out to her, but she didn't go over to talk with them. As conversations buzzed in the air around them, Elise managed to distance herself.

Robert leaned close, questioning softly, "Is there going to be a lynching tonight? Is it me? Are people angry that I want to buy the old library?"

Elise looked at him blankly, then she shook her head. "No, this is something else entirely. Do you remember what I told you about the body found at the lodge? The report on the cause of death came in today. People are reacting."

"What happened?" he asked curiously.

"It looks as if someone hit Margaret Ingalls on the head very hard."

Robert glanced at the people around them. "And you don't approve of people talking about that?"

"I'm concerned for Judson. I don't like the idea that a few people spreading rumors could . . ."

The members of the town council entered the room. All but one found seats at a long table positioned at the front of the room. Elise stopped talking and Robert straightened away from her.

A nice-looking woman with ash-blond hair and a slim build—Elise whispered that she was Nora Gates Forrester—remained standing. She was forced to bang the gavel twice to call the meeting to order. Finally the last voices in the assembly trailed off.

The woman gave everyone a level look. "I realize there are some present tonight who have never attended a council meeting before. Well, I'm here to tell you that we're not a clearinghouse for gossip. If you want to gossip, go outside." She paused. Feet shuffled but no one got up to leave. The woman smiled. "All

right,'' she said approvingly. "Now, since Mayor Ing-
strom has been called away on business again, in my
capacity as mayor pro tem, I'll be chairing tonight's
meeting. Our first order of business is..."

What followed was an interesting experience for
Robert. He had attended a few civic meetings before in
support of his work, but they had always been big-city
affairs with huge meeting halls and various, almost
professional, special-interest groups. In Tyler, most
people seemed genuinely concerned with the good of the
town and the problems were of a much smaller scale.
The stop sign people were there, pro and con, and the
angry man fumed about his chair. Finally, near the end
of two hours, Nora Forrester brought up the sale of the
library and turned the meeting over to Johnny Kelsey.

Robert felt his stomach muscles tighten. All afternoon he had been on pins and needles, railing against
the enforced wait. He had seen his lawyer and put into
motion the terms of his offer, then checked to be sure
that the offer had been extended to the town government of Tyler. The process had gone smoothly; the only
possible hitch would be if Martin Olsen decided to
counteroffer.

Johnny stood up and addressed the group. "As Nora
said, we've received an offer for the piece of real estate
we presently use as our library. The offer comes from
the man who's helping us build our new library, Professor Robert Fairmont of Milwaukee. He's made this
offer even though he's seen the place." There was a tit-
ter of laughter and Johnny allowed a dry smile. "He
says he wants to renovate it. Personally, I think he'd be
better off tearing the place down and starting over, but

that's between him and his pocketbook. Now…as a few of you know, someone else has been interested in the old library for a couple of years. Not the building, the land. Martin? Are you here? I can't see you out there in this crowd."

A man stood up, the same one Robert had seen earlier in the backyard of the library. His mop of thick red hair was hard to forget. "I'm here, Johnny," he said, then sat down.

Johnny continued, "I thought it only fair to give Martin a chance to have his say if he wanted. He told me he needed to think it over. Have you thought it over long enough, Martin?"

Martin stood up again. Robert held his breath. The man frowned, shifted his feet, then said, "I'm gonna pass on it, Johnny. The time's just not right yet."

Relief flooded through Robert's body. Still, he knew he wasn't completely out of the woods. It was possible the council might want to hold out on the off chance that, in the year before the new library was completed, the real estate market might perk up and they could get a higher price.

"Professor Fairmont," Johnny Kelsey said.

Robert stood up. He felt Elise look at him, pulling for him. He straightened his shoulders. "Call me Robert," he said.

Johnny smiled. "Would you mind answering a few questions, Robert? Some council members are curious about what you want to do. You said you want to renovate the place. Why?"

"Because it's a beautiful example of its period. Houses of that type are rare. And I'd hate like hell to see it torn down."

"You realize the condition that it's in. As an architect, you know the problems you'll face. The expense."

"I do."

"Yet you still want to buy it."

"I do."

Alyssa Baron spoke up. "You also realize that it won't be available until the new library is completed?"

Robert smiled. "Which gives me incentive to hurry construction along."

Nora Forrester expressed Robert's private fear. "But if we contract to sell it to you now, there's always the possibility that the real estate market will improve over the next year and prices will go up. We'd lose money."

"The market could just as easily go down," he countered.

Elise rose to her feet at his side. "I'd like to address that subject, please," she requested.

Johnny motioned for her to continue. Elise took a breath. "I think we're all forgetting the debt we owe Robert for his work on the new library. You know he's not charging a fee, when he easily could. If it weren't for him we'd be in a much worse position than we are. Sometime in the next week or two we'll be presenting the modified plans for the council's approval . . . and I can tell you right now, it's exciting. I believe everyone in Tyler is going to be pleased." She took another breath. "As for his reasons for buying the old library, do we really have to know? Isn't it enough that he wants it? As the place stands now, it's an eyesore—not so much on the outside, but that's only a matter of time. It's being held together by wishes and prayers.

"I can't tell you how many times I've heard people say they want Tyler to move forward into the next century but not by losing the historic character of the town. Well, this is a perfect opportunity. Beautifully appointed houses of another age are always attractive to people. They like to see them when they visit, and sometimes the fact that the people of a town care enough to preserve their history convinces people to move to that town. The Friedrich house is part of our history. I say we let Robert preserve it."

The weight of Elise's words when she spoke about the library was impressive. If Robert had not been aware of it before, it would have been readily apparent to him now why the people of Tyler showed her such respect. He saw it in their faces, heard it in the cries of support that followed her address.

The members of council conferred among themselves, then Johnny Kelsey grinned broadly and said, "If you want it, Robert, it's yours."

Applause burst out across the room. Several people seated nearby turned to shake Robert's hand and welcome him to their community.

Robert accepted their greetings, then, still standing, he said, "I don't want anyone to feel indebted to me. That's not the way I operate." He glanced at Elise. "I realize it's going to be some time before the house is mine, but I'd like to do something for Tyler straightaway. I'd like to put a new roof on the library—to preserve the books and to preserve the interior."

The offer was enthusiastically received. Elise looked up at him with glowing eyes. When he sat down, Robert took her hand as he continued to receive the good wishes of his new neighbors.

The other was enthusiastically received. Erica looked up at him with growing eyes. When he sat down, he reached back her head to be positioned to receive the next shake of his ever-to-shoulder.

CHAPTER ELEVEN

ELISE WAS QUIET as they drove back to her house. She was happy for Robert that he had won what he wanted. And she was happy for herself—if he purchased a home in Tyler, it meant that his tie to the community would be stronger. Also, she was glad that the library would get a new roof. But somehow she just couldn't muster much enthusiasm. She had been on a roller-coaster ride of emotion all day long. From euphoria to depression, she had touched all bases. At the moment what she felt most was exhaustion.

Still, she didn't want to go back home to Bea. She didn't want to have to brush her hair. She didn't want to have to defend what she had done this evening or to fight about her plans for tomorrow night.

She glanced at Robert. In the half-light from the street lamps lining the roadway, she could see that his expression was thoughtful. He had been elated when they'd reached the car and had asked her to go somewhere with him to celebrate, but Elise had declined, citing Bea. After looking momentarily disappointed, he'd rallied to say that they would celebrate tomorrow night. Since then both had been quiet, prisoners of their own private thoughts.

Elise sighed as she looked away, an action that drew his attention.

"Are you tired?" he asked.

"Very," she murmured, deciding to be honest.

He checked the street ahead, then turned back to study her. After a moment he asked quietly, "Elise, are you happy? And I don't mean right now, at this moment. I mean every day...in your life."

The unexpectedness of his inquiry disconcerted her. "I—I suppose," she stammered. No one had ever asked her that question before. No one had ever probed so deeply.

"Only suppose? I ask...because I don't believe you *are* happy. And I wonder if I'm partly to blame. Living with Bea isn't easy—you've told me that. And I couldn't have helped the situation by antagonizing her the other day. If I made matters worse for you, I'm sorry. I'd like to talk to her, but I don't know if she—"

"No!" Elise interrupted, instantly alarmed. She didn't want Robert trying to talk to Bea at this point. The thought of what Bea might say or do unsettled her. "At least, not right now. You haven't really done anything. She...Bea..."

Robert glanced at her again and what he saw made him pull the car off the road. They weren't far from Elise and Bea's house, but he obviously didn't want to wait. He switched the engine off and faced her. "Then tell me what's bothering you," he requested.

His voice was so gentle, his concern so real. A ball of emotion burned through Elise's body before finally finding a way to burst free. She had kept such tight rein on herself over the years. Kept the secret that only Bea and herself knew about. She had told no one. Not Donna Cook, who had been her best friend at the time; not even Josephine, who became her best friend as an adult. It was a secret shared only by the two sisters, even if most times it lay buried in the not-so-quiet past.

Elise tried to hide her tears, but Robert forced her face into the light. When he saw that she was crying, he made a soft sound and gathered her into his arms.

Elise tried never to cry in front of other people. Since she was a small child her tears had been reserved for when no one could see them. But held against Robert—feeling the strength of his arms around her, absorbing his warmth—she felt a sudden lifting of that restriction. As on the first day she'd met him, he had a way of endowing her with hope that nothing was as dark or as impossible as she had previously thought.

His voice was shaken as he tried to persuade her to stop crying, but fresh evidence of his tenderness only made Elise sob harder, made her cling to him with greater need. Forty-two years of pain had to be excised. Forty-two years of guilt.

"Elise..." He whispered over and over.

Finally she grew calmer, and the silence that stretched between them was broken only by an occasional shuddering breath. He continued to hold her, allowing her the privilege of deciding when she wanted to pull away.

Moments later she did, but only enough to dab at his dampened jacket with her fingertips. "I've ruined your suit," she murmured.

"A suit can be cleaned," he said.

She sniffed and chanced a quick glance at him. He looked pale beneath his natural tan, unsettled, the light in his yellow-brown eyes filled with compassion. She avoided being caught by his gaze, her attention instead returning to the dampened area of his jacket.

"Elise," he prompted softly when he saw that she wasn't going to look up again. "Tell me what it is. If there's any way that I can help..."

She shook her head. "It all happened such a long, long time ago."

"*What* happened?" he insisted.

Elise played with the point of his collar, unaware that she was doing so. "Bea's accident. She—she blames me for what happened. That's why she...why she—" She couldn't go on. Tears again rushed into her eyes.

Robert remained very still as he waited for her to steady herself.

At last Elise continued, her voice a whisper. "I've never told this to anyone before. I was too ashamed. Her accident really was *my* fault. If I had done what I was supposed to do, it would never have happened. She...when I was eleven, my job was to keep the steps clear of snow in winter—the two leading down from the porch to the sidewalk in front of the house and the ones that led to the garage in back. I did it. I shoveled them all the time. Except once."

Mentally, Elise was no longer with Robert. She was back at the house where her family had lived from the time she was five and they first moved to Tyler. Shrubs guarded the two steps to the tiny porch and were positioned along the sidewalk to the street. In winter, snow made the front yard a wonderland. She and Donna had already built one snowman and had decided to move on to Donna's house to create another. Then they had become involved with some other children in the construction of a snow fort and the time had passed quickly.

"I didn't shovel them," Elise said, shaking her head. "The one time I didn't... We'd had a bad storm the day before, snow and ice and wind. My parents wouldn't let me go outside. The next day was better—it only snowed lightly a couple of times. I played outside all day." She drew a ragged breath. "I was late coming home. I saw snow on the front steps, but I decided it wasn't that much. I didn't want to take the time to clear it." She paused, still caught up in the past. "Bea had a date that evening... she always had a date. She used to get into trouble about that with our dad. He didn't like her going out so much, especially on weeknights, but Bea was determined. They argued and Bea ran out of the house. Her boyfriend was waiting in his car. Dad didn't like that, either. I saw Bea pause and wave to her boyfriend, then she ran down the steps...and when she did, she fell. I saw her. I knew immediately what had happened. The snow I left on the steps must have melted a little, and when the temperature dropped, it turned to ice." She looked at Robert, her gaze pleading for understanding. "I didn't mean not to do it. I was just afraid I'd be in trouble if I came in late. I didn't mean for Bea..."

Robert drew her back into his arms and stroked her hair. "Shh," he soothed. "No one could believe you meant it to happen. It was an accident, that's all. Just an accident."

Elise pulled away. "But Bea..."

"Would you blame her if your positions were reversed?"

"No, I'd probably blame myself, but—"

"So would most people. Under the circumstances you described—a bad storm the day before, snow showers that day—Bea should never have tried to run down those steps. Ice can form in a matter of minutes. How old was she—sixteen, seventeen? You said she was dating."

"Seventeen," Elise whispered.

"Definitely old enough to know better."

"But it was my job!" Elise repeated.

Robert looked at her. He could see that she would never shirk her duties. Responsibility had been drummed into her from an early age and reinforced by what she considered to be her failure to her sister. "Does that mean you have to pay for your mistake the rest of your life?"

"Bea does! She can't walk!"

"Bea's partially responsible for what happened."

"Then we both pay!"

"Why are you getting angry?"

"I'm not angry! I just..." Elise stopped. Her hands had curled into fists against his chest and she realized that she had hit him. Instantly she jerked away, reaching for the door handle. He had tried to help her and look how she repaid him!

He caught hold of her arm. "Elise, don't."

"No! I..."

"Elise, look at me!"

Elise's struggles ceased, and after a moment she did as he requested.

"You don't have to be a slave to Bea all your life. She can have a full life if she wants to. So can you. It's never too late."

"Sometimes I think it is," Elise whispered, her throat tight.

Robert smiled. "No, it's never too late. I saw my friend go through something very much like this. It's not been easy for him or for his wife, but they managed."

Elise continued to look at him, her hair mussed, her cheeks splotched with tears, and Robert didn't think he could remember a more beautiful sight. In such a short time, this woman had come to mean so much to him. What he felt for her was more than mere attraction. He shied away from putting a name to it, yet he knew that it was more than friendship. She had trusted him with a secret from her past, something she said she'd never told anyone. That knowledge humbled him.

He touched her cheek with the side of his finger, gently stroking the soft skin. "You're tired," he said. "Why don't I take you home so you can get a good night's rest, and we'll talk about this tomorrow. I appreciate the honor of your confidence, Elise. I'll never tell anyone. Not unless you ask me to."

Elise managed a smile, and long after dropping her off at her house, Robert carried the memory of that tremulous response.

THE NEXT MORNING Elise awoke with a feeling of rebirth. Her guilt about the burden Bea must carry through life had not lessened, but it had undergone a subtle change. Even to herself the evolution was hard to describe, but it had to do with her attitude toward herself and toward Bea. It was as if she were seeing the two of them through different eyes. No longer was she a woman looking at the situation from a child's viewpoint, with a child's sensibilities. A terrible thing had happened to Bea, something that had shaped her life. But it wasn't the only thing that would shape her life. And if, until this moment, they both had allowed it to be, there was no reason why, with careful prodding, that fact shouldn't change.

Elise tapped on her sister's door when she was ready to leave. She had tried to be kinder to Bea over breakfast, tried to be more patient. She didn't feel quite so trapped when she was in her presence or quite so intimidated. As a result, Bea had looked at her oddly, as if trying to gauge what was going on.

"I'm leaving, Bea," Elise called through the door. Buttercup twined about her ankles, purring and mewing at the same time. "Buttercup is here. I think she'd like in. May I open the door?"

The door opened. The cat scooted inside. Bea sat in her chair, glowering. "Thanks," she said shortly.

Elise knew that the day was going to be hectic. Many of the books that had been transported to Fellowship Lutheran were ready to be brought back to the library. But instead of coming home to make a quick lunch, she decided to do something different. "Bea, I was wondering. How would you like to go out to lunch today? It's been a long time since we've done anything like that together."

"Are you getting tired of cooking?" Bea demanded shortly.

"No. I thought you might enjoy getting out of the house. We can start doing it every Tuesday, if you like. Maybe Tuesdays and Thursdays. We could even go shopping in Chicago sometime...spend the night, paint the town. What do you think?"

Bea frowned. "I think you've been sniffing too much library paste!"

Elise laughed. "Well, think about it," she said. "After we eat, we can stop by Worthington House and you can see Inger Hansen. Isn't she the person you used to like to talk with about dolls?"

"Yes..." Bea replied slowly.

"So, as I said, think about it. I'll give you a call in a couple of hours and see what you decide. If you'd rather not, that's okay, too."

Bea continued to eye her with suspicion but she said nothing.

Elise smiled to herself as she turned away. For once her sister seemed speechless.

THE BIG NEWS at the library featured several events: Robert's plans to buy the old building and his promise to reroof it, the Ingalls family's continuing saga of troubles, the transfer of a great portion of the now-dry books back to the Biography Room and, to top the day, the engagement of Marge Peterson to Dr. George Phelps. Marge ran the town's only diner, and when she sported a huge diamond solitaire on the appropriate finger of her left hand, word spread fast. When Elise heard, she immediately thought of Mary and was glad that the poor woman's daughter had spirited her out of town the day before.

The news that Robert intended to purchase the library was met with approval by all. He already had a number of acquaintances in town, just from his short visits—especially the first, when he had plunged in to help with the book rescue.

Elise examined the old building with new eyes, trying to see it as Robert did. It was old, it needed tons of work, but she supposed that it had character. She had always had a soft spot for the place herself, even through the darkest days. Still, it concerned her that he might have acted too precipitously.

Bea declined her invitation to go out to lunch that day, which gave Elise pause to wonder if possibly *she* might have acted too precipitously where her sister was concerned. A change had occurred in *her* outlook to life, but nothing of the sort had happened to Bea yet. Had she pushed her too hard too fast? But instead of concentrating on the negative, Elise determined to concentrate on the positive. She would continue to prompt her sister to get out of the house and into the world because it was the right thing to do. Only she would use care not to overwhelm her.

CLINGING TO THE POSITIVE proved difficult, though, when Elise was met by the force of Bea's negative determination. By evening Bea's black mood had deepened and her suspicions increased. She didn't say much, but she watched Elise closely, quietly analyzing her every word, her every gesture.

As evidence of her distraction, Bea put up very little resistance to Elise's proposed date with Robert. Her only comment was, "I hear the police want to question Judson again. If I were him, I'd worry." After her halfhearted attempt to upset Elise failed, she lapsed back into silence.

Elise wanted to look her best that evening. This was such a special time, their first actual date. She wore a becoming aqua print dress, white shoes and belt and little white pearls in her ears. Her body tingled with anticipation.

The doorbell rang and Elise hurried to answer it. Her smile was enough to take Robert's breath away. He actually stood there as if stunned before quickly gathering himself to step into the house.

With him, he brought a gift and a bouquet of flowers. He handed the flowers to Elise and delivered the gaily wrapped package to Bea, who had just rolled into the front room.

"What is it?" Bea grunted.

"Open it and find out," Robert replied.

Elise arranged the flowers in a vase but kept a wary eye on her sister.

Bea made a tiny tear in the paper, tore it a little more. "It's a doll," she said coldly.

"A Hildegard Günzel. I don't remember you having one in your collection. She's my sister's favorite doll designer and I thought you might enjoy having one by her as well."

"I don't *want* a Hildegard Günzel."

Elise felt the old nervousness try to reassert control. She had to bite back a plea for Bea to behave properly.

She knew she couldn't allow herself to play that kind of game anymore. "Possibly it will grow on you," she murmured. Then she added, "I may be late, so don't wait up," before she turned brightly to Robert and asked, "Are you ready?"

As they left the house, Elise felt like a butterfly newly emerged from its chrysalis. Her wings were still damp but they were definitely growing stronger.

"I made a reservation at Timberlake Lodge," Robert said as they approached the car. "But if you like, we can cancel it and go to a little place I know in Milwaukee. I'd like to show it to you."

"That sounds wonderful," Elise enthused, her eyes shining.

THE RESTAURANT was Moroccan and specialized in roasted lamb, with entertainment by an amazingly talented belly dancer who had mysterious dark eyes and tiny cymbals on her fingers. The people who worked in the restaurant all seemed to know Robert, and their meal was interrupted by frequent friendly inquiries as to whether they were enjoying their time there.

"I taught their son a few years ago," Robert explained. "The dancer is his sister, the chef is his father, the hostess is his mother and everyone else seems to be a cousin. It's a family-run business."

Elise nodded, her expression reflecting her enjoyment of the evening. It had been light and fun, yet with an edge of awareness that made everything exciting.

After they'd stayed at the popular restaurant for as long as they felt they should—a group of people had gathered in the vestibule to wait for tables—Elise experienced a momentary sadness. She didn't want the evening to end.

Robert must have felt the same way because, after settling behind the wheel of his car, he turned to ask, "Would you like to see my apartment? It's only a few blocks away."

When Elise hesitated, he gave her a quick smile. "I promise I won't do anything rude."

"I didn't expect you would."

He took her answer as yes and drove to an apartment tower just off the lake. Everything was new and modern, from the parking garage to the elevator. They were whisked to the tenth floor and stepped onto sound-absorbing carpet in the corridor.

Elise waited as he unlocked the door, then moved inside after he switched on a light. His apartment was just as she had imagined it. Sophisticated, with clean lines and abundant good taste, it was pleasing to the eye. It also claimed a spectacular view of Lake Michigan through a row of windows that formed the outside wall.

The only article of furniture that seemed out of place was a drafting table at one side of the large, open room. Robert saw the direction of her gaze and shrugged. "Tools of the trade," he said.

Elise walked over to the table and found numerous sheets of drawings and diagrams. Some looked finished, others were not. All were of the new Tyler library. "You've been busy," she murmured. A partially completed ink drawing of the finished building held her attention longest. "This is beautiful," she said. She ran a finger over the distinctive hand lettering near the bottom of the page. "How long did it take you to learn to do this? To make these letters?"

"A long time. Some people think it comes naturally to an architect, but most times it doesn't. Some architects take as long to letter a sheet as to draw it."

"Is that the way it is for you?" she asked curiously.

He smiled. "It comes fairly easily now."

Elise nodded and went to look out one of the windows. She heard him move behind her but didn't look to see what he was doing. Soon he came to stand at her side, a glass of champagne in each hand.

After offering one to her, he toasted, "To you, Elise. For your help in achieving my dream."

"To your dream," Elise murmured and touched her glass to his.

As they sipped the bubbly liquid, their eyes met over the rims. The promise of the evening was at hand, but Elise glanced quickly away. She wasn't ready yet. "I thought about what you said last night," she murmured. "About Bea and myself. And I think maybe you're right. Things have to change. I tried to make a start today, by being nicer to her, but with Bea..." She shook her head.

"I didn't mean for you to be the one to do all the trying."

"I know." She took another sip of champagne, her gaze on the dots of light that ringed the edge of the lake below. "But change has to start somewhere."

"You've always been the one to do all the trying, haven't you? You work at the library, then go home to take care of Bea. You've given up your life... and all because you feel responsible for your sister's accident.

Haven't you ever wanted to do something different? To do something that didn't involve Bea or the town?''

Elise moved uncomfortably under his questioning. She felt that he was censuring her, making light of all that she had accomplished.

Sensing her thoughts, Robert said quickly, "I'm not condemning you. On the contrary, I admire you for what you've done. Not many people would have that kind of courage. But if the opportunity presents itself, what would you do? Would you take it?''

"I don't know. Right now, Bea needs me. She—"

"What if you had the chance to go to Europe? To Spain, or Italy, or France?''

When Elise placed her glass on the table, the tremor in her hand almost caused it to spill. "I don't know," she said faintly.

"With me," he continued. "What if I asked you to come with me?''

Elise lifted tortured eyes. "Don't say that," she pleaded.

"Why not?''

"Because you're not serious!''

"What if I am?'' He stepped closer.

"Robert—''

"We could take a month. After the town council approves the modifications, I'll be turning the project over to the firm to have the construction documents redrawn. They should take about that long to complete, possibly a little longer. We'd be back in plenty of time to oversee the restart of construction.''

"No," she whispered. "I can't.''

"Only because of Bea?''

A muscle pulled in Elise's cheek. "Partly," she admitted.

"What's the other part?" he asked.

Elise turned away, not wanting him to see into her too closely. She loved him, but did he love her? He hadn't said anything about love.

It was on the tip of her tongue to expose her true feelings, to tell him the truth and see what he said. But something made her hold back. An echo of Bea's warning? A memory from another time, when the man she thought loved her had hurt her so badly? She was ashamed of her hesitancy but couldn't seem to get around it.

She gazed at Robert, and a jumble of thoughts ran through her mind. It would be so easy to reach out to him, to fire the beginning of a physical relationship. She knew it could happen. And the fact that she had such power staggered her. She was Elise Ferguson, librarian. In no way, shape or form could she be mistaken for a model or a film star. She was normal, ordinary.

And Robert? There was no way Robert could be termed ordinary, not with the way the room's lighting played on the silver threads in his black hair and made his beautifully colored eyes seem even more unusual. The way the light emphasized his natural coloring and caressed the lines made by his smile. The way he stood, confident, fit. When she'd seen him that first time at the library, she'd been a little afraid of him. Was it because she had sensed the meaning he could come to have in her life?

She stood very still, torn by the possibilities. Then she discovered that she'd waited too long. The decision was taken out of her hands when Robert shifted and said, "Maybe we should get out of here. I don't want to keep you out too late."

Elise didn't need an interpreter. "Maybe we should," she agreed, her voice taut with control.

She looked for her purse and found that she hadn't put it down. It still hung from her shoulder just as it had when they came in, a small rectangular afterthought in white.

CHAPTER TWELVE

LITTLE CONVERSATION passed between them during the trip back to Tyler. The sound system in Robert's car played a pleasing variety of music, but Elise paid scant attention. As the miles crept by, she remained immersed in her thoughts. Had she made a mistake in turning down Robert's invitation to go to Europe? Had he expected her to make some kind of move to let him know that she wanted further intimacy? Had he been disappointed when she didn't? Was that why he had wanted to leave his apartment so suddenly?

She chanced a quick look in his direction. His expression showed very little of his thoughts. In fact, he didn't even seem to notice that she was there, whereas she was extremely aware of everything about him. She knew his every move, his every breath. She was aware of the way he sat, comfortable yet in charge. Once or twice she thought she heard him hum along with the music, but she wasn't sure.

She forced her gaze to remain straight ahead. She should say something! At least tell him that she'd had a nice time. But after what had happened in his apartment, banal words just wouldn't come.

When finally they turned into her driveway, she wondered what he'd do if she made a mad dash for her house. Write her off, most likely.

He cut the engine and turned toward her.

Elise felt like a tightly twisted rubber band. She rushed into speech, saying exactly what she had kept herself from saying earlier. "I had a nice time. Thank you for asking me."

His gaze was quizzical.

"I—I truly did enjoy myself," she hurried on. "The restaurant..."

He was not destined to learn her opinion of the restaurant, nor did he seem to care. As if she hadn't said anything, he murmured, "This seems like a fairly safe place," and reached out to draw her close, lowering his mouth until he could take command of her slightly parted lips.

At first Elise didn't respond. She was too surprised. Then, like Sleeping Beauty, she awakened to the passion of the man who kissed her. With her heart tripping wildly in her chest, she wound her arms around his neck and allowed her body to melt against his. Meeting need with need, hunger with hunger, she kissed him back, reveling in the intimacy of their caress. She thought of nothing except him and the pleasure they shared. For that moment, whatever he wanted she was willing to give. There was no hesitation, no holding back.

When their lips moved apart, it was as if a portion of her died. She moved slightly, swaying toward him, but he held her back.

"Then again," he murmured huskily, "maybe I was wrong."

Elise's eyes fluttered open to meet his smoldering gaze. She had no idea what he was talking about.

She came back to reality with a jolt. Inching away from him, she ran unsteady fingers through her hair, trying to bring order to the tousled strands. "I—I should go," she said, not wanting to.

The light in Robert's eye hadn't lessened. Still, he agreed, "Yes, maybe you should."

She reached for the door handle, but Robert stopped her. "Wait," he said and got out of the car to come around.

The night air was cool against her heated skin, but Elise wasn't sure if that was what caused her to shiver or if the cause was the feel of Robert's fingers on her arm. He saw her to the porch.

Elise used the excuse of searching for her keys to keep from meeting his gaze. When she found them, she hung on to them like a lifeline and gave him a quick, rather plastic smile. "I, uh, I suppose I'll see you again sometime in the next few days?"

Robert, too, held himself stiffly. He shook his head. "Probably not. As you saw, I have a lot of work to do at home. I think I'll hang around Milwaukee and get it done."

"Then when...?" She stopped herself. She wouldn't beg!

"Next Monday. I should be finished by then. Maybe we can arrange to show the modifications to the council. I'll give you a call."

She hadn't meant to look at him, but she did. For the first time since she'd known him, she would have described his look as brooding. The teasing light that usually dominated his expression had disappeared. There were no laugh lines, only a deep frown. Elise looked away, her heart heavy.

She opened the door and started to step inside. Robert stayed where he was, but he said, "Elise?"

Elise turned back.

"Take care of yourself, all right? Don't...don't work too hard. And don't let Bea..." He stopped, swallowing what he would have said next.

Elise made no reply and closed the door softly behind her.

HER SHOULDERS SLUMPED once she was inside the house, and her face crumpled with distress. Had she lost him before she had even won him? Was this all there was going to be to their story? The next time they met, would he treat her with utter politeness while she treated him the same way in return? Somehow it just didn't seem possible.

She walked tiredly across the hall and switched on the stairwell light. It was then she saw Bea, sitting cross-armed and angry in the doorway that led to the family room. Her eyes were narrowed, her lips pursed.

"I heard you drive up fifteen minutes ago," she challenged curtly.

Elise closed her eyes. She didn't think she had the energy to deal with Bea after what had just occurred. As quickly as she could, she schooled her expression to protect herself from Bea's prying eyes, but it was too late.

"You don't look exactly happy," Bea said. "What's the matter? Have a lovers' spat?"

"We're not lovers."

"Not because you aren't willing! Do you realize you're the laughingstock of this town? Oh, they won't show what they think to your face, but believe me, they do after you turn your back. Just ask some of your friends. Ask Josephine, if you don't believe me. Everyone's talking about you." She wheeled closer to Elise, examining her in more detail, as if hoping to find traces of blood from her barbs.

Elise would not be drawn out.

Bea smiled, if you could call it a smile. It was more a smirk. "He's only interested in one thing. And you're more the fool if you give it to him. You won't see him again. Just like Kenneth Faraday, he'll be gone when you wake up."

"Leave me alone, Bea," Elise warned coldly.

"Ohh! What's happened to all the sweetness and light you were so intent on conveying earlier—doesn't make it through the first rainstorm? I thought you wanted to do more things with me. Get me out of the house.... Get me into Worthington House! Wasn't that the object of the little visit you proposed for today? It took awhile, but I finally worked it out. You've met a man, I'm in the way and you want to get rid of me. You want to put me in a *home!* But I won't be gotten rid of so easily, Elise. I'll be a millstone hung round your neck for the rest of your life! Because it was *you* who put me in this chair! *You* who made me what I am today! You took away my life and left me with nothing but a bunch of silly dolls! Well, this is what I think of his doll...." She reached for the box that still sat on the hall table and reared back to throw it.

Elise was galvanized into action. She leaped across the distance separating them and grabbed hold of the box to keep Bea from throwing it. Bea tried to wrest it away, but Elise wouldn't let go. Bea was amazingly strong for her size; it was all Elise could do to hold on.

Bea grunted and puffed and murmured imprecations beneath her breath. Still Elise would not let go. For both women the doll had ceased to be a doll and had become instead a symbol of power.

The box tore open. A doll's leg stuck out, a hand. Bea screeched when she saw them. The chair rolled, swung around, scraping Elise's knee. The hall table shuddered from being hit and the vase of flowers teetered, then fell, crashing to the floor in a shower of flowers and glass.

Elise cried out in pain, not because she had been cut, but because those were the flowers that Robert had given her at a time when life seemed brighter.

"You won't put me in a home! You won't! *You won't!*" Bea cried.

"I'm not your slave!" Elise cried in return. "What happened to you was an accident! I was a *child!* You should have looked before you tried to run down the stairs! It wasn't totally my fault! *You should have looked!*"

Bea jerked on the box again and this time Elise let go.

When Elise stood back, her chest was heaving as she gasped for air. Bea was little better off. Her hair had come unclasped from its knot and fell in a tangled stream across one shoulder. Her face was flushed, her eyes feverish. And for the first time, Elise saw fear in her sister's expression. It was there, unveiled, for only a second. Still, she saw it.

Drawing back to the stairs, Elise collapsed on the runner and buried her face in her hands. Too much had happened today. Too much had happened this week . . . this year! She remembered a time when Tyler was a sleepy little village where nothing much went on, where people stayed pretty much the same and little unexpected occurred. But had there truly ever been such a place? Or was she using a child's innocent memory to recall something that had never existed? A stranger, looking at Bea and herself today would see two sisters—one in a wheelchair and one not—who shared a middle-size house in a middle-size neighborhood. The sister who walked worked at the library; the other sister was not very friendly. And they had been like that for years. That stranger would be unable to see the conflicts that raged between them, or sense the changes that were actually taking place.

She lifted her head and looked at Bea, who was carefully placing the doll's exposed appendages back in the box. Her gray face and drab dress made her look much older than her years. Her expression remained bitter.

Bea caught her look and the old flare of anger returned. "The family relied on you to shovel the steps," she said spitefully. "It could easily have happened to any one of us—Mom, Dad. Just think how you'd have felt if it had been one of them. We all had jobs to do."

"I don't remember you doing your chores very often. Mom always had to do them so that Dad wouldn't find out."

"I can't help it if I was popular!"

Elise dropped her head again. Bea was impossible to argue with or to feel compassion for. She saw things the way she saw them and there was nothing anyone could do to convince her otherwise. "I'm not going to argue with you, Bea. I can't believe that we..." She motioned to the disturbed hall.

"I told you from the beginning that man was bad news. Look what he's already done! He's sown trouble between us, between you and the community—"

Elise stood up, her action cutting off her sister's words. "I don't want to hear any more," she said. Then, partly as an act of defiance, she bent down to collect one of the flowers that were strewn over the floor and turned to take it upstairs with her.

"Is that all?" Bea demanded. "Aren't you going to clean up this mess?"

Elise paused to look at her. After all the years of being made to feel guilty, all the years of tiptoeing around Bea's sensibilities, giving in to her and subjugating her own will, she said quietly, "You know where the broom is." Turning, she went on up the stairs.

The delicate yellow rosebud went to bed with her. She looked at it for a long time before finally falling asleep. But her dreams were troubled ones. She twisted and turned, and in the morning when she awakened, the petals were scattered everywhere.

ROBERT MOVED restlessly around the apartment. He couldn't keep his mind on his work. He had told Elise he wanted to remain in Milwaukee so that he could complete the project, but now that he had ample opportunity, he couldn't do it. And the reason was that he didn't want to *be* in Milwaukee. He wanted to be in Tyler... with her!

The previous night had been the hardest he had ever spent. He knew when he left her that she was upset, but so was he. He had been shaken by the depth of his feelings for her. Challenged in his apartment, in his car... it had taken every ounce of willpower to maintain control. And he hadn't done a particularly good job.

Did he love her? In some ways the idea terrified him. He had been on his own for so long. For most of his fifty-seven years he'd had no one to answer to, no one to please. He could come when he wanted, go when he wanted... see whom he wanted. He had never been tied down. He was completely free.

On the other hand, there had been times when he wondered what it would be like to have someone share his life—someone to come home to, to travel with, to go to bed with each night.

Robert groaned as he moved away from the spot by the window where she had stood last night. He sensed that she had come close to reaching out to him. He knew he could have forced it, forced her to respond. But that wasn't the way he wanted it to be with her. He wanted her to *want* to be with him... maybe for the rest of his life. Did that mean he loved her?

He felt alive when he was with her, more alive than he'd felt in years. He'd gone to Tyler many more times than he actually needed to to discuss the plans for the library...just because he had found himself wanting to be with her. He worried about her, was concerned for her. He cared about what happened to her. He was even willing to try to get along with that harridan of a sister, Bea!

He dropped onto his soft leather couch and leaned his head back to stare at the ceiling. He stayed that way for what must have been hours.

AS ELISE WENT about her work in the library, she was conscious of whether people looked at her oddly, or if they whispered behind her back. She didn't sense anything unusual, but couldn't be sure. She knew she shouldn't listen to Bea, but couldn't shake the thought that this time her sister might be right. Elise had done little to hide her feelings for Robert. They were there, exposed, for anyone to see.

With her spirit still tender from what had happened the night before—both with Robert and with Bea—she held her chin up as best she could and tried to get on with the job. She went to Fellowship Lutheran to check the last of the drying books and made arrangements with Pastor Schoff that they be moved to a smaller room so that the church could have its meeting hall back. At this point, the library staff would have to go through the more severely damaged books individually, sorting the ones that could be repaired and rebound from those that would have to be discarded. She thanked him profusely for his help through the crisis, a message he said he would pass along to his church members.

When Elise arrived back at the library, it was to find Josephine waiting for her.

Josephine's sharp eyes quickly saw that all was not well. "I came to ask if you'd like to get a cup of coffee," she said. "I haven't seen or heard from you in a few days. But from the look of you, you need more than coffee. How about a meal at my place tonight?"

Elise shook her head. All she wanted to do when she got off work was go hide in her room.

Josephine urged. "It will do you good. No hassles, no pressure. Just a nice, peaceful dinner in convivial surroundings. I'll even stop by your house and talk Bea around. Take her some of my spaghetti."

Elise's face tightened. "It will take more than her favorite food to bring Bea around today."

"You two have had another argument?"

"More than that, I'm afraid." Elise rubbed her brow. "Look, Josephine, I really think I want to pass on dinner tonight. I appreciate the offer, but I—I'd just like to be on my own. I'm sorry."

Josephine shrugged. "I understand. I have days like that myself." She examined Elise closely and, lowering her voice, asked, "Is Bea still upset about Robert?"

A flash of pain crossed Elise's delicate features. "You might say that." She looked at her friend. "Josephine, I have to ask you. Are people talking about Robert and me? Are they saying that I'm a fool to think that someone like him could—"

"Who told you that?" Josephine interrupted sharply. Then she answered her own question. "Beatrice! One day that woman is going to pay for all the—"

"She's paying already. She thinks I'm going to move her to Worthington House."

"And maybe you should! I'm serious!" Josephine insisted when Elise looked shocked. Then she went back to the previous question. "No one in this town thinks you're a fool. There's been a little talk, yes. Especially after the council meeting. But it's all *good* talk. People are happy for you. They like Robert, like what he wants to do with this old place. They think you make a nice pair. There's not one person who wouldn't enjoy seeing you get together."

Elise closed her eyes. Her body was as tense as a bowstring. It had been all day. "Thank you," she said after a long moment. "I needed to hear that."

Josephine patted Elise's shoulder, then turned to leave. "Call me if you need me. You know I'm always available to help."

Elise watched her friend walk away. After another moment, she went to the circulation desk to relieve Pauline for her lunch break.

THE NEXT TWO DAYS elapsed without incident—at least, without incident for Elise. While her life seemed stuck on hold, she watched as others in the community moved from one point to the next.

The entire Ingalls family held their heads high and tried not to notice the cyclone of speculation that swirled around them. Especially Judson. He continued to go to Marge's Diner for breakfast and then on to the F and M and his other favorite haunts.

He stopped at the library one morning to thank Elise for the concern she'd expressed when he was under the weather. A tall man with high cheekbones and a commanding nose and chin, he held himself with pride and dignity. To Elise he had always seemed the epitome of a gentleman. Nearly eighty now, he'd been more affected by his recent troubles than he wanted to admit. His eyes looked tired, his step a little less confident. He didn't tarry, but delivered his message and left. That he had taken the time, though—considering the circumstances—underscored Elise's faith in him.

Another person who came to the library, one Elise had seen only rarely since his return to Tyler, was Edward Wocheck. He was a few years younger than Elise, and her memories of him were of an intense young man who had left Tyler a number of years before, determined to succeed. That he had was evidenced by the fact that he now controlled the Addison Hotels group and had been instrumental in its purchase of Timberlake Lodge. He came to the library looking for Alyssa Baron.

When Alyssa and Edward were young, they had once been in love. But the course had not run smoothly for them, and rumor at the time had it that Alyssa's rejection of him was the true cause of his departure. Now, upon his return, no one knew what to expect. But here he was, looking for her.

"I heard that she'd be here," he said to Elise. Still very intense, Edward had acquired a tough, no-nonsense edge from his years at the helm of a worldwide conglomerate.

"I haven't seen her," Elise replied. She looked around, to check with someone else. "Have you seen Mrs. Baron, Delia?" Delia shook her head.

Elise shrugged. "Would you like us to give her a message if she comes in?"

Edward frowned. "No, that's all right. I'll catch up with her eventually." Then, as an afterthought, he added, "Thanks."

Elise had no way of knowing for sure, but the few times she had seen Edward he didn't seem happy. He had gained success, but at what price?

On the way out of the building he almost collided with Britt Hansen, who was coming in the main doorway. After a quick word, he stepped aside to allow her to enter before going on himself.

Britt, a pert strawberry blonde, looked back over her shoulder as she approached the circulation desk, her thick rope of braided hair swinging over her shoulder. Dressed in jeans and a thin cotton shirt, she could have posed for a poster of the all-American farm girl. Only she was a little older than a "girl," being a widow with four children, one almost a teenager. "My goodness," she said to Elise. "Mr. Wocheck's in a hurry."

"He probably has an appointment," Elise commented.

"Just like me...only mine's with the shoe store for Matt. I hope this pair lasts longer than the ones before. It seems like we were there only a month ago."

"He's at that age," Elise said in sympathy.

Britt's laugh was brittle. "Tell me about it. I can't keep him in clothes, either. And right now I just don't need the extra expense." Her pretty face took on a harried look. Then she forced another bright smile. "But...I can't put a rock on his head to hold him down, so we'll just have to make do."

Elise was aware that Britt was trying desperately to hang on to the hundred-acre farm that had been in her family for four generations. Times were bad, and to help bring in a little money, Britt made the cheesecake that was served at the lodge—the cheesecake Robert had enjoyed so much the first time they went out together.

That thought caused Elise a flash of pain. She straightened, busying herself with a stack of returned books.

Britt frowned and glanced at her watch. "Matt said he'd meet me here," she murmured. Then she looked up and saw him coming across the room. "There he is!" With a quick farewell to Elise, she set off to collect her son.

ELISE LAY IN BED that night thinking of all the people in town—how one person's troubles and joys affected so many others. Like the pattern on a quilt, their lives were tiny, interconnecting pieces that formed a whole. If one or more, through the stresses and strains of life, began to tear or fray, the entire structure was weakened. Only careful stitching could make the quilt whole again. And the thread used was mutual concern.

Judson, Edward, Alyssa, Britt...herself. Disparate people, but all were connected in the intricate pattern that was Tyler.

CHAPTER THIRTEEN

ROBERT STARED at the purchase agreement for the Friedrich house, which had been delivered in the morning mail. Just a few short days ago, gaining ownership of the house had been all that he could think about. Spurred by the possibility that he might lose it, he had gone to the Tyler town council and, with Elise's help, had received permission to buy it. Now he was faced with the consequences of change.

The house was still important to him, but it wasn't *as* important. Also, he was bothered by the fact that he hadn't told Elise of his suspicions, that he hadn't told the council. Could his actions be termed in any way deceptive? When examined dispassionately, he feared that they might.

To anyone who didn't know him, *he* could seem a profiteer. He had found a house of possible worth and had not informed the owner—the town of Tyler; his employer, in fact. And instead of telling that owner, he had rammed through his own purchase of the property. The scenario didn't look good.

Yet the truth was complex. It was possible that he might one day profit by his action—not so much momentarily as in prestige. But it was just as possible that he would not. Either way, a goodly sum of money would be spent. And he would end up spending even more if the house *did* turn out to be a Stephen deVille/ Frank Lloyd Wright collaboration, because of his commitment to restore it to its original state.

How would the people of Tyler feel about him if the house did indeed turn out to be historic? Robert pushed the contract away and moved to the windows that overlooked the lake.

With that question, he felt on firmer ground. If he hadn't intervened, the house would have been torn down and no one would have known what they had destroyed... which was frequently the case with old houses. As it was, if the house was historic, Tyler would have something it could be proud of. Once restored, such an addition to architecture's trove of treasures would lure aficionados from around the world. Articles would be published, pictures taken, the house would be publicized far and wide. So, too, would Tyler. The townspeople would have to be pleased with that.

But was it the townspeople's opinion he cared so much about, or Elise's? What would *she* think? What would *she* say? Would she understand?

Robert returned to the sofa and picked up the contract. As he saw it, he still had only one course of action: to do as he'd previously planned. When he gained confirmation from his friend—*if* he gained confirmation—he would immediately tell Elise everything.

He reached for the phone to call his lawyer.

THE SISTERS had barely spoken since their stinging argument. They lived like strangers in the same house, sharing the kitchen and the family room, but not with any friendliness. Once Elise had tried to draw Bea out, but she would not respond.

Elise knew Bea wanted to make her feel guilty again, wanted her to accept all the blame, wanted her back under her thumb. But she refused to resume her accustomed place, and Bea's cold anger increased.

Elise continued to make her sister's meals, to change her sheets, to wash her clothes. Everything else, though, Bea insisted upon doing herself. She wouldn't let Elise do her dishes, arrange her feet or brush her hair. She did it all herself—out of spite.

Elise was on her way upstairs for an early night when the telephone rang. She answered it to find Robert on the line.

"I've finished," he said. "A couple of days earlier than planned. The council says they can fit us into a special working meeting tomorrow night if we can make it. I can. Can you?"

His voice sounded so achingly familiar. Elise cradled the receiver closer to her ear. "What time?" she asked.

"Seven o'clock."

"I don't see why not."

Buttercup rubbed against her ankles and she automatically bent to stroke her.

"I've missed you," he said after a short hesitation.

Elise's hand stilled on the yellow fur, then started to tremble. Her whole body trembled. Her knees grew weak. She reached for a chair.

More seconds passed. "Are you still there?" he asked.

"Yes," she whispered.

Again more silence. Neither seemed able to find the proper words.

Finally, Robert broke off the call. "Tomorrow night, then," he said softly.

"Tomorrow night," Elise breathed, and she had the strong feeling that she had just committed herself to something much more significant than a simple meeting.

ELISE GREETED the new day with a burst of energy. Because it was Saturday and her usual day off, she cleaned house, then went grocery shopping, and even managed to have some enthusiasm left for the interlibrary loan meeting she was scheduled to attend that afternoon. Unlike the previous few days, she found herself humming to herself frequently, and a smile was never far from her lips. As she drove to Madison, she found it hard to concentrate on anything except the night to come.

Robert also found it difficult to wait until evening. He wanted to see Elise more than he had ever wanted anything in his life. Frequently, when he was young, he had wondered what it would be like to fall deeply in love. His perceptions of that state had fused with childhood memories of soldiers returning home from war, to be greeted by the women who waited for them. His own father and his uncles had virtually disappeared for the better part of four years, to be welcomed back in a haze of joy and glory. As a result, love had seemed to be something that burst upon a person so vividly it was impossible to ignore. That memory had faded when Robert grew up...until its recent resurrection. His love for Elise had not started in a burst of feeling, but it had grown quickly. Now it was so intense and so glorious that he knew he could never go back to the life he'd led before.

The telephone on the table at his side rang and he quickly answered it, hoping it was Elise. When he heard masculine tones, he couldn't disguise his disappointment. Then, as he recognized the identity of the caller, he sat up, at instant attention.

"Max! Hello!" he said. "When did you get back? How was your trip? Great. Great," he enthused as he listened. Minutes passed as his friend continued to talk, explaining why he had come back to Chicago sooner than expected. Finally he wound down enough to ask Robert about the message he'd left. "Well, yes. Actually, it was important," Robert said, and he told his friend about the house.

"When can I see it?" Max wanted to know.

"How soon will you feel like traveling again?" Robert asked.

"For something like that, I'm on my way right now."

Robert laughed, pleased at his response. "Then I'll meet you there in, say... two hours. At twelve o'clock. That should give you enough time for a leisurely drive."

"Great. You can buy me lunch."

"It's a deal," Robert agreed.

After he hung up the phone, excitement had him on his feet in a second, and he began to gather all the materials he would need to take with him to Tyler.

TWO AND A HALF HOURS later Robert stood with Max Prescot on the front porch of the library. Max was small in stature, not much over five feet tall. He had dark fuzzy hair and intense dark eyes and looked as though he was in desperate need of a good meal. He was also one of the country's foremost authorities on members of the Prairie School—architects who designed buildings in the metropolitan Chicago area between 1890 and 1917 and who shared a common, original style. Frank Lloyd Wright was the most famous. Stephen deVille was Max's personal favorite.

The entire time they were in the building, Robert felt his friend's excitement grow. So he wasn't surprised when Max turned to him and said, "You've got a winner here, Robert! An absolute beauty. Definitely deVille and definitely Wright!"

Robert beamed his pleasure. His first thought was to tell Elise. But his friend demanded payment.

Rubbing his hands together, Max said, "I'm starving! I haven't had a good steak in months. I hope your pockets are deep today, Robert. We're going to celebrate! Good wine, good food, good friends!"

"I know just the place," Robert replied. "Not far from here... beautiful scenery. I haven't had a steak there, but the trout amandine is fantastic."

"I don't want to see a fish again for a month! I'm a meat eater, a carnivore...."

"Well, I had thought of sushi," Robert teased.

Max gave a terrible grimace that made Robert laugh.

"Come on," he said. "I'll give you a ride. You can tell me all about your South Seas adventure."

"Only if you tell me how you found this place. My heavens, you're a lucky man!"

At this moment, Robert thought himself the luckiest man alive. But he didn't tell his friend the most important reason he felt so.

BEA HAD DECIDED at the last minute to go out. She had at first thought to stay at home, hoping to elicit Elise's concern, but Elise was in another world that day, happy and busy, and she didn't seem to notice Bea's petulant withdrawal. Elise also was scheduled to attend a meeting and wouldn't be home all afternoon, so there was no reason for Bea to remain alone. She called her friends and told them she had changed her mind.

For lunch they decided to go to Timberlake Lodge. It was not a frequent stop of theirs, as the prices were a little steep. But Jenny and Ann and Rebecca thought they should splurge in honor of Ann's recent pay raise at Ingalls F and M.

Bea often felt out of place with these women, even though she had known two of them for years. At times she wondered why they asked her along on their regular outings, as they had so little in common now. Each of them worked, had a husband and children and was interested in concerns she knew nothing about. The idea niggled that they did it more for Elise than because they liked *her,* but Bea tried to keep that thought to herself. When she talked, they seemed interested. Occasionally, they even laughed at one of her semicaustic jokes. On most occasions she enjoyed their excursions.

A chair was removed from the table so that Bea's wheelchair could be put in its place, leaving the eating surface a little high but manageable.

"Isn't this a beautiful place?" Jenny Lewis said, craning her neck to look about the room. "All homey and rustic and...rich. Look at that pine breakfront over there. I'd die to have that piece in my house. So would my husband, if he had to pay for it!"

Bea gave the antique cabinet a cursory glance. She didn't see anything special about it.

"I like what they've done with the curtains," Ann said. "I wonder if I could do that in my dining room. Say, isn't that Professor Fairmont over there? See? At the table by the window. He's with a boy...no, it's a man. See, Rebecca? You've met the professor at the library...isn't that him?"

Rebecca craned her neck. "Sure is. He's certainly a hunk, isn't he? I can see why Elise..." She stopped and glanced uncertainly at Bea.

Bea's gaze swung to the table, her eyes narrowing. Their expression grew suddenly arctic. "Yes, that's him," she confirmed.

Her companions gave an uncertain laugh or two. Bea was aware that she had chilled the previously affable moment, but she couldn't help the way she felt about that man. He had disrupted her life, been the cause of Elise— Someone tapped her arm. A young woman handed her a menu. Bea took it, but her attention wasn't diverted for long from the man she hated most in the world.

ROBERT LAUGHED at his friend's humorous tales of his adventures in the South Pacific. Max had been his roommate in college and they had been fast friends ever since, even if they met only one or twice a year because of their complicated schedules.

"...Then she waved a hand in the air and said—" Max stopped. "Well, maybe I'd better not say what she said here, but you get the idea. Made my whole vacation worthwhile to hear her say it. I thought I was getting too old!"

Robert shook his head. Max had always had a way with women, despite his diminutive stature. Many a larger man stood in awe of him. "One day, Max. One day."

His friend grinned. "Let's hope not until I'm in my nineties."

Robert helplessly continued to shake his head.

Max took a sip of his drink, then said, "Okay. So you've now got yourself this special house. What are you going to do with it?"

"Renovate it, what else?"

"Do you have the original drawings?"

"I was hoping maybe you could help me there."

"Well, I do know deVille's daughter and granddaughter. They have most of his papers and drawings. I could take a look."

"Great!" Robert said. "I'd like to stay as close as possible to the original."

"You say you couldn't find any papers here—no builder's contract, nothing?"

"They had a fire. Papers are missing...if they were ever filed. I haven't looked through everything yet, but I doubt it's here. I thought possibly I could authenticate the place before you got back, but it didn't work out."

"And deny me the pleasure of seeing it? I'd never have forgiven you."

"I'd have asked you down." Robert smiled. "Just to show off."

"For which you have every reason. Do you realize what's going to happen when news of this gets out? You've really pulled off a coup, Robert. This place will create a sensation! And to think the people here were ready to tear it down—a building by Stephen deVille and Frank Lloyd Wright!"

Robert didn't respond to his friend's excitement. His gaze was locked just off Max's shoulder, on the woman who rolled determinedly up to their table. Her face was a mask of spiteful anger, her body held rigid in its dowdy dress. He was surprised to see her there. Shocked.

She looked from Max to him.

"Bea," Robert said, pushing to his feet. "Is Elise—?" He made a quick visual search of the room.

"No," Bea said abruptly.

Robert glanced at Max, who was looking at Bea with undisguised curiosity.

"Ah...Bea, I'd like to introduce you to my friend Max Prescot. Max, Bea Ferguson."

Max extended a hand, but typically, Bea ignored it. Instead, she skewered him with her gaze. "May I ask what you do, Mr. Prescot?"

Max handled the situation with aplomb. "I teach architecture at the University of Illinois in Chicago."

"Humph," Bea grunted.

She turned her gaze on Robert, but when she continued merely to look at him, he asked, "Is there something we can do for you, Bea? Would you, uh…like to join us?''

Bea laughed, but the sound wasn't pleasant. "I'd sooner eat with a snake than eat with you. I only came to tell you to *leave Elise alone*. You come around here with your fancy title and your fancy ways of doing things, and you think you can carry on as you please. Well, that doesn't include making a fool of my sister. Leave her alone. Leave *me* alone. We don't want you here!''

So saying, Bea backed away from the table and whipped her chair around. Her arm thrusts against the wheels were jerky but powerful as she moved back across the room to a table where three other women were watching her with varied expressions of dismay. Since Bea hadn't bothered to keep her voice down, the entire room was aware of her feelings. A moment later the women left, following Bea's wheelchair like a small parade.

Red-faced, one woman looked back at Robert. He recognized her from the library. She made a small gesture of apology, to which Robert etched a tiny salute. What Bea did wasn't the woman's fault, both of them seemed wordlessly to acknowledge.

Max shook his head. "You're definitely in her bad books. Who is she, anyway? And who is this Elise?''

"Elise is the chief librarian in Tyler.''

Max's dark eyes took on an added gleam. "And you're supposed to 'leave her alone.' That tells me you haven't up to this point.''

"No. And I don't intend to.''

"Then if I were you, I wouldn't turn my back, because that lady who just left would gladly plunge a knife into it."

"More like a machete," Robert murmured. He smiled at his friend's hoot of laughter, but the smile didn't fully erase an underlying sense of apprehension.

BEA WAS CAUGHT UP in her own dark thoughts on the drive back to her house. She barely noticed the strained silence in the car or the tight words that occasionally broke that silence. She already knew she was the object of the other women's censure, but she didn't care. She had something far more important on her mind.

Really pulled off a coup... create a sensation... the people here were ready to tear it down—a building by Stephen deVille and Frank Lloyd Wright. Bea didn't know who Stephen deVille was, but she sure as anything knew the name Frank Lloyd Wright. It was hard to grow up in southern Wisconsin and *not* know who he was. He had been born in Richland Center somewhere around the mid 1800s, and had built a hideaway of some kind in Spring Green. And even though he had been dead a number of years, his name and image were like a sacred trust the state still proudly proclaimed.

What "building" were "the people here ready to tear down"? Bea's brain worked on the teaser. The man was Robert's friend.... The *library!* It had to be the library! Did that mean that the library had been built by this Stephen deVille and Frank Lloyd Wright? It was a coup, his friend had said... which meant that Robert had somehow done what others, if only they'd known, would have liked to do, too.

Bea was anxious to be rid of the women around her. She wanted privacy to think, to act. When the car pulled into the driveway, she accepted her friends' help into the house with gruff impatience. She didn't even say goodbye when they left. She didn't think to. She was already on her way to the telephone.

ELISE LEFT the meeting in Madison with plenty of time to spare. She wanted to go home, make a light dinner for Bea and herself, then have time to shower and get ready for her meeting with Robert.

A pleasant sensation of excitement had surrounded her all day, and it seemed to grow as, minute by minute, the afternoon ticked away. Additionally, her intuition that something of great import would occur that evening had grown stronger. She looked forward to seeing Robert, wanted desperately to be with him. She almost ached with a physical need.

She turned into the drive, parked the car and hurried into the house. She stopped only long enough to check the messages on the answering machine before she went upstairs to change out of her suit. Whenever she was away from the house for an extended period, she liked to make sure that she wasn't needed at the library. Bea hated to answer the telephone, so the machine served them well.

When she saw that there were no messages, Elise shrugged. Usually there were one or two calls, even if they only involved telephone sales solicitations for magazines or light bulbs. Today must have been a quiet day for everyone.

She was gathering vegetables for a stew when she heard the wheelchair roll softly across the floor into the kitchen. Because Bea had avoided being in the same room with her for most of the past few days, Elise instantly looked up.

Bea wore an odd expression, part amused, part malevolent. From years of living with her sister, Elise raised her guard. "Bea," she greeted cautiously.

"Elise," Bea returned. That and nothing more.

Elise turned back to the potatoes and carrots, but she was very much aware of what her sister was doing. Bea rolled over to the counter and pulled a paring knife from the wooden block.

"Why don't I help?" she offered.

Elise blinked. Her caution increased. Bea had never offered to help make a meal before. "Do you know how?" she asked.

"Of course I know how! I've helped Mother cut vegetables before."

"Oh," Elise said. She wanted to add, *But that was years ago!* but held her tongue. What was Bea up to?

She washed and peeled several large carrots and put them aside for her sister. Bea placed the cutting board on the lowered section of counter and began a slow but acceptable job of slicing the carrots into small pieces.

"I used to like to help Mother," Bea said. "You're nothing like her. You may look like her, just as I do, but I'm more *like* her than you are, if you know what I mean."

Elise wasn't in the mood to play games. "Just say what you mean, Bea."

Bea looked at her with pretended innocence. "Why, I thought I was." She continued, "Do you remember how Mother dealt with that old man who used to come to the house one summer? The one who pretended to have been hurt in a train accident? She used to give him odd jobs to do from time to time in exchange for a meal, and then one day she caught him going through Father's desk drawer, remember? Well, she told me she'd had a bad feeling about him from the beginning. She put him in the study deliberately, then watched from outside the door. And sure enough, he started looking through the desk drawer for something to take. She caught him in the act. But the important thing was she had enough sense to suspect him. He could have stolen us blind and we wouldn't have known a thing until long after he'd moved on."

"Bea!" Elise snapped. "Get to the point! I'm sure you're not telling me this as a form of entertainment."

"All right, I will. I've caught someone else in the act. Your Robert. And he's not content just to steal from us . . . he's stolen from the whole town."

Elise carefully placed a peeled potato in a water-filled bowl. "One day, Bea, someone's going to actually believe what you say and you're going to find yourself in a whole lot of trouble."

"I have proof," Bea claimed smugly.

"Don't be ridiculous."

"I do!" Bea cried.

Elise shut off the tap and went to stand in front of her sister's chair. She took the knife from her hand and placed it on the counter. "All right," she challenged her. "Show me your proof. But I'll bet you're not going to be able to do it. Because everything you say about Robert is a lie. You don't like him because you're afraid of him. You're afraid that if I fall in love with him, I'll either abandon you or put you in Worthington House. But it's too late, Bea. I've already fallen in love. I think I did that first day. And if it's unseemly to you that someone my age and with my looks did something so foolish, then that's just too bad. I love him and there's nothing you can do about it!''

Bea's mouth twisted. "Then you love a criminal! Ask him about the old library. Ask him why he was in such a hurry to buy it. I heard what happened. I heard how he practically forced the sale down everyone's throats—with your help! It was a masterful piece of showmanship, a coup! He must have been laughing all the way to the bank.''

"The old library is practically falling apart, Bea. I tried to stop him from buying it."

"Then why didn't he listen?" Bea countered insinuatingly, again giving that aggravating smile.

Elise straightened. "Because... he wanted it. He's always wanted an old house to redo. He loves old houses."

"Especially if they were built by Stephen deVille and Frank Lloyd Wright."

"I don't know what you mean," Elise denied, frowning.

"I overheard him talking with a friend today. They were having lunch at the lodge, just like the girls and I were. They didn't know I was anywhere around. They were laughing about the wonderful strategy Robert had used. How he had gotten the place for a song when it's worth a million, maybe two!

"I didn't know who Stephen deVille was, either, but I found out. The *friend* Robert was talking to is a professor of architecture in Chicago. I called his school and learned that he's an expert on this deVille man and also on Wright. I even called Taliesin, just to be sure—that's Wright's compound at Spring Green. The people who work there were happy to answer my questions. I found out that there are people who scour the country in search of Wright artifacts, because anything designed by him is worth a fortune—a door, a window, a lighting fixture, a chair. Some people have even been known to buy one of his houses and tear it down for parts, because it's worth more that way than as a whole. Do you think that might be what Robert has in mind?"

She waited for Elise to say something. When she didn't, Bea continued, "This deVille man is popular in his own right, too. Some people think he's as much of an original as Wright himself. He was one of Wright's pupils and was on his way to fame and fortune when he died. He built only a small number of houses, which means that the houses he did build are extremely rare and very expensive . . . *if* you can ever buy one! Collectors don't like to let go of them." She eyed Elise. "So what do you think of your precious Robert now? How do you feel about being *used* by him? Because that's what he did. I tried to warn you, but you wouldn't—"

"I don't believe you," Elise whispered, her color receding.

"He's little better than a common thief, Elise. Who owned the Friedrich place? Tyler. Who should he have told if he knew the place was worth a fortune? The people of Tyler. But he didn't, did he? He kept that little piece of information to himself. Then he bought the place . . . oh, how heroic!" Bea mocked. "A house that everyone was glad to get rid of. Do you think they'll feel that way when they learn the truth? I don't.

"And think about something else. . . . He knew how bad the financial condition of the town was. He knew we barely could afford to build the new library. He *knew* the money from the sale would solve that problem . . . and yet he still let you dither and dather, cutting this and that, when you could have had everything you wanted. The atrium! Extra space! The quality materials you worked so hard to get in the first place. Tyler could have had it all, with tons of money left over for other things!

"And now you tell me that you love him." Bea laughed. "What a joke! If the town was laughing at you before, think what they'll do now. You love him!" Bea laughed again and this time she didn't stop. She seemed to find the whole situation amazingly hilarious.

With her sister's laughter echoing in her ears, Elise shook her head. "No," she said hoarsely. "No." But she didn't sound convinced.

CHAPTER FOURTEEN

ROBERT SPENT the afternoon in growing frustration as he tried to contact Elise. When he called her home, he reached only her answering machine. And when he talked with the library staff, he found that she was at a meeting in Madison and no one knew when she would return. It might be early, they said, or it might be late. They would tell her to call him the instant she came back, they promised helpfully, only Robert didn't know where he would be so that she *could* call him. He refused to drive back to Milwaukee. When he told Elise about the house, he wanted to do it in person, not over a telephone, and he didn't want to have to wait the hour's drive to get back here for the council meeting. So he stayed in Tyler, passing time in the library, in a diner he discovered just off the main square, at the site for the new library—which he had visited several times before but was drawn to again. He couldn't settle in any one place for long. Finally, after making numerous telephone calls to her house, all to no avail, he got in his car and drove out to the country. He knew he would see her at seven.

At five-thirty he could stand it no longer. He turned his car back toward Tyler and didn't stop again until he pulled up in Elise's drive. He was prepared to wait there for her return, but upon seeing her car, knew that he wouldn't have to.

He parked the Mercedes behind the Escort and got out. During the afternoon some of the tenseness that had been with him since lunch had lessened. But as he approached the house, it returned stronger than ever. Robert wasn't one to believe in intuition. Clairvoyance and cold hard fact were difficult for him to reconcile. But if ever he had experienced a sense of impending adversity, it was now. An invisible hand reached out to squeeze his throat, and his heart rate doubled. Something was wrong. He knew it.

He rang the bell, then had to ring it again before the door swung open to reveal Bea. His eyes widened when he saw her. He had never known her to greet a guest before, especially one she found unwelcome.

Little had changed since their earlier meeting at the restaurant, except now, instead of an expression of fury, she wore a dark smile that was unmistakable in its claim to victory. She kept her chair planted firmly in the doorway, blocking his entrance.

"Is Elise here?" he asked, trying not to notice the gleam of hatred in her eyes.

"Oh, yes. She's here," Bea said. She didn't move.

Robert wanted to brush past her, to claim the right to ignore her nastiness and speak only to Elise. "Would you tell her I'm here, please?"

Bea's smile grew. "Actually, I don't believe she wants to see you."

"What do you mean?" Robert demanded.

"Just what I said. She doesn't want to see you. She knows the truth about you now, you see. I told her. I told her how you bought the Friedrich place for your own nefarious reasons. How you cheated everyone in Tyler out of what was rightfully theirs. How you used her to get exactly what you wanted and—"

"That's not true!" Robert denied, taking a short step forward.

"Oh, I think it is." Bea braced herself by locking the wheel brakes and placing her hands against the doorframe. "I heard you this afternoon, you see. You didn't think I had, but I did. And with a little checking, I know all about Mr. deVille and Mr. Wright. I know how you worked your wicked little con game on this town and took it for everything that it... *No! You can't come in!*" Her voice rose as Robert erased the space between them. She struggled to hold herself in place, screeching as first he released the brakes, then grabbed hold of the arms of her chair in order to push her back out of the way.

Bea's hold on the doorframe was tenacious. For a short space of time her strength matched his. But as seconds passed, her potency faded, and one by one, her fingers lost their grip. "You *bastard!*" she screamed as he rolled her back into the hall. Her nails dug into his arms through his sleeves. "You can't do this! I won't let you! I'll call the police! I'll—"

"Go ahead!" Robert challenged, returning her glare. "Call them. But if anyone deserves to go to jail for what they've done, it's you. You're a hateful, spiteful woman who'll do anything to keep Elise from being happy."

"With you?" she spit. "All you are is an opportunist! You don't care anything about Elise! You only care about yourself, about what you can get out of it! I'm glad I was at the lodge today! I'm glad I was able to save my sister from a life of pain and misery with someone like..."

Her hate-filled words continued, but Robert didn't wait around to hear their finish. He turned his back on her and started to search the lower rooms of the house. "Elise!" he called. "Elise, you have to listen to me!"

He moved from the family room to the kitchen and then the room he knew to be Bea's. Elise was not in any of them. He went back into the hall. Bea had positioned herself at the foot of the stairs. Her eyes told him she was prepared to struggle to the death to keep him from getting past her again, but he didn't give her that opportunity. With one quick move, he vaulted over the banister and landed lightly on the stairs just above her, out of reach. Again, she screeched in rage.

Then she cried, "Elise, run! Get away! *Get away!*"

Robert's worst nightmare was coming true. He'd known he was vulnerable to criticism. He'd known that the situation could be made to look as if it benefited no one except himself. He'd known that he could be made to look the villain. But he hadn't expected it to play itself out in such a horrible manner: with Bea downstairs screaming for Elise to protect herself as if he were some kind of crazed killer, and Elise hiding away as if she believed everything her sister said. His portent of adversity had proved to be true, and he was unsure how to deal with it to keep it from turning into tragedy.

Only one door upstairs was closed, and it was to it that Robert went. He knocked as he twisted the knob. "Elise! Please! Let me in. What Bea's told you isn't true. Please... let me explain." Even to himself he sounded winded, anxious.

A voice came from inside the room. "Go away, Robert. I don't want to talk to you."

"But what she said isn't true! At least, not in the way she said it."

Bea still could be heard downstairs, throwing things, bumping against furniture, taking her anger out on the house. Robert pressed his body against the door. "Please, Elise. Let me talk to you. I love you!"

Only silence came from the room. Then again, quietly, she said, "Go away."

Robert's features twisted with pain. "I could break down the door!" he warned. When she made no reply, his body sagged. Enough violence was being done downstairs. He couldn't bring himself to do more. He took several deep shuddering breaths.

"If nothing else," he said after a minute passed, "I'm going to talk. You can listen if you want, and I hope you do.... I know it looks bad, Elise. But it's not what it seems. I had no idea whether my suspicions were true or not. I didn't *know* the house was built by deVille, I only thought it *might* have been. I had no idea when I bought it. I was taking a chance. Everything happened so quickly. If I hadn't acted when I did, the place might have been bought by Martin Olsen—you know that. And he planned to tear it down. I couldn't let that happen—so I acted. None of this was planned. I didn't come to Tyler with the idea of making a profit. I came to *help* the town."

The doorknob turned beneath his hand. Robert's heart jumped. Did she believe him?

Her skin was pale, almost translucent, her eyes large and hurt as she stepped into the hall. When she looked at him, Robert's spirit sank. There was no understanding in her gaze, only dullness. "I have to see to Bea," she murmured. "Before she hurts herself."

Robert grasped her arm, holding her back. "Elise," he said huskily.

Without a word, she pulled away.

ELISE'S BODY might have been broken glass, the pieces held together by willpower alone. If she thought she had been shattered by betrayal before, it was nothing to what she felt now. At first she hadn't wanted to believe Bea, but everything she'd said had the ring of truth. Her sister couldn't make up a name like Stephen deVille and create a history of him working with Frank Lloyd Wright. She'd also mentioned Taliesin, just as Robert had once done. Then, moments before, Robert had unknowingly confirmed the story when he said that he hadn't been sure that the house was built by deVille. Until then, Elise had held out hope. Now that hope was gone.

She held herself perfectly erect as she went downstairs. She didn't seem to notice the mayhem around her as she moved toward the noise coming from Bea's bedroom. She was aware that Robert followed a short distance behind her, but she tried to numb herself to that fact.

Tears were streaming down Bea's cheeks as Elise pushed open the door. Her complexion was blotched with red. Any object within reach had been swept to the floor, and even her dolls had not escaped her fury. They lay like crumpled bodies, their colorful dresses and hats mute evidence of the unexpectedness of their fate.

With her body shaking uncontrollably, Bea might have been an object of pity except for the angry fire that leaped into her eyes the moment she saw Robert. Uttering a sound of primal rage, she pushed her chair toward him, but a wheel got caught on one of the dolls and her chair tipped over and fell.

Uttering a cry, Elise tried to reach out to catch her but she was too late. Her sister sprawled on the floor and was still. Elise fell to her knees at Bea's side, whispering her name and trying to get her to open her eyes.

She was vaguely aware that Robert had dropped to one knee beside her. She, too, was shaking, and tears flowed freely down her cheeks. None of this seemed real to her! She was like an observer of some terrible play who had somehow been caught up in the action.

"Bea!" she heard her voice cry hollowly. "Bea!"

Robert gently eased her out of the way and bent to examine Bea more closely. "She must have bumped her head," he said, his fingers moving over her skull, searching for an injury.

At that, Bea jerked away. "Get away from me, you...!"

"Bea!" Elise cried. She was shocked to realize that her sister had been pretending.

Bea looked about the room, then at Elise before directing her gaze back to Robert. She struggled to sit up. "Look what you've done," she accused. "Don't you think it's enough? Look at Elise! Look at me! Look what you've reduced us to!"

Elise tried to help her sister back into her chair, but when they encountered difficulties, Robert took over. He swept Bea up in his arms and placed her in her accustomed seat. Bea wheeled as far away from him as she could possibly get the instant she regained control.

Act two, scene two, Elise thought. She wanted to run away. From Bea. From Robert. From this house. From this town. And if she could manage it, the universe.

When Robert touched her arm, she made the mistake of meeting his eyes. A little of the unreality receded and pain took its place.

"Elise," he said quietly. "We have to talk. We have too much to lose if we don't."

"Don't listen to him!" Bea directed from the corner, a note of hysteria still in her voice.

"Elise," Robert urged.

Elise closed her eyes. The delicately poised pieces of glass that comprised her essence were near disintegration. Much more and she would be a heap on the floor. She looked from Robert to her sister. Bea shouldn't have pretended to be hurt; it reminded Elise of all the other times when she had been manipulated. She drew an unsteady breath. "I'm going away," she said flatly. "I have to think. And I can't think here."

"But what about me?" Bea cried. "I can't stay here alone!"

"I'll call Josephine."

"Where are you going? How long will you be gone?" Bea paused, then suddenly demanded, "Not with him!"

"No, not with him," Elise said, her gaze flickering toward Robert. He stood very still, watching her. "And

I don't know for how long. A few days, a few weeks. I won't be back until I'm ready.''

"But Elise..." Bea protested.

Elise walked out of the room. The family room was in almost as bad a state as Bea's bedroom, and she had to follow the cord to find the phone. When she called Josephine, she explained very little. Still, Josephine agreed to come.

After hanging up, Elise turned to find Robert across the room. Had he been there the whole time?

"I won't stand in your way, Elise," he said quietly. "But while you're gone, just remember...I love you and I'd never do anything to hurt you or, through you, to hurt this town." He held her gaze steadily before he turned to walk away.

ELISE DIDN'T EXPECT to find peace in the tiny cabin she rented for the week, but she did. Away from the stress and strain, for the first few days all she did was sleep and stare off into the trees. Then, finally, she began to notice the birds and the animals of the forest and the delicate summer flowers that struggled to give new life. With nothing to do except think, she found the situation that had previously tied her into emotional knots came slowly into perspective.

Bea had talked of Robert using her. But what had Bea done since her accident? If that wasn't using her, what was? Bea also talked of being concerned for her...but wasn't Bea only concerned for herself? As far back as Elise could remember, her sister had never once put another person's welfare first. Even before the accident, she'd been primarily concerned with how a situation would affect *her*. How *Bea* would manage. How *Bea* would feel. Never Elise, or their parents, when they'd been alive. And she'd often lied to get what she wanted. Elise knew she had; she had seen her do it many times. So why this time, concerning Robert, had she listened?

Did it all come down to the substance of her own fear? Had she believed the worst because she doubted herself—doubted her ability to attract and hold him? Had she used Bea as a handy excuse? And was that the first time she had done such a thing? Kenneth had wanted her to marry him, but he had also wanted to move away from Tyler. He couldn't go on living there, he had told her. The small-town atmosphere stifled him; he needed more room, more stimulation. And she had refused to budge...because of Bea. At least, she'd told him it was because of Bea. She had been crushed when Kenneth eventually left. Or had she been?

Wasn't life safe when you were faced with few choices? When the person closest to you manipulated you, but did it in such a way that you knew exactly where you stood from day to day? There were no surprises, no nasty jolts. A nice safe job, a nice safe town, nice safe friends...

Then Robert had come into her life. Almost too late, but he had come. He'd made her impatient with what she knew, with what she had previously accepted as her lot. And he had also frightened her...because he was beyond her control. He wasn't safe, he wasn't secure. He was thrilling and exciting and he made her feel wildly alive. And he made her wonder, *Why me?*

He'd said he loved her. Elise hugged the memory close to her heart. He had told her that twice—once from the other side of her bedroom door and once in the disarray of the family room. She had been too upset then to listen. But he'd said it.

Had he betrayed Tyler? He swore he'd meant no harm, that he'd only come to help the town. Elise remembered him standing across from her in the family room, so proud, so noble.

She moved restlessly in her chair on the narrow veranda, and soon the peace and isolation of the cabin was not enough.

THE DAY HAD SETTLED uneasily into dusk by the time Elise arrived in Milwaukee. She spent a while locating Robert's apartment complex, but once she did, she moved quickly into the lobby on the heels of another tenant and soon stood outside his door. Not giving herself time to reconsider, she raised a determined finger and pressed the doorbell.

When he opened the door and saw her, his first expression was clearly one of shock. Then he reached out to pull her inside. "Elise!" he said, relief and happiness blending in the one word. She could see that he wanted to continue pulling her until she was in his arms, but her stiff body made him hold back.

His hand dropped away, but that didn't prevent his gaze from devouring every detail of her face, of her form.

Elise skittered far enough away from him to feel somewhat safe. She, too, wanted nothing more in the world than to press herself against him and be enclosed by the security of his strong arms, but she had come here for something more. "I—I came to talk," she said.

For the first time in his company she had paid little attention to how she looked. Her hair had been given only a cursory brushing; she wore a minimum of makeup—a little mascara to darken her pale lashes, a touch of blush. She wore jeans and a faded cotton shirt and an old pair of walking shoes.

Her gaze slid over him. He, on the other hand, looked nicely turned out in a pair of tan cotton slacks and a dark gold shirt that fitted loosely. But then she hadn't expected to find him shabbily dressed. He just wasn't the sort. He had good taste in clothes, and the knowledge of how to wear them was second nature.

When he closed the door behind her, the room seemed too small. Swallowing tightly, she continued her earlier statement. "About the library. About Tyler. About us . . . in that order."

His golden-brown eyes, their color emphasized by his clothing, held on to her. "Would you like to sit down?" he asked politely.

She shook her head. She felt more in control on her feet.

"Do you mind if I—?" He indicated the leather couch, and she nodded jerkily. "What would you like to know?" he asked.

"I want to hear what you have to say. You said you could explain. . . . I'd like for you to do that."

"It's not easy."

"I don't care."

Robert sighed. "Then I'll start with the most important point: I didn't *use* you, Elise. Whatever else you might think of me, I want you to believe that. Bea was dead wrong on that score.''

"But she wasn't on the others?"

"It all depends on how you look at it. She wanted to believe that I did wrong. 'Nefarious' plans was how she described it. But there wasn't any plan. Things just happened. I tried to explain last week, but you and Bea—"

"Did you know the house had special value before you bought it?"

"No. I suspected that it might, but I didn't know."

"Why didn't you tell someone? Me . . . the council?"

"Because I *didn't* know. If I'd said anything... Let's just say I didn't want the house torn down, either by someone who didn't know what they had or someone who did. I want to renovate it, put it back as it was. Make it beautiful again."

"So you don't want to tear it down yourself?" Elise remembered what Bea had insinuated.

"No! Why would I go to all the trouble of putting a new roof on it if I wanted to do that?"

Elise was quiet, then she asked, "What if the house didn't prove to be valuable? What if it was just an ordinary house?"

Robert gave a tight smile. "I wish it were, now. Then I could do as I planned without anyone questioning my motives. Without you thinking that I—"

"You'd still renovate it?"

"Yes."

"Because it's your dream?"

He nodded.

Elise sat down gingerly on the edge of a chair cushion. "Bea said the house is worth a lot of money. That the man who designed it is famous and also that Frank Lloyd Wright..."

"Contributed. Yes. But in its present state, it's more valuable torn apart. Only someone dedicated to preserving the vision of the architects who designed it would do what I want to do. Most others would..." He shrugged.

"Because it will cost so much to refurbish."

He nodded.

Elise looked down at her hands. Bea had put her own personal slant on what Robert had done. After hearing his reasons from his own mouth, she didn't think his actions seemed nearly so reprehensible. "But the town lost a lot of money," she said.

"It will gain more in the end. To be able to claim a house built by Stephen deVille and Frank Lloyd Wright is a windfall, and architecture fans will come from far and wide to see it. Stephen deVille built very few houses. The ones that remain are treasured by his devotees. And Wright! I don't have to tell you about Wright."

Elise thought of the building she had worked in all these years. Rolled book carts through, driven nails into the walls of, complained about... And all the time it was a *treasure*.

She lifted pale blue eyes. "But why didn't you tell me?" she pleaded softly. "Didn't you trust me?"

Robert sat forward. "It wasn't that! Everything just...evolved. One discovery led to another, and then I heard that Martin Olsen was thinking of buying the place. I had to act. My friend, Max Prescot—he's the person Bea heard talking the other day. Anyway, he's a big fan of deVille's. I wanted Max to confirm what I thought I'd found. I was afraid it was a fake, an imitation. But Max was out of town and I had to wait.''

"That's the reason you went through all the town records . . . why you asked if I knew who had built the place."

"I was trying to get confirmation. I wanted to tell you, but I didn't want to say anything until after I knew for sure. Then Olsen . . ." He drew a deep breath. "Last Saturday, after Max saw the house, I tried to contact you all day, but you were in a meeting. I left messages on your answering machine, I went to the library and talked to your assistants—"

"Messages?" Elise repeated blankly. She remembered clearly that she had checked for recorded messages and found none.

"At least ten or twelve. No one at the library knew when you'd return, so I just kept trying."

Elise frowned. "There were no messages. I checked. I remember thinking that it must have been a quiet day for everyone. Then I went in to make Bea's din—" She stopped abruptly and closed her eyes. "Bea . . ." Bea must have erased every attempt he'd made at communication.

Robert said nothing.

Elise's eyes slowly opened, pain again filling their depths. "She must hate me so very much," she murmured.

"She hates me," Robert corrected her.

Elise shook her head. "No. It's me."

Robert leaned forward to take her hand. Elise let her fingers curl around his. Finally she asked softly, "Did you mean what you said the other day?"

"I love you, Elise," he repeated without further reference.

She bit her bottom lip to keep it from trembling. "Why?" she whispered. She motioned to herself and then to him, to the sophistication of his apartment and then toward Tyler.

"Do you love me?" he asked quietly, rubbing her fingers while keeping his gaze on them.

"Oh, yes!" she breathed.

"Why?" he asked. And when he looked up, Elise saw that there wasn't one solid answer for either of them. One soul had reached out to another and kindled an answering warmth. Why it happened as it did, why both had been made to wait so long . . . were questions that had no answer.

Elise's white teeth could no longer stop her lip from trembling, and Robert could no longer resist taking her into his arms. Falling to his knees in front of her with a low groan, he held her tightly against him, as if he would never let her go.

"You don't know what you've put me through this week," he said unevenly in her ear. "I was afraid I'd lost you."

Tears rolled down Elise's cheeks, but they were tears of dawning happiness, not sadness. "I had to get away," she said. "I was being torn in two—Bea on one side, you on the other. I thought about a lot of things while I was away. How my life has always been, how I want it to change. I'm not a saint. Much of what has happened is my fault, but much of it isn't. And I'm not talking about Bea's accident," she rushed to explain. "I mean . . . other things. Things you don't know about." She pulled back to look at him, to look at the face of the man she loved so much. She trailed her fingers through his hair, letting the black and silver strands run loosely over her skin before falling back into place. "But mostly I realized that I love you."

Robert sat back on his heels, his hands sliding down her arms, his yellow-brown eyes glowing with happiness. Then he stood up, separating himself from her only for a moment as he offered her his hand, and she, rising, accepted it. "You'll have to marry me," he murmured as he led her across the room toward a door she had never entered before.

"Why do you say that?" she asked.

"So we don't outrage the town."

"What—what are we planning to do that would outrage the town?"

He swept her into his arms when they stopped just outside the door. Then he pushed it open. "Oh, lots of things," he teased.

Once inside the bedroom, Elise didn't have either the time or the inclination to ask more questions.

CHAPTER FIFTEEN

"ELISE!" Josephine said as she stepped onto the porch. "I heard the car, but I didn't really expect it to be you. People have been calling or dropping by all week, wanting to know what's happened. I told them what you said—that you had been called away. But I didn't say anything else. Not even to Pauline at the library. That seemed to satisfy all but the worst." She ushered Elise into the house and looked her up and down, her sharp eyes seeing what others might miss. "You look . . . happy."

"I am," Elise said. She glanced about the tidy front room and hall and remembered the mess she'd left. "Josephine, I'm so sorry."

"It was no trouble."

"Nothing a good friend wouldn't take care of. I hope you remember this the next time I want to help *you.*"

Josephine made a dismissive motion.

"How is Bea?" Elise asked, her tone changing.

"Quiet."

"How do you mean?"

"She just sits in her chair. It's as if she's waiting for something."

"Did you have trouble with her after I left?"

Josephine shook her head. "Not at all. She was almost... docile. Actually, I've been a bit worried about her."

Elise frowned. "Where is she?" she asked.

"In the family room having lunch."

Under normal conditions, the instant Bea heard their voices she would have wheeled into the room and demanded to know where Elise had been, what she'd done and if she ever planned to do it again. But these weren't normal conditions.

"I'll go talk with her," Elise murmured. She started to draw away, but Josephine stopped her.

"Are you back? I mean... do you want me to pack my gear? If you need me, I can stay longer."

Elise smiled at her friend's generosity. "I won't take advantage of you any longer. Robert and I have worked things out. I'll stay here until everything is settled with Bea."

"You and Robert?" Josephine queried, her brows arching.

Elise's smile grew. "We're getting married. Just as soon as we can."

Josephine's thin face beamed as she hugged Elise and gave her a congratulatory kiss on the cheek. "I'm so *glad* for you. For a time, I was worried."

"So was I," Elise returned. Her smile dimmed as she looked toward the family room. "I'd better go. We can talk later. I'll tell you everything... well, almost everything."

"It should take me about a half hour to pack. If you need me—"

"I won't."

Josephine nodded, but her expression held concern.

No sound came from the family room. No television or radio voices, or noises of everyday life. The entire house was silent.

Elise found her sister in her usual place. Instead of holding reign, though, Bea seemed to have shrunk into herself. She stared dully at the empty television screen, her lunch untouched on a tray at her side. She seemed not to notice Buttercup spread languorously on her lap, although, after a moment, she did notice Elise.

"So... you're back," she said quietly.

Elise had not known what to expect, but she hadn't expected this. "Yes, I'm back," she said, equally quiet.

Bea turned away and resumed staring at the empty television screen. Finally she said, "And? What have you decided?"

"Robert and I are getting married."

Bea flinched but did not protest. "What about me?" she asked after another moment.

Elise drew up a chair. "Bea, I want to talk to you."

"Why? I've lost. You'll do with me what you want. Just tell me what it is so I'll know."

"Bea! This isn't a war! It never has been."

Bea roused the cat and prompted her to jump to the floor. Then she pivoted to face Elise. "Tell me!" she demanded, some of her fire returning.

"We can't live together anymore, Bea. And with Robert... It just wouldn't work."

"So you're going to put me in a home."

"No."

"Why not? Then you'd be rid of me."

"I don't *want* to be rid of you!"

Bea snorted and rolled away, but she didn't go far, only a few paces. "Why don't I believe that?" she asked, swinging around.

Elise had known this was going to be difficult. She struggled for words. "You're not an easy person to live with, Bea. You never have been. Even before the accident you liked to have your own way. And afterward..."

"Now it's all *my* fault!"

"No. But it's not all mine, either! I don't want us to get upset again, but we have to talk about this. Otherwise—"

"Just tell me what you're going to do with me," Bea snapped. "Have that much mercy, at least."

"I want it to be *your* decision."

Bea laughed shortly. "The condemned woman gets to choose between the rope or the guillotine."

"I've lived with you for a long time, Bea, taken care of you. Now it's time for you to take care of yourself."

"That sounds like Robert talking."

"Maybe it is," Elise agreed. "But he helped me to see the truth. I'm not doing either one of us a favor by letting you stay dependent on me, by letting you blame me for what happened. Neither of us can move forward if we don't let go of the past. And we should move forward."

"That's easy for you to say. You can walk!"

Elise shook her head. "There are plenty of people in the world who find themselves in your position, Bea. And they go on. They make a life for themselves. Look at the park ranger in California last year who climbed that mountain. He didn't let physical impairment stand in his way."

"I'm supposed to climb mountains?" Bea echoed incredulously.

Elise clung to patience. "I'm not saying that. I'm telling you that you *can* make a life for yourself. You love to collect dolls...so get out, meet other people who like to do the same thing. You like to sew . . . so join the Quilting Circle."

"At Worthington House! The Quilting Circle is at Worthington House! I don't want to go there, Elise. Please! Don't make me do that!"

"I never said..." Elise drew a steadying breath. Pleading was so out of character for her sister. It showed how deeply she was shaken. "Bea, please, listen to me. You don't have to *go* anywhere. You can stay right here if you want. It's up to you."

"But you said—"

"This is as much your home as it is mine. I won't turn you out of it. When I marry Robert, I won't be living here any longer. I'll live with him."

"But—"

"If you want to stay here, we'll hire someone to help you with the things you can't do. We'll talk to Patsy Conners. She retired from the hospital recently, and since her husband's death, she's all alone. I know she's looking for another place to live, preferably with someone to keep her company." Elise saw Bea relax slightly. She continued, "I didn't mean that you had to move to Worthington House to join the Quilting Circle. Emma Finklebaum doesn't live there. Neither did

Rose Atkins before she died. They just showed up for the meetings. You could, too."

"How would I get to all these *meetings?* I don't drive. Someone would have to take me. You're always so busy. And you'll probably be even busier after you marry *him*. How would I get there?"

Elise murmured, "You could always learn to drive."

"Me?" Bea repeated, and this time her incredulity was real.

Elise smiled. "Stranger things have happened. They sell specially fitted vans, you know."

"But the money."

"Robert and I could buy it for you."

"As a sop for a guilty conscience?"

Elise sighed. "I've told you from the beginning, Robert isn't what you think. His motives are honorable."

"Even concerning the library? I don't believe that for a moment."

"Well, you should, because it's true."

Bea began her special brand of pacing, pushing herself back and forth, her head bobbing. Then she stopped. "I can't learn to drive. I'm too old!"

"People older than you have learned."

"I'd be afraid."

"You?"

Bea paused to look at Elise. She gave the smallest glimmer of a smile, which disappeared as quickly as it emerged. "I have to think," she said.

"I'm not rushing you. I'll be here for a month."

"And after that?"

"I'll be married to Robert."

"This is all settled?"

"It is."

"Then it doesn't really matter what I decide."

"It does matter!" Elise contradicted her. "Because through it all, Bea, you're my sister. I care about what happens to you. And you should, too."

Elise wanted to say more. She wanted to make things instantly right between Bea and herself, to erase the years of contention. But change would take time. It wasn't something that could be forced.

She stood up. "I have to go out for a while this afternoon. Will you be all right?"

Bea nodded tightly.

Elise started to leave the room. Then she turned back and bent to kiss her sister's cheek. She was surprised when Bea didn't pull away.

ROBERT WAITED for Elise outside the council chambers. He hadn't wanted to let her come back to Tyler alone, but she had insisted. She wanted to talk to Bea and didn't think he should be present. He had been apprehensive ever since. When he saw her pull her car into a parking space not far from the Mercedes, he felt both elation and relief.

"You look like you survived," he murmured dryly, opening her door.

"Only just," she replied, leaning into his kiss.

Robert still couldn't get used to the idea that she was his, even after the night they had spent together. But it helped to see the warm light of love in her eyes and the delicate flush on her cheeks as she pulled away.

"How did she take the news?" he asked.

"Fairly well, actually. I think she was preparing herself for the worst."

He grinned. "Me."

Elise patted his arm in commiseration. "*And* being turned out on the street. I told you she'd think that."

"You set her straight?"

"I tried."

"Is she still angry?"

"Probably. Something like that just doesn't go away. But she's quiet now. She even smiled once. And—she let me kiss her cheek. That's a lot, Robert. For Bea. It makes me feel as if—"

"Elise!" Alyssa Baron called from the sidewalk, then immediately started toward them.

A tall, nice-looking young man and an equally nice-looking young woman followed her more slowly. They resembled each other enough to be brother and sister and probably were, Robert thought. He hadn't seen them before.

"We were all so concerned for you," Alyssa said. "Josephine was very closemouthed. She wouldn't say a thing other than that you were called away." Then Alyssa registered the air of intimacy between Elise and Robert. "Oh," she said. "Oh!" she said again as she put the pieces of the puzzle together. "Did you two...? Are you two...?"

"Mother, you're embarrassing them," the young woman cautioned.

Alyssa herself became embarrassed. Her perfect skin flushed and she fluttered nervously. "I didn't mean to intrude."

Robert spoke up, giving a slow, charming smile. "Actually, you can be the first to congratulate us. We're engaged."

"Oh, how wonderful!" Alyssa exclaimed. "It couldn't happen to two nicer people. Is that why you called and asked to meet with the council? To tell us the good news?" She looked curiously at Robert.

"Actually, no. It's something else," he evaded.

Elise's hand crept into his. To help deflect the moment, she introduced Jeff and Amanda. They were brother and sister, and Robert liked the look of both of them. The doctor was carrying a manila envelope, which he tucked beneath his arm in order to shake hands.

"What *is* that, Jeffrey?" his mother asked with barely restrained patience. "You seem to have been holding on to it for hours!"

"Just something I gave him, Mom," Amanda said, placating her. "Those old photos Liza found at the lodge. I had them at my office. It's nothing important."

When a shadow passed over Alyssa's face, brother and sister exchanged a worried glance. Immediately, as if to do a little deflecting of her own, Amanda took Robert's hand in greeting. "Mom has shown us the plans for the new library, along with your estimation of the lower cost, and I think you're an absolute genius! Thank you." She flashed a smile. "Now, I have to go. I have an appointment in ten minutes and I can't be late. Elise, Professor Fairmont…congratulations." The two women exchanged a warm glance.

Jeff, too, made his excuses. "I've got to go, as well. Mom, we'll see you later this evening?"

Alyssa's smile was tight. "Of course. I don't have any meeting scheduled for tonight. I'll be at home."

"Good," Jeff Baron said. "Professor Fairmont... Elise. All the best!"

As her children walked away, Alyssa Baron watched them with eyes that brimmed with love and pride but also with a tinge of fear. "They never truly grow up," she murmured softly. "To a mother, her children are always children, and when the world starts to close in..." She paused. "I'm so glad that Edward's here now. He makes me feel...safe." She shook herself, not seeming to fully realize what she'd said. Then she looked at Elise and Robert and invited brightly, "Shall we go inside?"

ELISE CONTINUED to hold Robert's hand as they waited for the rest of the council members to arrive. When he'd phoned, Robert had told them the meeting would be short.

Johnny Kelsey was the last to show up. He wore his Saturday overalls, splattered with different colors of paint. "Sorry," he apologized. "Time got away from me. I thought I'd better get myself over here rather than take time to change."

Nora Forrester dismissed his appearance as unimportant. "I can only be away from the store for a half hour tops. Robert, would you mind?"

Robert stood. It wasn't necessary, but it made him feel better. What he had to tell them was difficult enough. "You may have heard some rumors..." he began, immediately capturing everyone's attention. "Now I'd like to set the record straight." Which he did. In as clear and concise a manner as he could, Robert told them everything. He told them about the house, about his discoveries, about his suspicions as to its history as well as his doubts. About his panic to buy, about Max. Then he told them what he thought would be a fair solution. It was something he had come up with on his own while waiting for Elise. "Most of you aren't aware of this, but Elise and I are going to be married next month." Murmurs of surprise interrupted him. "We know we'll never have children to bequeath the house to...so I propose that we deed the house to Tyler after our demise. On one condition: that it never be torn down. It will be our gift to Tyler, to be passed on to the generations that follow."

He looked at Elise, a bit uncertain of her response. He hadn't had time to discuss his plan with her. But he needn't have worried. She caught his hand and squeezed it tightly, smiling through her happy tears.

His announcement was met by the others with stunned silence. Johnny Kelsey was first to react. He let the front legs of his chair fall to the floor, then he stood up to shake Robert's hand. "In my opinion, you don't need to be ashamed of a thing. You found yourself in a tight spot and you did what you had to do to get out of it. If it weren't for you, we wouldn't be looking forward to a fine new library and we wouldn't have a house that will make all the other small towns around here turn green with envy. And now you're offering to give it back to Tyler." He pumped Robert's hand again. "I'd say we've come out pretty good in the deal."

The others agreed. First Alyssa, then Nora, spoke warmly to Elise and Robert, congratulating them on their upcoming nuptials and thanking them for their generosity before they hurried back to the jobs they had left unfinished.

ONCE THE MEETING was over and they had gone outside, Robert bent to kiss Elise lightly on the lips. Emotion changed his intent, however, and he lingered longer than he'd planned.

Elise was breathless once they broke apart. She looked up at him and blinked, then glanced quickly over his shoulder. "People will see," she cautioned. They were standing by her car, just off the street.

He grinned. "Let them! The phones are undoubtedly busy right now with the news. We might as well give everyone a little proof."

His hands were at her waist, his body touching hers. His expression was irresistible. "I don't want to let you go," he murmured near her ear, causing her to shiver.

"Robert," she sighed. Her fingers toyed with his tie. It was perfectly obvious that she didn't want to release him, either.

"This is going to be a long month," he teased. He tried to kiss her again, but she slipped away.

"Robert . . . stop!"

He smiled at her nervousness, then he smiled even more broadly at the woman who walked past on the sidewalk. The young boy with her kept jumping from gutter to curb and back again. In his hand was a picture book. The woman looked slightly startled when she recognized Elise, but she soon smiled in return.

"People..." Elise tried to explain. "Everyone knows me...."

Robert stopped her. "Hush, it's all right. I understand."

Elise's blue eyes glowed with her love for him. "You always have understood, haven't you?" she murmured. Then she said, "What you did in there...it was wonderful. To give the house back to the town."

"It just seemed the right thing to do," he said easily.

"I was so proud."

He shrugged, but he was pleased.

She looked at him. "Amanda said something earlier, then Johnny seemed to confirm it. You've given them the plans for the new library?"

He nodded. "While you were away. We missed the meeting last Saturday night, but I thought..." He paused. "It was the one thing I could do for you. No matter how things turned out, I wanted you to have the new library...and the atrium. I put it back in. It's smaller, but..."

Elise held his gaze for so long and so steadily that Robert became uncomfortable. "If you don't want it," he said, "I can—"

She placed her hands along either side of his jaw. "Hush," she breathed. And as she pulled his face closer to hers, she didn't seem to care anymore that people might be watching.

EPILOGUE

ELISE BRUSHED her fingertips through her short pale hair, fluffing it. Her new permanent had been nicely done, the curls casually tousled as they fell softly about her face. Her makeup had been applied with a light hand to enhance her looks, but the glow was supplied internally. A short veil became the crowning touch to a beautiful cream taffeta dress.

Josephine fussed with the soft bow at the back of Elise's waist, trying to get it just right. Finally she stood back and, through narrowed eyes, examined Elise from head to foot. "Beautiful!" she concluded.

"Thank you," Elise murmured.

Josephine kissed her cheek and handed her the bridal bouquet. Then she checked her watch. "Are you ready?" she asked.

Elise's stomach tightened. She bit her bottom lip. "Yes," she breathed.

Josephine walked with her from the Tyler Room, where she had gotten ready, to the stairs that led to the large room below.

The Friedrich house barely looked like a library this festive day. For the first time since Elise had become chief librarian, it was closed on a Saturday. Flowers and garlands and paper birds graced every available surface. And in place of the card catalog and tables in the middle of the room, chairs had been arranged to flank a center aisle. On each chair abutting the aisle was an arrangement of white flowers. At the end of the walkway were more flowers in the form of a bower in front of the huge fireplace. Volunteers had done everything. In the month that had passed since the announcement of Elise and Robert's engagement, everyone in Tyler had been busy.

Elise stopped for a moment to gaze at all the people who had come to witness their vows. Each face had a history, each life was a thread interwoven with everyone else's. Her friends from Tyler were there, along with Robert's family and associates. She had met his parents, his brother and sisters, many of his nephews and nieces, and they had welcomed her into their family. She had even met Max Prescot, his friend from Chicago. People looked back at her and smiled their good wishes.

Her gaze moved on, to the minister who waited...and then, unable to resist any longer, she looked at Robert. And she caught her breath. He looked so handsome in his tux, crisp and sophisticated in black and white. Her heart became so full she thought it would burst.

Josephine touched her arm. Soft music began to play. She took a deep breath and started down the stairs again.

There was no place she would rather have had her wedding. When she'd first thought of it, she'd wondered how the idea would be received. But Robert had approved and so had everyone else. It was as if any other choice would be inappropriate.

She paused at the base of the stairs and looked to her right. There had been only one lingering question about the day. Her grip tightened on her flowers, then she saw her. Bea had decided to come after all.

Elise's smile was tremulous as Bea rolled slowly toward her. Not only had she come, but she was wearing the new dress Elise had picked out. Her hair was perfectly combed into a bun, and she even wore a touch of lipstick.

Bea met her look. A tear escaped Elise's eye. Her sister offered her a lace handkerchief.

"Thank you," Elise whispered as she took it. She dabbed beneath her eye, then slid the soft cloth into the sleeve of her dress. *Something borrowed,* she thought, and hugged the moment.

Josephine started down the aisle. Then it was Elise's turn.

She must have floated, because she was barely aware of her feet touching the wooden floor. Her gaze had locked with Robert's, and within a heartbeat she was at his side.

Elise heard the flowers she carried make a fluttering sound, but she wasn't aware that she was shaking until she looked down. Soon Josephine relieved her of the burden.

Robert took her hand and Elise's nervousness instantly stopped. With him she had nothing to fear, nothing to dread. He was warm and kind and had such strength of character. By tomorrow afternoon they would be in Paris.

He smiled. He knew that she was thinking of Paris. She could see it in the teasing look that danced in his yellow-brown eyes. Then his expression grew serious as the minister addressed them.

The traditional questions were asked, the usual responses given. Finally Robert turned to her and lifted the short veil.

"For always, Elise," he murmured softly.

Then, under the new roof of the home they would one day share, and in front of the people who would continue to be part of their lives, Robert took Elise into his arms and they sealed the vows that united them for eternity.

And now,
an exciting preview of

MILKY WAY

by Muriel Jensen

the ninth installment of the
Tyler series

When Britt Hansen develops a low-calorie, low-fat goat's milk yogurt recipe to save the farm that has been in her family for four generations, it changes her life—in more ways than she'd expected. Jake Marshack, representative of a powerful dairy conglomerate, tries to acquire Britt's product for his company—and Britt and her four children for himself.

CHAPTER ONE

JAKE MARSHACK TURNED his red Ford Explorer off the highway onto the gravel side road marked with the Wisconsin Department of Transportation's official brown-and-yellow Rustic Road designation. The signs identified stretches of thoroughfare that retained the charm of days gone by, when life and travel were slower, when there'd been time to smell the wildflowers and listen to the birds. But the rich verdant pasture spreading out to his left, dotted with grazing Holsteins, and the tall, lush green crowding in on his right went unnoticed. He didn't see the gray clouds against the stormy spring sky, heralding rain, or the fat black-and-white Canada geese flying toward Timber Lake, a quarter of a mile away. His mind was ticking over figures.

As Winnebago Dairy's sales manager in southeastern Wisconsin, Jake spent most of his time in a Chicago office. But several times a year he went on the road to collect outstanding receivables. He could be charming and firm, understanding but unshakable in his resolve to have the district with the best numbers. Still, the percentage of collectible debt was growing among the smaller farms in his district, and the struggles of their owners to hold on to what little they had left touched him as few things in life did.

But business was business. However much he hated this part of his job, he had to do it. When the big red barn and the white Victorian farmhouse beyond it came into view, he pulled over to review his notes.

"Hansen widow trying hard, but still unable to pay," Buckley, the sales rep, had reported after his last call at Lakeside Farm. "Renting out large parcels of pasture in March and promises to pay outstanding balance at that time."

Jake checked his printout. March had come and gone and there'd been no payment. In fact, there'd been no payment since the previous September. Policy was clear. The widow Hansen was cut off pending payment in full.

Jake closed his folder with a groan. Great. A widow. He had to stop feed delivery to some little old arthritic thing who'd probably lose the farm before the year was out and be forced to move in with one of her kids.

He shook his head as he pulled back onto the road and headed for the lane to the house. He'd never understand why generation after generation of farmers broke their backs and very often their hearts over a piece of land that was subject to every joke God, nature and the government could play. It was masochistic and senseless. He couldn't imagine dedicating one's life to something as completely unpredictable as a harvest.

Now, numbers made sense. Columns that balanced were easy to understand. A future that depended solely on what an individual could do was the only course worth plotting, as far as he was concerned. Needing and depending on others or on the beneficence of nature always led to a predictable end—disappointment.

Jake didn't believe in disappointment. He believed in success.

He pulled to a stop behind a muddy blue GMC truck at the side of the house. A yellow Lab lying at the top of the porch steps raised an intelligent face to watch him. Jake leaped out of the vehicle, careful to miss a puddle, and took a moment to look around.

The house had a peaked roof with gingerbread finials and a wraparound porch. It was tidy but in need of a fresh coat of paint. A heart-shaped wreath of dried flowers hung on the front door, and scarlet May-blooming tulips and bright forget-me-nots trimmed the foundation and the porch steps. He imagined the little widow kneeling on a rug and pampering her flowers.

Maybe he'd get lucky, he thought, and she wouldn't be home. He could send her a registered letter telling her she was customer non grata. No. He had the best numbers in the company because he dealt with people face-to-face. He made things turn out his way, but he did it openly.

He took two steps up toward the porch and was greeted by a hair-raising growl from deep in the Lab's throat and a clear view of impressive canine incisors. The dog hadn't moved, and Jake got the distinct impression it was because she didn't feel she had to.

Accustomed to a fair amount of hostility, Jake had perfected an understanding manner and a conciliatory tone of voice that usually worked on dogs as well as people. He extended a cautious hand and asked, "Good dog?"

The Lab changed demeanor instantly. Rolling onto her back, she tucked her feet in in eager surrender, her strong tail wagging madly. She whined in helpless adoration as Jake reached up to scratch her sturdy mound of a chest. An upside-down tongue flicked at the sleeve of Jake's suit jacket.

Jake laughed. "You are a good dog," he praised. "You're not much of a security system, but I'll bet you're a great friend."

The dog rolled onto four big feet and followed him as he went to the front door and knocked. She sat on his right foot as he waited . . . and waited.

BRITTANY HANSEN STOOD on tiptoe on top of an eight-foot wooden ladder and groped for the shingle that was just beyond her reach. She growled impatiently when the tip of her longest finger refused to close the gap.

"Come on!" she said aloud. "One more shingle! I am not going to climb down and move the ladder again for one more shingle!"

She withdrew her aching arm and studied the shingle with hostility. Rubbing her aching biceps, she tried to remember why repairing the hole in the porch roof had seemed so important this afternoon. Because she wanted to put the porch swing out, she reminded herself, and a large drip had developed where she usually placed it near the kitchen window.

And because Jimmy had always brought the old swing out for her at the first sign of spring, and she wanted to prove to herself that although he wasn't here to do it, it would still get done.

Sneaky, strong emotion rose up to sting her eyes and clog her throat. Having it out would be no fun, and she'd probably choke up every time she looked at it, but it would be in its place because *she* had put it there. It would be one small victory after a long dark winter of silent, corrosive grief.

Britt drew a deep breath, leaned her weight against the roof and stretched her right hand out as far as she could reach—and felt the toe of her right foot push the ladder out from under her.

She screamed, the palms of her hands scraping over the rough tiles as she slid down, then caught the rain gutter with her fingers.

Great, she thought with a gallows humor she was surprised to find had survived the winter. *Hanging by my fingernails. Literally. The bank should see this.*

She groped with her feet for the porch railing, but the extended roof had her too far out of reach.

She considered letting go, but the drop to the ground was considerable. She could not afford a broken limb at this point in time, and the way her luck had been running, a multiple fracture was bound to result.

"Dammit, Jimmy!" she shouted at the air. "Do something!"

JAKE AND THE LAB, still waiting at the front door, were galvanized into action by a crash followed immediately by a piercing screech. With one loud *Woof!* the dog ran around the porch to the back of the house. Jake followed, his mind already in sympathy with the poor little arthritic old lady.

He jerked to a halt at the sight of a pair of long legs dangling at eye level. They were not arthritic legs. They were slender, shapely legs in snug denim. His brain took a moment to swap mental images and assimilate what was happening.

His eyes lifted to a baggy gray sweater and arms holding rigidly, desperately to the gutter. Pale blue eyes in a white face were wide with alarm and a curious resignation.

Jake wrapped an arm around a pillar to steady himself and reached out over the railing.

BRITT STARED at the man in the three-piece gray suit and wondered if her desperation had conjured him up. Before she could decide, he had a fistful of the front of her sweater.

"Kick a leg out toward me," he ordered.

She blinked. He didn't disappear. "Who are you?" she asked.

She heard his gasp of exasperation. "Does that matter at the moment? Kick a leg out."

Reflexively, she complied, and felt a muscular arm wrap itself around it.

"Now drop a hand to my shoulder."

She wanted to, but even the threat of falling couldn't blunt the effect of a large male hand wrapped high around her inner thigh.

"I haven't got a good grip on you," he said when she hesitated. "If you fall now, we're both going over. I don't know about you, but weeks of traction wouldn't fit into my schedule."

"I . . . can't hold on with one hand."

"When you let that hand go, I'll have you."

"You're sure?"

"Absolutely."

She believed him. She wasn't sure why. Possibly because she wasn't in a position not to. Closing her eyes, she dropped a hand and reached out blindly. She uttered a little scream as her other hand lost purchase and she fell, landing solidly against hard muscle. Sitting on his arm, she was swung sideways over the railing, then deposited on her feet.

For an instant she couldn't breathe or speak. All she could do was stare.

Her Good Samaritan was long-legged and lean, with just enough thickness in the shoulder to make her grateful he'd been the one to come along and not spindly Chuck Stuart, who rented part of her pasture.

With eyes the color of maple wood and dark blond hair side-parted and perfectly groomed, he bore a startling resemblance to Kevin Costner. His recent exertion hadn't disturbed his good looks at all. There was a confident, capable air about him that was both comforting and alarming.

She watched him shrug his coat back into place and straighten his tie.

She began to emerge from her trance when she noticed the subtle elegance of everything about him. His finely tailored suit probably cost more than her monthly food budget. And he wore cuff links—gold and jade, if she wasn't mistaken. Antiques, probably. His shoes were shined to perfection.

She pulled herself together and folded her arms. "You're from the bank," she accused.

"No," he said.

"An attorney, then."

"No."

She frowned, her shoulders relaxing. "Then who are you?"

Jake had never seen hair that color. It rioted around her face in soft curls and ended in a fat braid that rested on her shoulder. It was the shade of a ripe peach, a sort of pink-orange with gold highlights. He judged by the generous spattering of freckles on her face that the color was natural.

Aware that he hadn't answered her question, he offered his hand and a smile he was sure had to be at least a little vague. "Jake Marshack," he said. "And you are?"

She studied him uncertainly for a moment, then shook his hand. Her fingers were long and slender, but her grip was firm. "Britt Hansen. Thank you for rescuing me."

He indulged in a poignant memory of an armful of soft, round hip, then immediately dismissed it. "The...widow Hansen?" he asked.

She laughed lightly at the title. "One and the same. For a minute I thought you were the villain come to tie me to the railroad tracks. Instead you turn out to be a genuine Dudley Doright. Come on inside. A gallant rescue deserves at least a cup of coffee."

She beckoned the dog with a slap to her thigh "Come on, Daffy."

Jake hesitated on the threshold as she opened the back door. Dudley Doright he was not. "Mrs. Hansen..."

But the ring of a telephone at the far end of the kitchen made her hurry inside. She gestured for him to follow and pointed to a chair at a large round table. The dog settled under it.

Feeling an annoying little niggle of guilt, he sat. He'd left his notebook in the car because he'd found that official papers and copies of bills always made people defensive, and he wanted them willing to work with him. Of course, in her case, he doubted she had anything to work with.

Chatting happily to someone he judged by the conversation to be a neighbor, she washed her hands, poured coffee into two mugs, then walked the full extension of the phone cord to hand one to him. He stood and reached across the table for it.

"No, I was happy to lend it to you, Judy," she was saying, "but if you're finished with it, I'll come pick it up. I was trying to repair the porch roof with my short ladder and almost broke my neck!"

She grinned at him, and he heard a loud expression of dismay from the other end of the connection.

"No, no, I'm fine. Dudley Doright rescued me."

"Who?" came across the line loud and clear.

"It's a long story. I'll tell you about it when I pick up the ladder. I'm going to town tomorrow—want me to bring you anything?"

While she made notes on a pad stuck to the refrigerator, Jake sipped his coffee and studied the enormous kitchen. It was a large square room papered in a soft blue-and-cream pattern. The woodwork was Williamsburg blue and the high cupboards were oak. Children's artwork and schedules covered the beige refrigerator, and something with a rich, beefy fragrance simmered in a deep pot on the stove.

The table at which he sat was bordered on two sides by sparkling countertops. The third wall was painted creamy white and covered with what appeared to be antique kitchen implements and an ancient pitchfork that must have been hand-carved all of a piece. He was wondering who had used it how long ago when three kittens, one white and two spotted black-and-white, suddenly ran across the kitchen from the room beyond. They tumbled over one another in a rolling heap, then raced back the way they'd come.

He had turned his attention to the pitchfork again when the widow Hansen joined him at the table.

Pale blue eyes smiled at him over the rim of her cup. "My great-grandmother pitched hay with that," she said, "and once held an amorous neighbor at bay while my great-grandfather was off hunting. I believe her father carved it. Would you like something to go with your coffee?"

"Ah...no, thank you." He straightened in his chair. It was time to state his business. "Actually, I'm from Winnebago Dairy. I'm here to talk to you about..." He looked into her eyes and experienced a glitch in his thought processes. His brain disengaged and he couldn't remember simple words. All that seemed to work were his eyes, which couldn't stop looking into hers.

They were like Lake Geneva under a cloudy sky, softly gray-blue and suggesting unimagined depths. He felt pulled in, like a diver who'd forgotten to draw a breath before jumping.

"About?" she prompted. She lowered her cup and a subtle change took place in her cheerful, friendly expression. That helped him pull himself together.

"About your bill." He forced out the words and groped for his professional persona. "You're eight months overdue, Mrs. Hansen."

She looked at him levelly across the table, her eyes now like the lake in February—with a six-foot, impenetrable ice crust. "So you're not Dudley Doright, after all," she said, pushing away from the table.

Jake half expected her to order him to leave. Instead, she went to the sink, a deep old porcelain one with ancient faucets, around which a more modern counter and cupboards had been built. She looked out the window, and he supposed she could see the cows grazing.

"You're here to cut me off," she guessed.

He mentally went through all his options. It didn't take long. There weren't any. "I'm afraid so," he said finally. He added, "The moment you pay the outstanding balance, I'll send a truck out with the order you put in two days ago."

She turned and leaned against the edge of the sink, both hands behind her, gripping it. "I can't pay right now, but I've been to the bank about a loan. I should have an answer in a few days. And I'm getting a desserts business going on the side for extra money. I—"

"Our rep," he interrupted quietly, "said you thought you'd be able to pay when you rented out pasture."

She nodded. "It went to the mortgage. I thought having my payments almost current would give me a better shot at getting a loan."

Robbing Peter to pay Paul was a sign of real trouble. But Jake knew that was how half his customers made it from year to year.

He shook his head regretfully. "I'm sorry. We'll ship to you the moment—"

"But I could have the money for you in a week," she said, trying desperately to keep the plea out of her voice. She wanted to convey competence, reasonableness.

"Or the bank could turn you down," he said gently.

She tilted her chin. "I believe they'll approve me."

Jake stood. If he had to hurt her feelings, he felt he had to do it on his feet. "I've seen your credit file, Mrs. Hansen. I think you're deluding yourself."

Anger sparked in her eyes, which were suddenly like the lake in an electrical storm. "At the moment, hope is all I have, Mr. . . . ." She hesitated over his name.

"Marshack," he provided.

"Marshack," she repeated. "If you're going to tie me to the train track, let me at least hold on to the hope that the *real* Dudley will come along."

Jake wanted out of the warm, cozy kitchen and out from under her judgmental glare more than he wanted anything else at that moment. Yet something rooted him in place. He guessed the reason was that she looked so touchingly brave that he couldn't do anything cowardly.

So he decided to tell her what he thought. "Mrs. Hansen, small farms run by strong men are going under left and right. Why continue to fight the inevitable? We've offered to buy you out twice. Maybe it's time you considered it."

She was now rigid with anger, but he gave her credit for controlling it very well. Had their roles been reversed, he'd have had her on the porch by now, on the business end of the pitchfork.

"This is a heritage farm," she said, her voice very quiet. "It's been in my family for four generations—five, counting my children. I'm not interested in turning it over to a dairy that now owns more of Wisconsin and Illinois than the state park systems."

He nodded. "I've been empowered to raise the offer." He named the sum Stan Foreman, vice president of sales, had brought to his office that morning with the subtle reminder that acquiring her property for the company would speed Jake's rise up the corporate ladder. The offer was generous and was intended to knock her off her feet and out of her stubbornly negative stance. It didn't.

For an instant the blue eyes widened and he saw a flash of longing, then it was gone and he was treated once again to the February lake. "You don't understand," she said, her patience obviously strained. "Four generations of Bauers were born here. It's been like a gift passed from hand to hand. I couldn't sell this farm any more than I could sell one of my children."

"How are you going to provide for those children's education, Mrs. Hansen?" he asked. "You're in considerable debt already, with little chance of fighting your way out without selling—or marrying a wealthy man. Would you rather the bank got your memories?"

She paled, holding both arms rigidly to her sides. "How dare you worm your way into my kitchen—"

"You invited me in," he reminded her quietly, "after I prevented you from breaking your neck."

"—drink my coffee, then proceed to call me a deadbeat?" She was practically shouting toward the end.

This wasn't going at all the way he'd hoped. "I said no such thing," he denied, pushing the chair he'd occupied back to the table. "I mentioned only what is public record. If you sell, you can pay all your debts, buy a nice little place somewhere and still have enough left over to start four college funds."

She did not appear appeased. "You even know how many children I have."

"Details are an important part of my job," he said without apology. "You owe us a lot of money, Mrs. Hansen. One of us better do his research."

She marched across the kitchen, her braid flapping against her upper back. She yanked the door open and fixed him with a lethal stare, her cheeks pink, her voice wavering a bit as she said darkly, "I'm a 34B, I love silk underthings and mocha fudge-nut ice cream, and I root for the Milwaukee Brewers. Anything else you'd like to know?"

Jake tried to accept defeat gracefully. But his life and career were on a timetable, and her inability to pay her debts, plus her refusal to sell, were holding things up. The Winnebago Dairy board would be making the vice-presidency decision at the end of summer. He'd hoped to be district quota buster by then, or to have reeled in her property for the company so that he'd be the only possible choice.

On such short acquaintance he'd decided he liked her, even though she was making his life difficult. He'd try again. There had to be a way to reach her. But he had to regroup first.

He smiled politely and went to the door, resolutely keeping his eyes from the charming dimension she'd announced. "We'll deliver," he said, "as soon as your bill is paid."

He stepped out onto the porch, but was swept back into the kitchen when a wave of children collided with him, then carried him along as they burst into the house. He heard the four of them yell Hi, Mom. Four lunch boxes clattered onto the table, then the wave disappeared in four directions—the refrigerator, the cookie jar, under the table where the dog lay and to the small television in the opposite corner. A bouncy cartoon ditty filled the room. The kittens raced back in, seeking attention.

A slender boy about twelve or thirteen polished an apple and studied Jake from a careful distance. He wore jeans and a plaid flannel shirt open over a T-shirt. "Your wheels in the driveway?" he asked.

"Yes," Jake replied.

The boy nodded. "Cool." Then he looked from his mother's frowning face to Jake's unfarmlike attire and asked with an edge of hostility in his voice, "You from the bank?"

Britt put her arm around her older son's shoulders and forced herself to smile. She tried so hard not to let her financial woes affect her children, but money, or the lack of it, had become so large a part of her life lately that the subject intruded everywhere. Determined to keep it from gaining more ground as long as she could, she said cheerfully, "Matt, this is Mr. Marshack. We were just talking about...about Great-Grandma Bauer."

Jake saw the transformation take place on the widow Hansen's face as, snacks secured and the dog and kittens petted, the children gathered around her. He guessed it was maternal reflex at first; she didn't want them to know she was upset. Then the youngest boy and girl flanked her, each leaning in to her, and she seemed to visibly relax.

"This is Christy," she said, putting a gentle hand atop a pre-adolescent with hair the same shade as hers. The child wore glasses with red frames and had eyes that studied him with the same suspicion her mother's showed.

"David," she went on, moving her hand to a boy about eight. He was the only one in the group with dark hair, and his blue eyes verged on green.

"And Renee."

"I'm six," the plump little girl reported. She was the spitting image of her mother and sister, but with the rounder features of early childhood. She smiled up at him. "You look like Robin Hood," she said.

Britt's eyes met his and said without words, *But you're more like the Sheriff of Nottingham*. Aloud, she said, "Mr. Marshack was just leaving."

"Stay cool," Matt advised.

"Nice to meet you," Christy said.

David waved at him from his mother's side, and Renee followed him out to his truck.

"I'm in first grade," she said, hopping on one foot beside him, then racing to catch up as he got ahead of her. "My birthday is in October. You know, January, February, March, April..."

She went all the way through to October while following him around the truck and watching him open the door and climb in.

He let her go on without comment because he never knew what to say to children. He always got the impression that, despite the less-sophisticated vocabulary and the smaller stature, they were smarter than adults. And this one fairly glowed with curiosity and intelligence.

As he consulted his calendar to check his next call, she pointed to the portable office that sat on the passenger seat. "What's that?" she asked.

"Files," he replied.

"What's that?"

"Papers and stuff."

"Oh." Satisfied, she stood on tiptoe to study the dash.

"Renee, honey," the widow said, appearing from around the hood and taking the child by the hand. "Mr. Marshack has to leave."

She stepped away from the truck, pulling the little girl with her. "Goodbye, Mr. Marshack," she said, her eyes hostile again. "Next time you wish to speak to me, please write or phone."

Jake put the truck in reverse, checked that his rearview mirror was clear, then stepped on the gas, determined that the widow Hansen hadn't seen the last of him.

The sound of metal crunching and glass popping under his rear tires made him slam on the brake.